PASTEL REMEMBRANCES

A Collection Of Short Stories

Fimo Mitchell

WE ARE HOME BOOKS

ISBN: 978-0-9738822-2-3 (Paperback)

Cover art by Fimo Mitchell
Book design by Fimo Mitchell

To the hippie who named me, taught me, and encouraged me to see the world.

Pastel Remembrances
by Fimo Mitchell

Green, in food
Hunger, in hue
Our soil
Our blues
Waves seek refuge too
Rites bleed beneath shoes
While hands reach for thread
Watery eyes watch the needle
Life's patchwork
Reveals the fragility of size
The beauty in thorns
The repose in power
The suffering in memory
To honour time
We allow the tears
When silence sleeps
Walls collapse under speech
Bodies trapped under debris
Architects walk in deceit
Purchasing worlds of free
Their coronations
Love by another name
Their fragrances
Fear by a stolen gaze
Pastel remembrances
For their choices
Pastel remembrances
For our losses

CONTENTS

ENDINGS

I took the key off the metallic ring and placed it on the dining table. The defiant part of me that had blossomed in South Africa wanted to pick the key up and clip it back on the band. It was this same defiance that made me contemplate putting my clothes back in the closet, my shoes by the door, and my sketch pads on the coffee table. The coconut oil, face wash, and body soap would also return to their rightful spots in the bathroom. Instead, the sensible part of me that I had cultivated in England after Dad died remembered to take a deep inhalation and a long exhalation.

To a far lesser degree, leaving the key symbolized the end of a relationship, like dad's passing. Like everyone else who chose to feel, I had always struggled with endings and this one was no different. Tears that brimmed in my eyes finally flowed, streaming down my cheeks with a freedom I envied. A freedom I had relinquished by surrendering to his strong embrace.

He was closer in age to my mother with less than seven years separating them. His age never bothered me, but my own did unnerve him. I doubt he would have invited me out for dumplings if he knew my date of birth. When it came up over dinner, he laughed and declared that he was too old for me. Naturally, I disagreed and referenced Aaliyah in *Age Ain't Nothing But A Number*. He was impressed that I knew the song but told me that he had a niece who was my age. It wouldn't be the last time he brought up this fact. He also remarked that I hadn't gone through a season of promiscuity which he jokingly dubbed the "hoe phase." I wasn't sure how much of what he was saying was to discourage me from pursuing him or to convince himself that I was some sort of forbidden fruit. Either way, there was something about the way he looked at me that made dinner feel more like a date.

When he decided to pay the bill, I protested. Little did he know, the reason I came to China was to discover my independence. Having awakened it, I had every intention to contribute to the bill. He seemed taken aback by how firm I was. He told me just as firmly that next time I could pay.

After dinner we strolled to the beach, took off our shoes, and stepped into the sea. The tide was low and the water serene. The breeze danced around our bodies without overwhelming us. Although the mingling of clouds and pollution blocked the brilliance of shining stars, we had just enough light to see one another. As we stood side by side, we surrendered to the fragrance, the feel and the sheer power of nature. Amid such majesty, words were not needed, so we held onto the soothing quietness.

I was in no hurry to return home and neither was he. We sat on the sand, delighted to have the beach to ourselves. I felt fortunate to be where I was, especially considering the locations my peers were assigned to in ImmerTeach, an international program that placed applicants in teaching internships across China. Not only did Yantai have beaches, but the cost of living was also lower than in other assigned cities, and the air quality was better.

It pleased me to hear him say that Yantai was one of his favourite places in China. Having lived in five different cities and traveled to over twenty, his statements about the country and its people carried much weight.

To his credit, he didn't lecture me on what to expect in my first few months, nor did he judge my ignorance on key issues facing Chinese society. His observations were perceptive, and he followed them up with questions we pondered and tried to answer. He talked a lot, but I was hungry for new understanding, and so I didn't mind. Intellectual reflections with an attractive man on an empty beach beneath the night skies was a novel experience.

There was a purity to our exchange I found refreshing. But if I'm being honest, I wanted to feel his lips on mine and wondered if he had the same desire. It didn't take long for these thoughts to grow louder than his voice. Then, my more sensible side that I had cultivated in England after dad's death remembered to take a deep inhalation and a long exhalation. Already sitting crossed-legged, I closed my eyes and adjusted my posture while continuing to follow my breath. Time passed, I'm not sure how much, but when I peeked to my right, he was sitting in a half lotus with his eyes closed and his hands resting on his knees.

We stayed on the beach until it was late. Despite his heavy eyelids and having to teach in the morning, he offered to walk me home.

"Do I look like the kind of girl that needs protection?"

"Hold up, I wasn't trying to say that—"

I interrupted him by smiling and saying, "I know, and I appreciate the offer, but I'm good."

We shared a few nervous laughs as we hugged and wished each other goodnight.

"Call me the minute you get home."

He waved, I waved back, and then he set off. I watched him momentarily. His height, muscular frame, and stride made it hard to turn away. Eventually, I did.

On the way back to my apartment, I replayed the entire evening. I even revisited our first encounter at work a week earlier. I had been walking back to my office after having my lunch in the cafeteria when I spotted him eating at his desk.

Phyllis, an American intern who was quickly becoming a friend, had met him days before at a welcome dinner organized by some teachers at the school. She would later tell me that he and I were kindred spirits and was excited for us to meet. So, we did. I stepped into his office and introduced myself as he was chewing, fork in hand. He smiled and told me his name with his mouth full. It wouldn't be the last time he smiled or talked with food in his mouth. It was an awful habit that I would later rail against.

Mind you, what was left of his lunch smelled heavenly and looked nutritious. Phyllis had mentioned that he was a vegetarian like me, so naturally I was curious about his food. When I asked for the list of ingredients, he told me he was eating a kidney bean stir fry mixed with diced tomatoes, chopped onions, garlic, green peppers and cilantro. Beneath that stir fry was steamed millet. Sautéed cabbage was in the other container.

Playfully, he asked if my lunch was anything like his. I laughed, accusing him of being cruel since he knew the cafeteria didn't cater to vegetarians. He laughed too. He told me that I needed to follow his lead and start bringing my own lunch. To him, the food in the cafeteria was prepared without presence or love; as a result, it was of a lower frequency. Such food couldn't heal the body and might even be harming it he said. He then asked me if I believed in vibrations. I did, and with that, we got deep into a brief conversation about energy; brief because he suddenly remembered that it was Thursday, and he was supposed to be outside on duty.

I didn't hesitate to join him on a bench near the football pitch where he could keep an eye on the students: a group of boys who were kicking the ball around, four girls who were playing some variation of tag, and the older students who were walking around the track. We spoke at length about the bean sprouts he grew and his meditation. He infused humour into almost everything he said which helped to ground some of the more abstract concepts he expounded on. He was confident but not arrogant. His eagerness to speak was matched by an equal if not greater eagerness to listen. Our first conversation ended when the bell rang for the start of afternoon classes. He walked back to his office to gather teaching materials while I, curious about a man who sounded determined to live within the sacredness of each moment, lingered on the bench.

We didn't exchange numbers that day. Like everyone that I met in China, he used a messaging and calling app to stay in touch with friends. I had placed my phone over his to scan his QR code, adding him to my contacts list. In the days that followed, we would continue our conversations in person when our paths crossed at school and through the phone app. He seemed to enjoy leaving the occasional voice message – his American accent always made me smile – while I stuck to typed ones.

Five days went by before he asked me out for a second time. I sent him my availability and said that I was looking forward to it. He replied with two smiley faces that had hearts for eyes. Though I didn't know for certain how he felt about me, or what his intentions were, the emojis suggested to me he was interested in more than a simple friendship.

The idea of exploring something serious wouldn't have been a problem except for that I had just ended a relationship. My reasoning for coming to China was to explore life on my own. Since the age of twelve when boys discovered me, rare were the times when I wasn't involved with someone.

I told him that, having recently broken up with my boyfriend, I needed time on my own and was solely seeking friendship. There was also my confusion over Steve, a fellow ImmerTeach intern. During the program's two-week orientation in Beijing, I had spent most of my free time with him. We had shared a kiss and even though he was working in a city close to Shanghai, far away from Yantai, we continued to speak daily. This bit of information I didn't divulge. All he needed to know was that I was unavailable.

He thanked me for my honesty then explained that he already had a solid group of friends and was interested in cultivating something more than a platonic relationship. I respected his candor but maintained that I was in no position to embark on a new romance. He sent me a lighthearted voice message asking me what the protocol was for our situation since he wasn't sure how much time I needed before agreeing to explore possibilities with him. He also wondered if it was now inappropriate to request time alone with me. I responded that just as he was free to ask, I was free to refuse.

It took him only two days before he sent me an invitation for dinner, meditation, and some sketching at his place. I wasn't comfortable with the dining portion of the invitation but had no qualms about drawing or meditating with him.

We settled on Wednesday evening, which gave me ample opportunity to examine my motives and cancel if necessary. Yet, I never did. Instead, my anticipation for our soirée grew. I even considered joining him for dinner. On Wednesday morning we passed each other in a hallway, and he handed me a semi-detailed map he'd drawn that directed me from the school to his apartment. Truthfully, the map was quite rudimentary, but the mere fact that he took time to create something for me was touching.

He was not at the west gate of his apartment complex when I arrived late. I felt a bit anxious but knew he would appear at any moment. After standing around the entrance for a few minutes, I did briefly consider the possibility that I was being stood up. I remembered to breathe: a deep inhalation and a long exhalation.

Had I spoken Mandarin, I could have asked one of the security guards for his building number. Besides his features and physique, this man's complexion made him stand out in the city. I imagined it was the same within the Guoao Tiandi community.

When the uniformed men offered me a seat inside the tiny guard house, I thought they were showing me preferential treatment since I too stood out from the individuals entering and exiting the apartment complex. However, my load, a rucksack and a yoga mat, was not heavy enough to warrant me sitting. Besides, the trees that were planted alongside the sequestering fence captured my attention because of the intravenous-like plastic sacs that were attached to each one. I presumed the liquid was offering them nourishment, but I wondered why the nutrients and water they absorbed naturally through their roots weren't enough.

Maybe some trees, much like some people, needed more than what nature provided. Sensing that I was being watched, I stopped myself from hugging or even touching any of them.

When he appeared, he smiled and said that he was worried that I had changed my mind. It turned out he had been waiting for me at the west gate, but when I didn't show up, he decided to walk down the street and meet me at the corner. I admitted that, because I departed from my apartment almost a half an hour after messaging him that I was leaving, I decided to take a taxi right to the gate. He laughed as I confessed to having a problem with being on time. I still apologized even though he smiled and shrugged off my tardiness and the confusion it caused.

Stepping into his apartment, I was greeted by a fresh and slightly medicinal scent. I didn't know what I was expecting to smell, but it wasn't rosemary. He pointed to the large dome-shaped aroma diffuser on the coffee table that was projecting a steady stream of mist and said there was smaller one on the nightstand in his bedroom. The scent conjured memories of the women's retreat I attended in England when I was battling the demons of depression. Aromatherapy had been an integral element of that weekend filled with workshops and meditation.

The ambient sounds of outside didn't seem to penetrate the walls and windows of his spacious apartment. Inside, there were no paintings or decorative trinkets, not even a plant. I wondered how a man with tremendous effervescence could live in such monotony. In his living room was a dark grey L-shaped sofa that could comfortably seat six.

He told me that he hardly ever sat on it because he preferred to be on his meditation mat and cushion, which were on the floor facing the coffee table. When he wasn't there sitting crossed-legged, he was doing *asanas* on his yoga mat, which was rolled out by the sizable windows overlooking a decent view of the sea. He conceded that the pulp mill across the street did ruin the view.

I smiled when he told me how perfect life would be if the mill was magically replaced by a rainforest. The way his face lit up when imagining Amazonian trees populating his field of vision was endearing. I felt to ask him about the trees outside his gated community — trees that needed more than what nature provided — but didn't want to interrupt the mental journey he was taking into the wild.

Sitting on the sofa, I reluctantly handed over my sketch book, after much prodding. It was always nerve-wracking to have another person observe my work, especially when the person also drew. Though his feedback was flattering, I sensed that he might have been withholding criticism as he sifted through the pages. When I pressed him for a more visceral reaction, he raved about the boldness of my lines and my shading techniques.

After looking at the final piece, a portrait of my mother, he told me I should think less about my strokes and simply draw. I'm not sure why, but his suggestion stunned me a little. Picking up on my discomfort, he maintained that it was a beautiful portrait before cautiously alluding to what he believed was my self-doubt.

My relationship with my mother was uneasy. I was not her first or last child. I was, nonetheless, the only child she had with my father, a man almost twenty years older and who was once a geography teacher at her school. When her boyfriend got her pregnant during the last year of high school, Dad offered the kind of financial support her family could not. They were strictly friends for several years, until a series of events led to them living together. I was conceived a few months after the end of Apartheid. Under

Apartheid, my birth and their marriage would have been illegal. It was not love but rather a sense of honour and tradition that propelled them to the altar of an Anglican church in Johannesburg months before I was to enter the world. A week after my fourth birthday, mom gave birth to a baby boy whose father was not mine. Soon after, I was on a plane with Dad heading to England.

Growing up without my mother was not ideal, but that was all I knew. Over the years, I would overhear dad telling his brother, my favourite uncle, about some of her questionable behaviour, which only added to my growing resentment toward my mother. I was Dad's universe, yet at times I wanted her also to feel that way about me or at least not be fine with her daughter living so far away.

When I was twelve, dad got too sick to care for me. I was sent to back to South Africa to live with my mother and my brothers. Numerous times, mom told me how exciting it was to be reunited with me, but her actions showed otherwise. She worked long shifts that often began in the late afternoon and ended in the late hours after my siblings and I went to bed. And because I was the only girl in the house, I was expected to do most, if not all, of the cooking and cleaning in my mother's absence.

Then there were the parties that my mother hosted at our home. Although I enjoyed the music and the alcohol I secretly consumed, there were guests present that I shouldn't have been exposed to.

Dad would have never let anyone harm me, but my mother was too preoccupied with her own wants and needs to worry about shielding her teenage daughter from the vultures. A few years before I was to graduate from secondary school, I found out she used the money that dad's brother was sending for my school fees to buy a new car. Even more disturbing was watching her argue for a larger portion of dad's estate after he died. She had taken so much from my father when he was alive. How could she still want to take in his death?

I was intrigued by his observation and wondered if he had any notions about my relationship with the subject of my portrait. I couldn't bring myself to ask for fear he'd think I was a spiteful daughter. An uncomfortable hush settled around us. Gently, he closed my sketch book and placed it nearby on the coffee table.

"Let's draw," he said.

"What? No, wait. Show me your sketches first."

While promising to comply, he made one stipulation: I had to start with his most recent piece. Although I found his requirement a bit odd, I accepted. He rose to his feet, holding his sketch book with two hands above his forehead as if it was a sacred artifact. Bowing to one knee, he slowly placed it on my lap as I jokingly called him a certified lunatic. Rather than return to his meditation cushion, he sat next to me on the sofa and dramatically announced that he was prepared to hear whatever criticism I had of his work.

Her hair was a cloud of dark, kinky curls. She had a smooth forehead and slightly angled eyebrows that framed penetrating eyes. Her nose was delicately straight, and her nostrils were small. The soft contours of her cheeks dispelled any notion of her being underweight. Thin but meticulously shaped lips made her closed mouth desirable. Her chin pointed down to an elegant neck adorned with an African necklace that matched her earrings. She carried high her strength, beauty, and serenity—qualities I prayed were within me. Gazing at how he captured her, I struggled to find words to describe my appreciation and surprise.

"I don't know what to say," I murmured.

"You like it?"

"I do. It's soooo, like wow, I wasn't expecting that."

I was curious to know what it was about me that inspired his depiction but before the words could leave my mouth, he kissed me.

Despite kissing him back, I was terrified. We paused for a few breaths. He looked longingly into my eyes, leaving no doubt about what he wanted. In that moment, I no longer saw the man I meditated with on the beach and conversed with about the vibrancy of life and the need to bring more awareness into our daily activities. I no longer saw the man who seemed interested in engaging my soul through the sharing of art. Looking at me were the eyes of every man who had ever desired me.

Even with his tongue deep in my mouth and his hands aggressively stroking my back, there was opportunity for me to stop. But I knew men like him hated stopping, and their eyes made that clear. Over the years, I convinced myself that surrendering to their sexual desires was wiser than rejecting them and then enduring a situation that had the potential to become menacing. Although my instincts confirmed he wouldn't harm me, this knowing was overshadowed by his intense stare. If only I could have truly seen and sensed him, while clothes were being removed and wants were being expressed, I would have felt safe resisting.

He noticed the blood while I was in the bathroom deciding whether I wanted to sleep in his apartment or mine. When I returned to the bedroom and the bright lights revealed faint crimson smudges on the bedsheet, I was mortified. My period couldn't have come at a worst time. I wished I was invisible; I wanted the earth to swallow me up. Instead, there I was standing in the nude apologizing and feeling especially guilty for having soiled his only clean bedsheet.

He laughed it off and told me that it would take a lot more to upset or repel him. I wanted to stay with him, but I was worried about my flow completely ruining his bedsheet during the night. With ease, he grabbed a towel from his dresser and placed it on one side of the bed.

"Now don't roll off of it," he said, pretending to inspect the edges of the spread cloth with fastidious attention. "I don't want to wake up with blood on me."

His playfulness lessened the embarrassment I felt and calmed much of the anxiety I had about staying. He offered me a t-shirt and, when I accepted, he added that I no longer had any reason to leave. I enjoyed his confidence, although he was wrong. I should have returned home, but I chose to ignore the reasons why. Ignoring my gut instinct had become one of my worst habits; as I lay down next to him, I showed no signs of breaking it.

Waking up alone was no surprise. I knew he got out of bed at five a.m. on weekdays to do yoga, meditate and then draw, all before eating breakfast and getting ready for work. Still, as I rolled over onto my back, I wondered what would possess him to stick to his stringent routine after sleeping for no more than five hours.

I began to feel guilty for idling in his bed hoping that dawn would miraculously be delayed. It was an urge to use the bathroom that finally propelled me to my feet and out of the bedroom. Before relieving myself, I peeked into the dark living room where he lay in *Savasana*, Corpse Pose, on his yoga mat. I admired how his body looked free of tension. The longer I observed him, the more my feelings of admiration mutated into envy.

I had no problem with the balancing, bending, and twisting poses, but struggled with *Savasana*. It was a fact I reluctantly acknowledged but withheld from others, especially him. If he knew that I couldn't enjoy the state of active relaxation, he would, out of concern, ask a million questions trying to arrive at the root of my problem. Not wanting to disturb his stillness and not sure of how long he was going to lie there, I tiptoed into the bathroom. Even with the door closed, I worried that the sound of the flushing might reach his ears.

As I brushed my teeth with the toothbrush he gave me before going to bed, I stared at myself in his mirror, asking why there was no impulse to scurry out of his apartment. My reflection answered with a smile. It was the kind of smile that resulted from overflowing happiness in what life was giving me. Frustrated with her sudden amnesia – case in point: her recent breakup and a budding connection with Steve – I ordered her to leave. Slyly, she talked about staying for breakfast and possibly taking a shower. I got her to stop rambling and instead to breathe; a deep inhalation and a long exhalation. Still, she insisted on rejecting my reasons for leaving. She argued that being sensible would have meant returning to my apartment last night rather than running off the morning after.

When I stepped out of the bathroom, he was in the kitchen at the water dispenser, filling up a tall glass. Entering the kitchen, I wished him a good morning. He wished me the same as he dropped a thick slice of lemon into the water before offering me the glass. I thanked him. He chuckled at my bashfulness and told me it was essential to start the day with a cleanse.

Our eyes met. Holding his gaze, I noticed for the first time just how similar the shade of his brown pupils was to my own. They observed me with a gentleness and curiosity that erased whatever anxiety remained in my body. I basked in the warmth of his smile. When he pulled me into his arms and kissed me, I was already yearning for his touch and the thrust of his body into mine.

We ate oatmeal topped with bananas and hemp seeds for breakfast. I enjoyed the nutritious meal but when he told me that he ate the cereal daily, I couldn't understand how the sight of it didn't cause any repulsion.

"Oatmeal really became my thing when my dad told me that horses ate it," he explained. "I figured if such a powerful and majestic creature could thrive off oats, so could I."

As we sat side by side, crossed-legged on the sofa, he revealed that as a teen he read the entire series of *The Black Stallion* by Walter Farley and watched every episode of *The Adventures of the Black Stallion*. I was unfamiliar with the books and the television show, but his enthusiasm raised my interest.

I told him that I identified most with cats because of their independent and observant nature.

Grinning, he admitted that cats used to make him feel uncomfortable because of their uncanny ability to see through human phoniness.

I had to ask. "Are you a phony?"

His laugh was a burst of bright sound.

"Trust me," he said, smiling, "You and I are genuine fakes."

"Really?" I found the remark puzzling, so I turned to look directly at him. "What do you mean?"

He looked pensive for a spell, as if conjuring the right words.

"It's hard to explain but we just are."

With that, he went silent.

Later that morning, the most pleasant thoughts of him flooded my mind as I sat at my desk, avoiding any serious work. I sought to describe my inner happenings. What began as a few words mushroomed into an eight-line poem filled with the vulnerability and longing found in Emily Dickinson's and Maya Angelou's writings. I didn't recognize this young woman who meticulously folded her poem into a miniature rectangle and dropped it off on his desk while he was teaching. I didn't recognize the way she returned to her office to daydream about him until it was time for lunch.

When he messaged me, I was finishing up the food on my tray. "I love the poem," he wrote. "Please keep writing." Perhaps heartened by my words, his next text came seconds later: "I want us to spend every night together."

I went back to his apartment that evening after a post-workout shower and meal. He kissed me the moment I stepped through the door.

"I could barely wait for you to get here," he said. His sketch pad was opened with a graphite pencil on the page.

"Oh nooooo, what are we gonna do?" he asked, in a light-hearted manner when I told him that I forgot my pad in my bedroom.

"You can keep drawing," I suggested as I pulled out a book from my rucksack, "I'll just read."

From his expression, I would have thought I made the most ridiculous statement.

"What?" I asked with a nervous giggle.

"Don't you know there's nothing else in the world I'd rather do than to hold and kiss you?"

His words and the way he looked at me made me feel weightless. We reclined on his sofa and debriefed one another on our day. I was asking him about his supper when he suddenly divulged that it had been more than a decade since he felt excited about a relationship. I dismissed his words as ardent flattery because something in me didn't want to believe he was being sincere. What he saw in me I couldn't see nor could I touch. However, I kissed him and told him that he was becoming my world.

In the morning, I got out of bed a few minutes after him. We brushed our teeth together, and he prepared two glasses of hot lemon water before we meditated.

He set the timer for thirty minutes, but it felt like an hour. My mind would not settle. My thoughts kept wandering away from my breathing. Finally, the ringing of a gong on his phone signaled the end of the session, which was followed by him chanting *om* three times. I welcomed the serenity; it was as tangible as the cushion beneath my bottom.

It brought back memories from that women's retreat my aunt sent me to when I was battling the demons of depression after Dad's passing. There, in that space with those women and under the guidance of a compassionate facilitator, I experienced the most powerful sensation I had ever felt: tranquility.

As we sat in silence, I thought about sharing an affirmation that we could repeat several times. Repeating affirmations was a part of my morning routine but seamlessly he began a *metta* meditation. He first asked that we focus our attention on ourselves by repeating: "May I be happy, may I be safe, may I be healthy, and may I be at peace." Next, we sent loving kindness to a loved one, then to a person we barely know but see regularly, followed by an individual with whom we have a tension-filled relationship.

I wasn't sure if he knew that I was struggling to wish my mom happiness, safety, health, and peace, but he paused and suggested that we spend a bit more time reflecting on the person we don't get on with. After a few moments, my heart did soften a little. Still, I wasn't sure I succeeded in sending her loving kindness. We ended the meditation by focusing on all beings which was much easier for me to do.

While I showered, he prepared a bowl of oatmeal with walnuts and raisins for himself and a bowl of muesli with yogurt for me. He did this as he listened to a podcast about the recent rise of the extreme right in France. If we had never discussed his appreciation for radio documentaries and public lectures, I might have thought he was trying to show off his intellectual competence, especially considering the vast music library on his laptop.

I didn't know anyone else who cared to contemplate the history of intolerance and discrimination in France at six in the morning. His inquisitiveness about the world never seemed to wane. So immersed he was, between his blunt comments and rhetorical questions, that I felt as though he was in conversation with the podcast. He looked over at me – visibly concerned that I was feeling bored or possibly neglected seated next to him on the sofa – and asked if I would rather listen to some music. I smiled and told him only if he promised to maintain the same fiery engagement.

Before he went into the bathroom, I offered to iron his pants and shirt. He initially refused but after I insisted, he accepted. I got a great deal of satisfaction from pressing his clothes. Up until that point, I couldn't count one act of service that I had done for him.

Minutes later while I brushed my hair and he got dressed, he opened up about his reticence to accept help from a love interest.

"I've been single for so long," he said, his tone reflective. "I'm not used to any of this."

Before I could respond, he quickly added that he wasn't sure about the nature of our relationship, but he was happy to wake up next to me and to have me be part of his morning. I didn't know whether to believe him when he first said it: that my presence was a new experience. "Rewarding" was also how he described it. His words made me feel special and, being no different from the rest of humankind, I really wanted to feel special.

I spent the following two nights at his place, followed by one in my apartment where I video chatted with my favourite uncle and Steve.

Listening to Dad's brother rant about his ongoing divorce and the "uneducated" who voted for Brexit filled me with a sense of familiarity; so did conversing with Steve about a slew of quirky topics, like fake symbolism and hypothetical friendships with famous dead people.

Their English wit and sarcasm and their creative flair for profanity stabilized my inner world. There was a level of comfort that existed with them that, naturally, I had yet to attain with this new man in my life. Whether it was his tireless pursuit of truth or his obsession with being present and living a life free of vices, I felt nervous around him. It was nothing crippling, but it was noticeable in the way I tended to censor my words and actions. Still, I joyously returned to his place the following night because, after all, nobody is fully themselves in the early stages of a romance. And more importantly, the end of my period signaled I could have him again.

My shoes were still on when we began kissing. There was urgency, a hankering, in how we removed each other's clothes as we made our way into the bedroom; palms pressed against flesh and our mouths and tongues passionately engaged. We indulged in one another in ways that left us sweaty, exhausted, and with our skin humming.

In the morning, we found ourselves entangled with even more fervour. In our conjoining, steeped in the understanding that to truly receive pleasure one had to give pleasure, we became undone. Declarations like "I love you" were uttered more than once as were words that had the power to ameliorate or annihilate one's fabricated identity— promises that revealed our fear of life's transient nature. After such an unfiltered communion, somehow, we were able to return to our normal states of being.

We managed to get out of bed to meditate, albeit later than usual. For the first time, he followed me and repeated my affirmation about love and kindness being the answer in all situations. His voice echoed mine as I emphasized how eternally thankful I was for this truth that I practiced daily.

He lamented about having to rush off to school on my day off knowing I was headed back to bed where, ideally, he could have been joining me. I did want to sleep, but I longed first for more of his manliness. Of course, I made no mention of this but rather smiled and wished him a good day. I was told there was enough food in the fridge to sustain me for several days. And with that, he expressed his own desire: to see my beautiful face when he returned around five.

"I think somebody's being a genuine fake," I replied playfully.

He chuckled. "You're right, but this genuine fake really wants to wake up next to you every day."

Naturally, I didn't believe him, but when he pulled out a key from his book bag and offered it to me, I thought differently.

"You don't have to take it if you don't want it."

He made it clear that the key wasn't some spontaneous response to my disbelief. I'm not sure if my face emoted deep unease, but he continued to explain his offering like someone with great inquietude until I grabbed the key from his hand and kissed him.

I'm not certain why I accepted it. I had come to China to immerse into solitude and discover new dimensions of myself. He was completely unaware of my growing reliance on the nourishment I received by being with him; that I was certain of.

Soon, I was sleeping at his apartment four to five times a week. He told me how pleased he was to see my soap bar, shampoo bottle, and toothbrush case in the bathroom along with my hair wrap tucked underneath the pillow on the right side of his bed. Folded tightly on a chair in the bedroom, I left a few tops, panties, and socks, all of which thrilled him.

He made me feel wanted, a flattering and frightening sensation. To know that I was desirable to such a fascinating and unique man — someone who could choose to be with anyone far more remarkable — was unquestionably gratifying. At the same time, when I was with him, never did I sense that he was craving or even considering someone else. On more than one occasion he had told me that he was all mine. I could only express that same sentiment when he was pleasing me in bed. And equally terrifying was my growing apprehension whenever he wondered aloud why I couldn't spend all my nights with him.

I had told him about my plans to focus on drawing, working out, and completing an online class. One evening, I listed all my goals for the year which he wrote down on a brown notepad. Next, I wrote down his. His list had noticeably fewer than mine. Either he didn't feel comfortable disclosing all his plans, or he simply didn't have as many as I did. Part of me worried that he thought I was trying to prove something by being so ambitious.

I merely wanted my first year in China to be productive. After graduating high school, I had worked countless hours as an Avon representative in Johannesburg and then when I moved back to Kettlewell I waited tables or bartended. As an adult, the only accomplishment I cared to mention was my completion of the *Camino de Santiago*. Sadly, I had accumulated more problems than accomplishments. And yes, perhaps labeling my struggles as problems was a mistake, but all I knew was that I wanted to feel accomplished, and China was where that would happen.

In October, during the country's National Holiday I went to Qingdao to climb Mount Lao with Steve. The plan for us to spend the three or four days together had been hatched before I was swept up in a whirlwind relationship.

Steve knew about the man in my life, but I couldn't bring myself to divulge more than one or two details to him about Steve. What he knew was that I was going to do some hiking with a friend I made through the Immerteach program. He didn't know about the kiss Steve and I had shared in Beijing and how the defiant part of me that had blossomed in South Africa wanted another. If I was being honest, there was that moment on our way down the mountain when I thought he would press his lips hard against mine. Instead, we shared an awkward goodbye where he inadvertently walked away with my phone. I had placed it in his small backpack before we trekked up the mountain.

Not until I had returned to my hotel room did I realize what happened to my phone. I didn't know Steve's number and couldn't remember the name of his hostel or the part of the city where it was located. We had intended to meet up the following day but had not solidified plans. As much as I valued having a phone, I was filled with an incredible sense of independence without it. I would later learn that he, the man I was involved with, had sent me several voice messages the morning of my hike with Steve.

Knowing that I had a solid reason for not responding to him or anyone else, I allowed myself to be absorbed by the architectural feats of the historical mansions that were tucked inside a scenic area near my hotel. A single species of tree lined each street. And in the southern section of the grounds, a pristine beach offered the sort of serenity that my camera couldn't quite capture. For three days, I explored the terrain and did lots of sketching and journaling. I was alone and unbelievably content.

On my last morning at the hotel, I was in the lobby — checking out and leaving my backpack behind the front desk, so I could go out and enjoy my last day before a late-afternoon bus ride back to Yantai — when Steve appeared with my phone. He had searched almost every hotel on the coast and remarkably didn't seem at all aggravated. We had lunch and went for a long walk before returning to my hotel where we hugged and said our goodbyes. I wasn't looking for intimacy, and I don't believe he was either. We had developed an understanding and that was far more precious.

His flight from Shanghai was landing at a little after six o'clock, which would mean he'd be entering the apartment any time after seven. Standing in his kitchen, I was happily preparing a kidney bean and spinach stir fry with oven-baked sweet potato chips for dinner, all the while listening to a Ted Talk about time and space. Phyllis had suggested that I get a bottle of wine to celebrate what was going to be our first night together after one week apart.

I sent his friend Kyle a message.

"Should I go with red or white?"

"Red," Kyle texted back. "White wine would need to be chilled and he rarely puts anything cold in his body."

It was gratifying to put such effort and planning into our evening. Admittedly, guilt might have been the main catalyst. I felt bad for having him worry about me during his holiday when I hadn't considered him until my return to Yantai.

The moment he walked through the door, I pounced on him. With his backpack still on, we got reacquainted through a fiery exchange of kisses and caresses. Being in his arms again was so stimulating I almost forgot about the stir fry. He followed me into the kitchen. Instead of thanking me for cooking a meal, he playfully chided me for using the pot from the rice cooker to steam the spinach. As he left my side, perhaps out of a sense of obligation he told me that the food looked good. It felt like an afterthought. I tried not to let his lack of enthusiasm for the meal bother me, but it did. It seemed like the perfect time to open the bottle of wine, but when he returned to the kitchen, he told me he was only wanting one thing.

He lifted me onto the counter, pulled down my shorts, and lowered himself to place his face in between my legs. Breath tickled my thighs. Pressing his tongue into my warm and wet center while rubbing the sensitive flesh above it, he transported me to a realm of sublime arousal. The wooden spoon I was holding fell from my hand as I leaned back against the wall and firmly gripped the edge of the counter. My loud moans turned into pleas for him to continue. We moved from the kitchen to the dining table where he gave me all of himself with the kind of ferocity I was craving. It wasn't long before we were up against the wall, then on the floor, before coming together on the bed in the guest room.

The following morning after he meditated alone, because I was too tired to join him, we continued where we had left off. This time, since we both had to be at work and time was thinning, our lovemaking was even more direct and spirited.

I spent the next two nights in my apartment trying to regain that sense of freedom and purpose I had experienced during those three days I spent alone in Qingdao. Despite claiming to understand, he continued to send messages pleading with me to come over. I stayed with him on Wednesday night but not on Thursday and Friday.

In a conversation with Dad's brother, I was reminded not to forget about the goals I had set for myself right before coming to China. Uncle seemed genuinely supportive of the relationship I found myself in, but he was concerned about me getting lost in it.

On Saturday evening after my day of teaching, we went for dinner at a Thai restaurant to celebrate our month together. I don't know if he could sense that something had shifted, but throughout our meal he was overly chatty, even comical. He appeared almost desperate to draw laughter out of me. To be honest, his utterances served only to stall what was happening. I could have steered us into more serious conversation, but when I tried later that night at his place, I folded and allowed myself to be redirected into watching a movie not of my choosing.

I left his place in the morning to go to work and later returned before the sun went down. He asked me what was wrong as soon as he saw my face. I told him the kids were exhausting and that working on weekends was starting to irritate me.

This was true, but it probably wasn't what he saw in my eyes. As I walked across the living room, he asked again.

"Can you just give me a bit of time to organize my thoughts?" I asked, feeling an uneasiness rising.

"Okay."

I could sense his eyes on me as I paced around him. For different reasons, we both chose to avoid words. Slowing down at his sizable windows, I looked out and tried to imagine the rainforest that he wished was there. There were other things I tried to imagine but simply couldn't.

"I want some watermelon. You want some watermelon, right?"

He turned and walked into the kitchen without waiting for my answer.

I told him that I wanted to do some exercise before expressing myself. He proposed that we go for a run, pointing out that it was something we talked about doing on many occasions but never did. I thought about accepting but then imagined myself running to the point of exhaustion where collapsing on the beach and enjoying the sea breeze would become more appealing.

"I'll just do some *asanas.*"

Stepping onto his yoga mat, I decided to do a bit of stretching. From the kitchen where he was cutting a watermelon, he watched me do a few Warrior poses, a Shoulder stand, and a Bridge. I was doing a hip-opening exercise when he rejoined me in the living room. Despite my efforts to relax and stay present, anxiety gripped me.

Observing my agitation, he forced a smile.

"You'll feel much better when you release whatever it is you're holding," he offered.

Fidgeting on the sofa, I told him I needed time and space to figure myself out.

"And I just can't do that while I'm with you," I said, as gently as I could express.

He bit his bottom lip and grimaced but didn't say a word. What I told him next, I would later not remember. All I knew was that he was in pain and it was my fault. It didn't matter how much I stressed the depth of my feelings for him, or that I believed he would be the perfect guy for me in a few years once I worked on myself. Nor did it matter that I apologized for letting us become more than I could manage. And my insistence that I never intended to cause any grief didn't help.

When he finally did speak, his voice was low and stark. He conceded that it was probably not wise to invest so much of himself into our relationship. If he had maintained a more casual or indifferent attitude towards me, my announcement would not have been so painful, he reasoned. Sitting next to me on the sofa, he wouldn't glance over as he seemed to labour through his thoughts.

Before retreating to the bedroom, he pledged to return to his former ways as a single man on the prowl. His tone and his demeanour were unrecognizable.

Several minutes passed as I sat alone and let his words wash over me. I finally rose to my feet and walked into the bathroom to collect my belongings. Because I had covertly begun taking my clothing out of his apartment in the previous week, all I had to gather from his bedroom were two pairs of socks and a t-shirt. I quietly retrieved my items. He lay motionless on his stomach across his bed, his face hidden in his pillow.

On my way out, I placed his house key on the coffee table, squeezed a pair of canvas shoes into my rucksack, and put on my running shoes at the door.

Even with his bedroom door partially closed, I could hear weeping muffled by a pillow. To know that I had hurt a man to the point of tears was soul-crushing. Unable to control my streaming tears, I rushed out of the apartment, ashamed and unsure.

With his office less than ten meters from mine, not a day went by that I didn't glimpse him or hear his orotund voice resonating down the hallway. I was relieved that he didn't ignore me outright or avoid walking into places he knew I would be. Still, I had to admit it did pain me to realize that after a month of intimate sharing, our communication was now reduced to variations of "hello" and "bye."

When Phyllis asked if I was grappling with regret, I told her with as much pride as I could summon that my decision to end the relationship was a rare act of self-love. I sensed she wanted to believe me, but I'm not sure she did. Examining my sadness, I too had difficulty convincing myself that I was free of regret.

Free from his embrace, I dedicated myself to drawing, reading, and learning Chinese. I also used social media to set up a women's group that included teachers and other members of school staff. It was great having a space for us to connect deeply and truly support one another. By keeping busy, I avoided sitting around faulting myself for the relationship's failure. Not giving into blame granted me traces of peace, but I was still far removed from living in that beautiful state he appeared to abide in.

The voice that tormented me when I was growing up, that badgered me to a point of depression after my dad's passing, was still boldly ingraining its language of fear.

At the women's retreat in the UK, I had learned how to question the voice's sincerity and how to reject its typically dreadful judgment. On the good nights, I followed this technique until the chatter was silenced or hardly audible. But then there were nights where it wouldn't be denied, and I wound up believing whatever it said about me. These were bad nights; they produced the most unpleasant sensations made worse by the liquor I consumed to self-medicate.

Steve was the only person I told about my bad nights. Phyllis and another girlfriend knew of my past and, of course, the relationship I recently ended, but I never felt comfortable discussing my nights of suffering with them. Steve would listen without trying to fix me, which is something I didn't think my girlfriends were capable of doing. Also, he had spent years numbing himself with drugs, both legal and illegal, and now years later he still identified as an abuser. His philosophy resonated with me: *All things have a crack for light to enter.* We often spoke at length about our own fractures and wondered how much light they could host.

From my conversations with Steve and Dad's brother — and from my meditation practice, readings, and daily observations — my understanding of life's imperfections was deepening. I came to accept that living would most often be messy. It was this acceptance that prompted me to send him a message admitting a natural truth: I missed him. The combination of having seen him recently at a colleague's birthday dinner — he had worn a shirt that accentuated his lean torso — and the glasses of South African wine I gulped might have also contributed to my late-night brazenness.

Almost immediately, he replied: "I miss you too." We sent messages back and forth before he asked if he could call.

We talked and, with much laughter, we revisited our awkward interaction at that colleague's birthday dinner. This was followed by confessions usually reserved for diaries. To my surprise, I didn't hear any resentment or pain in his voice. Well, not until he announced that his love for me had not changed. When I struggled to respond, he told me that he shouldn't have made the revelation since I had probably moved on.

"I'm scared."

It was the truth and felt good to speak it.

"Scared?"

"Yeah, I'm afraid of losing myself in you," I answered, pausing to formulate my next thought. "There's still a few more things about me that I need to sort out."

With that, I hoped he understood why I wasn't with him. He didn't press for details, but he did ask why I wouldn't let him help me sort through my difficulties. I dismissed his offer by saying that I could manage it on my own.

"But I'm offering you my hand," he said.

The affection in his tone was loud and clear.

"Why do you keep slapping it away, I just wanna help you."

Feeling slightly cornered, I rebuked him.

"No man ever wants to just help me," I said bluntly. "You guys always want something in return."

He tried to deny it, but I cut him off to ask, "Tell me, what do you want from me?"

"Your love."

He responded so calmly and with such certainty, I had no reason to doubt him.

By the end of what had become our longest phone conversation ever, and our first since that dramatic Sunday in October, I agreed to grab his hand and let him guide me out of my own storms. I even agreed to meet him the following evening for dinner.

November's end was approaching. Autumn's cool sea breeze had changed into gushing winds carrying icy sea air. Most people I saw outside were wearing winter coats. Not him. He did however have on a wool hat and gloves when I met him outside the Korean restaurant. Immediately he noticed that I wasn't wearing any winter clothing.

"Did you walk here? Why didn't you just take a taxi?"

Mildly bothered by his questions, which sounded more like judgment, I barely smiled.

"It was fine, I'm not cold," I said.

I could have used an extra layer of clothing, but I wasn't going to admit it. The same way I didn't care to let him know that I had been regretting showing him some of my tattoos. After our second or third time together, he'd inquired about their meanings. Both times, his curiosity seemed feigned to cover his criticism. It was judgment that hit me right where my pride and independence met. Conceivably sensing what lay beneath my forced smile, he quickly backpedaled with a presumption that it was clever to delay donning heavier clothing to toughen up the skin. He suggested that a person with tough skin coped far better during the cold months than someone whose skin was paper-thin.

Throughout dinner, our exchange was pleasant and at times overtly flirtatious. The restaurant played the classics by Boyz II Men, Brian McKnight, and Joe. Korean R&B was also on their playlist.

The music and our cozy booth in the virtually empty restaurant ripened the conditions for rediscovery. When he reached for my hand, I offered it to him as willingly as the stars offer light to the night sky. He observed and caressed it as if he had never seen or held it before. Leaning over the table, we kissed with a longing that memorialized the moment. Before the bill was paid and possibly even before the *bibimbap* and *kimchi* pancakes were served. I predictably fooled myself into believing my night would end with me at home in my room and on the phone with Steve.

When the alarm on my phone roused me from sleep, I rolled onto my back dreading every single class I was scheduled to teach. Under my breath, I chided Sunday morning for its abrupt arrival and for ignoring my pleas to hold off for five, maybe six, hours. Not having to work, he was able to disrupt my half-hearted attempts to get dressed and leave the bedroom. Although my eyes were bleary, the sight of his naked body fueled a craving that I asked him to satisfy.

At lunch, he surprised me by bringing me a container of his hearty squash soup.

With my apartment less than a five-minute walk from the school gate, I was tempted to invite him over for a midday affair. However, I thought about the messy living room that my roommate was supposed to clean; empty bottles of beer were lined up on the kitchen floor next to the rubbish basket. I changed my mind and opted not to disturb his grocery shopping.

When I got home, I took a nap. Later, I woke up with every intention to visit him after making something to eat. Then Steve called.

He had just finished reading the book about nomadic life that I raved about for days when we first met in Beijing. Inspired, we discussed the advantages of living with no strong attachment to one place. And with the bulk of the story set in Mumbai, we imagined how life-changing it would be to backpack around India for a few months.

Steve and I had never been to the country described as God's raw land. It didn't take long before we considered making the trip together. Spending our days discovering the land where humanity displayed itself in a dizzying explosion of cultures, religions, and languages was a shared fantasy, a possible reality. We envisioned dedicating our nights to experiencing whatever states of being arose. When we ran out of words and finally succumbed to fatigue, it was after midnight.

The next day, I had some explaining to do. When I texted back that my conversation with Steve kept me away, he replied with a confused face emoji. Hoping to give him some more context, I called.

"With Steve, I don't know, we were just friends," I explained, trying to be as delicate as possible. "But over time the seeds of our friendship have blossomed and now I have feelings for him."

There was a tense pause.

"Did anything happen between you two when you met up in Qingdao?"

His voice was calm.

"I've never cheated. Steve has been nothing but respectful of my choice to be in a relationship with you."

He didn't seem convinced. And apart from my earnest words, I had no proof to offer.

"What are you going to do?"

"I really don't know. I'm so confused."

It was all I could say.

Phyllis believed that Steve was a better match because he was closer in age and at a similar place in life. She also figured it would be wise for me to continue along the path of self-cultivation without being romantically linked to anyone. I appreciated her opinions, yet I found myself undressing for him one night and on the phone with Steve the next, musing about love's manifestations. This went on until the following weekend when he asked if I was ever going to choose between him and Steve. I told him that I was torn and needed more time. In a roundabout way, he expressed his disappointment in my failure to realize that I wanted to be with him. I suggested that we just focus on enjoying another evening together, but he pressed for answers. Finally, out of frustration, I said, "I can't make up my mind because I love him. Alright?" Realizing the blow that I levelled, I apologized at once. With his eyes closed, perhaps searching for the well of composure within, he remained even-tempered as he asked me to leave.

I avoided him at work and presumed he was doing the same.
It saddened me to know that I had hurt him for a second time. Telling him that I loved Steve was thoughtless and totally unnecessary.

Only Steve needed to know, but I had yet to inform him, which was odd considering our friendship was founded on total disclosure. Maybe if I had told him, Julia, the brunette from New York, wouldn't have become such a fixture in his life.

He had met this woman through colleagues and lately we could hardly get through a conversation without him mentioning her. As delightful as she sounded, I kept wishing she would move out of the country or at least the city.

Steve was not the guy most women would flock to. He was not tall, muscular, or undeniably good-looking. In social settings like a bar, he was the quiet observer. His way of watching everyone and everything was imperceptible. Yet underneath his shy smile and awkwardness was a wealth of goodness. Steve rarely revealed this goodness to others which made me feel extremely special—that is, until Julia arrived in his world and got to feel special as well. For me, to have two souls find and take up space in my temperamental heart was a miraculous feat. It was this reality that made being alone pitiable.

I had my reservations about attending my work's Christmas banquet at an upscale hotel. There was little about the prospect I found appealing. Also, I knew that he would be there. Being in proximity to him would likely rehash the past.

It was Phyllis who managed to lure me to the event by emphasizing that she would be performing. The first time she graced the stage was for a Hula dance with her fellow kindergarten teachers. Less than half an hour later, she returned with a guitar and performed an acoustic cover of of Ed Sheeran's "Thinking Out Loud". Her soulful voice and masterful playing captivated the hall.

Standing only a few meters away from me, he appeared completely absorbed in the ballad, leading me to wonder if the lyrics brought back memories of us.

Toward the end of the staff showcase, Phyllis surprised me and everyone else by walking onto the stage during his choreographed dance number with Kyle. Her Beyoncé-esque moves added wonderfully to the comedy-filled routine, drawing laughter and cheers from the audience.

He was wearing his blue, fitted baseball cap, white tank-top, baggy jeans with a plaid shirt tied around his waist, and white runners. I generally don't like that sort of look, but the combination of his physique in that outfit and the way he moved effortlessly to the music aroused me. He had me blushing.

After, Phyllis said that she and a few other colleagues would be leaving once the showcase ended. I had planned to step out with them until he and Kyle hijacked the sound system to play some infectious beats. They got a group of children, whose parents were teachers at the school, to dance with them. Other members of the school staff soon joined in. I quickly placed my glass of wine onto the nearest table so that the music could take full control of my body.

When a hotel employee announced that the hall would be closing, the party was moved upstairs to the swanky bar on the ground floor. To be dancing without him was agonizing. That inebriated brash voice in my head tried several times to persuade me to end our standoff and to simply reach for his hand. I soon wound up in the bathroom in front of the mirror having a dysfunctional conversation with my dazed reflection.

He was standing at the bar alone for possibly the first time all night. As I re-entered the lounge, he greeted me with a courteous smile. I had trouble containing my excitement when he called me over.

We chatted about how enjoyable the evening had been and how our colleagues seemed bent on keeping it going. I complimented him on his performance with Kyle and Phyllis. While I was effusing about Phyllis's contribution to their performance, he looked into my eyes with more clarity than I imagined was possible after all the wine and spirits had drunk.

He asked me why I was so fearful. I shrugged off his question by teasing that he was summoning the clouds when we were basking in sunshine. He responded by affirming that the sun's power could never be blocked by clouds then repeated the bit about me being fearful. He added that I was terrified of what we could become if I decided to dive. I maintained that he was mistaking my prudence for fear which was insulting and made me want to retreat. He insisted that I close my eyes, breathe deeply and declare what I wanted. Cheekily, I followed his instructions then said I wanted more wine. He grunted.

"Oh, and to dance with you," I blurted.

Offering me a sip from his glass, he pressed me to take the exercise seriously. I called him annoying; he retaliated by claiming that I was still terrified. If we weren't in the presence of colleagues, I would have slapped him. Instead, I harshly announced that I was returning to the dancefloor.

"Fine, run away. That's what you're good at."

"I'm not running," I retorted, forcing myself not to run down a list of unfavourable adjectives that described his behaviour.

"I have no desire to play your silly game." Before I could walk away, he laughed, asserting that I was the queen of playing games.
He emphatically launched into an abridged but highly colourful version of the key incidents marking our history. He spoke with the arrogance of a lawyer in possession of the extensive and irrefutable evidence that would render losing the case virtually impossible. It was enraging being called the queen of games only because, to a certain degree, it was true.

Fed up with his simplified retelling of the past, I asked in an unapologetically confrontational manner: "So what do you want from me?"

"Your heart," he declared without a second's hesitation.

"My heart's a mess," I replied, softening my voice. "You don't want it."

I tried to deter him with self-loathing, but he repeated his wish until a tear broke through my walls and I allowed myself to be held in his love. The words of the Sufi poet, Rumi, could not have been better exemplified in that moment: "Love is the bridge between you and everything."

We kept our reconnection secret for about a week. When I revealed us to my friends, they were all supportive except for Phyllis. She was uneasy about me becoming enamoured with him again. She believed I would slowly forget about the projects I had been working on since our breakup. Bluntly, she told me, "You have more work to do before being ready for everything that comes with love." She argued that before I entered his well-established world, I needed more time to develop my own.

What did please me was hearing that Kyle and some others he had informed were excited for us. They could have easily advised him to keep me at a distance, and maybe they would have been wise to do so.
Unless he was lying about their reactions, they had more faith in me than I had in myself. Unquestionably.

After three consecutive nights of the most passionate lovemaking we had ever shared, we discussed the areas in our relationship that needed more attention. In talking about our need for greater transparency, he suggested that we forgo sexual intimacy for a week to focus on communicating our truths in ways that we never had. I fully supported his desire to strengthen our foundation, but part of me did wonder why we had to sacrifice sex. The music we were making with our bodies covered a multitude of genres and lifted me to heights I didn't know existed. Couldn't we come up with a way to do both?

Before planting a kiss on his cheek, I told him "This is going to be great for us."

He then leaned in and kissed me deep in my mouth. As he drew back, we exhaled.

"Only sex is forbidden."

One night before falling asleep, I told him that the next day would have been Dad's sixty-third birthday. When he asked me how I would mark the day, I answered, "By asking him for forgiveness." With tears welling, I recounted the terrible habit I had developed of not returning most of my ailing dad's calls; it happened during my last years of high school and first year of working full-time.

"Talking to him became so damn hard," I said, my voice breaking. "I couldn't handle what the disease was doing to his voice and to his mind."

I wanted to believe that I never stopped loving Dad, but if that were truly the case, how could I have treated him so coldly? My crying was loud and uncontrollable.
He held me close without trying to remove me from the clutches of my regret.

Though sporadic in nature, the tears continued for several days. Most of them were for Dad who had died less than a month after I had returned to England. To the bewilderment of family and friends, I had returned to my bland desk job after receiving the news. Dad was gone, but I wasn't ready to let him go. I didn't begin to mourn him until I was at that women's retreat, away from the fallacies of my daily life. Two years later, I was in a foreign land still mourning.

Since leaving South Africa, I could count on one hand the number of times I spoke to my mother. I'm not certain what I wanted from her, but there great pain in accepting our profound disconnection. Instead of foolishly consuming alcohol to avoid these emotions, I bravely confided in him night after night. The way he listened and offered encouragement made me feel valued. As appreciative as I was of his love, there was that voice within that frequently reminded me of how undeserving I was. When I told him about its taunting nature, he confessed to dealing with his own voice. His insisted that he was incapable of fully satisfying a woman's wants and needs. Despite knowing the voice was a liar, he said he found himself believing it at times as I did. We agreed to support each other against the crippling ridicule and vowed to strike it with our truths.

"I want you to know that I'm all yours," I said, as we laid in bed. "I'm not going to mess it up this time."

Without saying a word, he jumped out of bed and walked out of the room.

He returned moments later walking slowly and deliberately with an exaggerated stiff posture; arms stretched out in front of him and palms facing up as if he were making an offering to the skies. Reverently, he knelt by the side of the bed I was on, without moving his arms or hands.

"Oh, my word!" I exclaimed, grinning uncontrollably at what sat in his open hand. "I was wondering how long you were going to make a girl wait."

He seemed to find my excitement gratifying, laughing aloud when I told him that all week the defiant part of me that I developed in South Africa had been contemplating stealing the key.

Since meeting him in August, I had spent hours upon hours researching and attempting to understand the meditation technique taught during a ten-day course he had described as life changing. My enthusiasm to attend the course waned after I'd broken his heart in October. Hoping to forget about him, I dove into a couple of self-help books, which brought on periods of deep reflection. Yet, whenever I thought about that course, the lying voice within discouraged me from registering. It suggested I was too fragile and too volatile to endure ten days of silence and stillness.

Being reunited with him and experiencing consecutive days of breakthroughs did however lead me to email a center in Myanmar that was offering the course. A week later, I was overjoyed when I opened my inbox and read the response. They granted me a spot in the session starting on the first Friday in February.

Hearing this, he was delighted to know that I would finally experience the meditation technique taught by the Buddha.

"The only sad part is I won't be able to meet up with you and Janice in Bali," I said, disappointment sedating me. While we had been apart, he and his long-time friend Janice, who was from his hometown, had planned a trip to Beijing, Bangkok, and Bali for the Chinese New Year. Initially, I declined his request to join them because I didn't want to be the proverbial third wheel. However, his insistence made me reconsider. I began looking at flights to Bali.

"This means I won't see you for almost a month," I concluded after counting the days on his calendar. The thought of spending that much time away from his embrace was distressing.

I moved the bulk of my clothes into the closet space he had cleared out for me in September. For months, he had kept the space free, hoping that I would return. The bathroom looked incredibly feminine with my skin and hair products scattered around the sink, along with my exfoliating bath gloves and flowery bottle of body wash in the shower. I stored my sketch pads and notebooks with quotes, affirmations, and random thoughts inside the empty drawers of his coffee table. In addition to the aloe vera I gave him, we went to a flower shop and bought three more plants. We rarely slept apart and even rarer were the mornings when we didn't eat breakfast together. In an intentional manner, our lives were becoming increasingly interwoven.

Yet sharing so much time with him had one major downside: I could no longer hide my most unpleasant traits. One afternoon, a few days after Christmas, I was sitting on the sofa watching a documentary about black holes while pressing a hot, wet rag into the right side of my neck to ease stiffness.

He was in the kitchen preparing lunch and making some lemon and honey tea to combat a cough that had been with me for a month and showed no sign of leaving. When the rag lost its warmth, I called out for him to come fetch it and put it back in boiling water. To avoid spilling any tea, he approached cautiously before gently placing the mug on the coffee table next to the laptop and asking if my neck was improving.

"Not really, no," I answered dryly as I handed him the rag without lifting my gaze from the computer screen. Though he didn't comment on my behaviour, I knew it bothered him – something I found satisfying. He went back into the kitchen and returned almost ten minutes later grinning and singing a Bob Marley song as he placed the steamy rag on the throbbing area of my neck. I didn't pause the documentary or thank him. Next thing I knew, I was coughing. It prompted him to caress my shoulder and offer an empathetic sigh.

"I'll be fine," I said starkly, hoping that my chilly tone would repel him. It didn't. He, being true to his motivational nature, claimed that I was going to be more than "fine" then reminded me to take my cough medication.

Rather than tell him to fuck off, I turned up the volume on the laptop while he was talking about the importance of following the doctor's orders.

"There's no need to be rude."

"Well, there's no need for you to lecture me about taking my medicine."

He defended himself by maintaining that he was just trying to help, especially since I routinely forgot to follow the prescription.

"I can look after myself just fine, okay!" I declared, pausing the documentary, to look up into his eyes.
He smirked, perhaps having endured enough of my ungratefulness, and asked: "Are you sure?"

"Whatever," I said, dismissing his words as I pressed play on the laptop. Clearly agitated, he said the problem was that I didn't know how to receive his advice or encouragement. He went on for several moments without any response from me.

"Damn! Who hurt you?"

If his goal was to strike back at me and get me more upset, he succeeded.

"Oh, fuck off!" I shouted, getting up from the sofa, marching into the bathroom, and slamming the door. I was livid. I wanted to punch him in the face. Instead, I lit an incense and took a deep inhalation and a long exhalation.

The day before New Year's Eve, he traveled to Shanghai to meet up with old friends. While he was bringing in the new year at a massive party, I was lying in his bed reading a book about reincarnation. Before closing my eyes, I regretted not joining him out of my own worry about being a tag along especially since his plans were made before we got back together.

I left him a series of voice messages boldly declaring my love and admiration for him. In one message, I thanked him for giving me another chance and begged him to hurry back so that we could create our sensual music.

Waking up on the first day of the new year without a hangover was a new experience. If I had been with him and his friends, it would have been a challenge not to drink. It was for this reason I came home after dinner with my friends rather than continue the festivities at a downtown bar. I had achieved my goal of starting the new year sober, yet I still wasn't content.

Although I had a slight cough, my body felt stronger than it had in weeks. My sketch pad was filling up with solid pieces, and I was writing poetry that I could see myself sharing. For the first time in my life, I was surrounded by individuals who inspired me to learn more about myself and my environment. In a little over a month, I was going to start a life-altering meditation course and if all this wasn't enough, he, a man with so much life in his words and deeds, loved me in the most terrifyingly pure manner.

I should have talked to him about my lingering unhappiness. We did vow to be open and transparent about whatever thoughts, feelings, and needs manifested themselves within us; but it seemed a little silly to share stuff that I didn't even understand.

Given my history of living with dark emotions, I didn't want him to worry about me or worse, pity my condition. The mere mention of feeling discontent would have spurred him to rack his brain in a valiant attempt to identify the cause. But perhaps for the time being, I didn't want to know. Perhaps I knew, but convinced myself otherwise, so that I could be the person I needed to be for us to flourish. Still, on the first night of the new year we made love with abandonment experienced by only the most reckless and hedonistic of people. He satisfied me; at least, that's what I told myself. After a bit of talk and laughter, he fell asleep and left me alone with my feigned satisfaction. My frustration prompted heavy tears before giving way to a hostile sleep.

I wasn't expecting the call from Steve. Our interaction had been reduced to texting, so hearing him voice my name and ask how I was doing released a rush of heat into my cheeks.

There followed other involuntary reactions that would be too embarrassing to mention. Steve wasted no time telling me that he and Julia were no longer an item. He categorized his affair with the American brunette as a lesson in inauthenticity. He explained, how she carried herself as a free-thinking seeker with little interest in participating in the perilous games formed by social climbing. But upon close inspection, he realized that she was no different from the people she claimed to abhor.

I laughed when he labeled her has as a sheep in rebel's clothing. I missed the way Steve made me laugh. Knowing that it would have been inappropriate to tell him this, I kept it to myself. I did tell him about my unhappiness, but quickly maintained it had nothing to do with my very committed relationship.

"It's most likely the result of unresolved conflicts from my past," I said. Maybe sensing how much I wanted to believe my self-assessment, he listened without questioning my perspective.

My break for the Chinese New Year began almost two weeks before his. I had planned to focus on my personal projects during the day so that my evenings were free to share with him and my friends. My plans were nixed however when I accepted an offer to work at a winter camp in the city.

I told him, and myself for that matter, that I took the job for the extra money. My plan to increase my savings was a fact. Truthfully though, it might have been the thought of him wanting to monopolize my evenings that propelled me to accept the position.

He seemed to support my decision even though my seven-day work week — made worse by the long commute there and back — meant that we would have considerably less time together.

Given that we were on the verge of being apart for a month, it was disconcerting that I had no deep longing to be in his arms. In the days leading up to his trip with Janice to Beijing, Bangkok, and Bali, I did my best to assure both of us that our decision to reunite was proving to be fruitful. As evidence, I talked up the new entries in my sketch pad and the completion of my weekly reading assignments for the online course I had started. I also mentioned my decision to contact my mother and a few other family members in South Africa. All proof.

"Because of you I meditate every day," I said, as we sat on the sofa eating dinner. "I wouldn't be going to Myanmar if we weren't doing this love thing, so I'm filled with gratitude for you and for us."

He teased me about being a sweet talker, then told me that he was inspired by my commitment to growth. Next thing I knew, his hand was on my thigh, and he was looking deep into my eyes.

"Since meeting you in August," he said, clearly wanting me to feel every word, "you've been the only person I want to be with."

We kissed and very soon found ourselves tugging at clothing while placing our plates on the coffee table. That night, and the following nights and mornings, I gave myself to him in ways that I hoped compensated for the other parts of me I was withholding.

I was beginning to suffocate under the weight of the words that I knew would crush him.

It was not my intention to disrupt his holidays. But what was I to do when my unfulfilled needs continued to produce thoughts that demanded verbal expression? After all, there was, in my opinion, no appropriate time or method to communicate my truth. And considering how intuition and presence were guiding forces in his life, a part of me was baffled by his obliviousness. Perhaps he knew all along yet preferred to believe that I was the woman he painstakingly drew in his sketch pad. So many times, I had tried to warn him about putting me on a pedestal, but he wouldn't be dissuaded.

When he called from Beijing, where he was enjoying time with Janice, he was bold.

"You make everything in my life better," he said. "I love you."

It was too much. Hearing Janice gush about her friend's affection for me, I felt obligated to return the sentiment, even though I felt an unpleasant mix of emotions. If he could see my strained expression, he would have known that it wasn't a good time to discuss how difficult the next month would be without me. I wanted him to stop with all the sappy utterances but wasn't comfortable making the request, so I lied.

"I need to call my uncle back," I said.

The following morning, I sent him a message stating that I was no longer certain about our relationship. As I feared, he responded with shock then anger.

He wanted to know exactly what I was uncertain about and if my uncertainty signaled the beginning of our end. I told him that I wasn't sure what it meant which did not sit well with him.

While he seemed to relish the unpredictable nature of life when it came to personal growth, career, and relationships with family and friends, he had great anxiety when it came to love, and more particularly, me. He needed to know how I felt and why I felt what I felt when I felt it.

My appeal for space was swiftly rejected. He sent me a voice message questioning my mental state and accusing me of deliberately seeking to cause him pain. Then, he sent a second message demanding that I retrieve all my stuff from his apartment and to never contact him again. When I sent him a reply, pleading for calm and understanding, it didn't go through. He had deleted me as a contact.

The sensible part of me, that I started nurturing in England after Dad died, remembered to take a deep inhalation, followed by one long cleansing exhalation.

KARNEVAL

The driver looked at Darian in the rear-view mirror, hesitated, then offered one fact about the assailants: they weren't German. He repeated this information a second time in a way that could only be described as priggish. Darian wanted to challenge the man's perspective, but Anna was already speaking in German and English about an article she had read on the victims.

The driver seemed eager to show how much he knew about this infamous incident that was getting national and international coverage. He chimed in to describe how one man felt guilty when he was unable to protect his partner and fifteen-year-old daughter from the drunk and predatory crowd.

"Those monsters grabbed their breasts and butts and even touched them between their legs."

Nodding her head, Anna added that many victims reported being verbally abused by the perpetrators.

"They shouldn't be allowed to come here and do that to our women."

The driver ranted about the attackers; he said they developed damaging views of women in their native countries where he claimed misogyny and abuse were fully acceptable. He told Anna and Darian that all the boys and men entering Germany from countries he tagged as 'backwards' needed to be re-educated and taught that violence against women would not be tolerated. The longer he spoke, the clearer it became how much his mentality was rooted in divisiveness.

Anna brought the conversation back to the victims. She had watched an interview with a university student who resorted to keeping a small knife with her whenever she stepped out of her apartment. The driver interrupted Anna to add that many of the young women were petrified to leave their homes and were even withdrawing from their university studies. He warned that unless the country's political leaders and law enforcement responded with stern measures, there would be more incidents in the future.

"Prison or send them back to their country."

Self-assured, the driver explained exactly how the attackers ought to be punished. He spoke entirely in German looking at Darian in the rear-view mirror and noticing for a second time that he had turned his face toward the window. Anna could sense her friend's frustration but continued to listen and respond politely.

When they arrived at their destination, Darian jumped out of the car before the driver could finish wishing them a joyous Karneval with a reminder to keep safe.

"What an idiot!"

Darian had been thinking it for the past hour and was relieved to finally be able to say it aloud. If the driver's window was down, the insult might have reached his ears as he drove off—something which seemed to worry Anna.

"Not so loud."

Darian didn't appreciate being reproached, especially when he was stating what he believed was a fact. Walking into her friend's building, he asked why she didn't hush the driver when he was spewing his brainless rhetoric.

"Or maybe you don't think he's an idiot."

Anna paused going up the stairs and kindly asked him to forget about the driver. They were about to enter the home of a childhood friend, she said.

"Someone who would like to celebrate Karneval and not debate that man's intelligence."

"This is not a debate. I'm just asking you a question. Was the driver an idiot, yes or no?"

She ignored Darian as she continued up the flight of stairs. Arriving at a door, she knocked. Seconds later, her friend opened it and the two women hugged and held onto each other, speaking in their native Bavarian tongue. Darian, still bothered by the driver, found their unbridled excitement endearing. Anna's friend pulled him inside and hugged him warmly. In English, she told him that she hoped he got enough sleep during the ride from Munich because the next three days were going to feel like a never-ending party.

"Leave your stuff here, we need to have a toast."

Darian and Anna dropped their belongings at the door and followed their host into the kitchen. She handed him then her friend a bottle of *Kölsch*, picked up one for herself and, poised to sip, announced that Karneval had officially begun.

They stood around the island in the kitchen where Anna's friend had placed a large bowl filled with pasta salad and platters of cold cuts, meat balls, and cheeses. Next to the food were two bottles of red wine and a carton of fruit juice. The fridge was stocked with more ale, bottles of white wine, and champagne. As their host opened her laptop to play some Karneval music, she declared, "The weather might be bad, but we will have a good time!"

Once the first song blared through her Bluetooth speaker, she raised one hand in the air and swayed from side to side. Anna joined in with equal enthusiasm. Apart from throwing out occasional lyrics, they mumbled through the verses, especially Anna. Still, they made up for their failure by belting out the chorus.

"I only listen to these songs during Karneval."

Darian knew Anna shared his taste in music, so he wondered why she would torture herself each year with such racket. Despite how discordant he found the vocals and cadence, he smiled respectfully to avoid offending their host. His appreciation for the melody grew somewhat after Anna and her friend translated a few lines and explained their playful nature.

"Karneval is the time we break all the rules."

Agreeing with her friend, Anna added that mocking the individuals who made the rules was always a popular practice during the festival.

"For the next three days my rule is to have no rules."

Anna followed her words with a gulp of beer that almost emptied her bottle. Her friend and Darian raised theirs in support and took large swigs.

"Yeah, no rules is the best way," their host announced before finishing her beer. She reached inside her fridge for three more.

"Oh boy, this is gonna get messy," Darian said. The exaggerated look of concern that flashed across his face made the two women laugh. It also prompted them to confess that their rallying calls were mostly talk and very little action.

"Every year we say something like this."

"But then we never do anything crazy."

They got to talking about last year's festivities and how embarrassing it was that they needed a full week to recover; for them, it was evidence of their depleted youth. As they laughed, the doorbell rang. Their host jumped up, rushed to the wall panel, and immediately buzzed the caller into the building. She flung the door open and shouted into the corridor something that got an equally loud response from the person climbing the stairs.

Darian was pleased to see Anna's former teammate walk into the apartment. He recalled their drunken push-up contest and the copious trash talking that had coloured their first meeting almost a year earlier. Greeting her now, he was quick to inquire if she was prepared to experience another loss. As she bent down to pull off her boots, she asked Anna how Darian was even granted entrance into the country.

"I told the customs officers straight up that I was here to shut up a loud-talking basketball chick from East Germany."

"And what did they say?" she asked, positioning her small suitcase next to Darian's and Anna's belongings.

"Something like, 'Thank God! We've been waiting for someone to do it.'"

They laughed and hugged long despite barely knowing each other.

Their host was the only person in the room who never played competitive basketball. She was also the only one among them who was a resident of Cologne, a city that was far from being the mecca of the sport. Yet her enthusiasm for a possible one-on-one match between Darian and Anna's former teammate was unrivaled.

"The game must happen before we go to party, yes?"

The others entertained the idea through more talk but took no concrete action.

"There's too much alcohol and food to leave now," Anna's former teammate conceded while digging into a plate of pasta salad.

Knowing that he would be leaving for Berlin after Karneval, Darian asked Anna's former teammate about the train ride.

"It was a fine. It took about four-and-a-half hours," she told him. "There was a lot of police at the train station."

"Oh really?"

"Yeah, I have never seen so many officers in one place."

Anna followed that statement with a remark in German that sparked a conversation between the three women. Darian munched on slices of ham and wheat crackers topped with pieces of Brie as he waited for a translation.

"But it's perfectly understandable."

He learned that Anna's former teammate supported the heavy police presence inside and outside the train station after what transpired on New Year's Eve. Anna agreed, but their host had a different opinion. She interpreted the city's resolve to have officers patrolling the station throughout the day and night as a show of force. She said it only deepened the already stark divide between Germans and refugees.

"A few weeks ago, about one hundred Syrians were there to protest against sexism."

She also mentioned the signs they carried which read: "We respect German values" while others handed out flowers to onlookers. Darian scoffed at the protest. It was unnecessary, he claimed.

"Like sexual harassment and rape didn't exist in Germany until 'they' arrived."

Anna explained that the police chief labelled the crimes committed on New Year's Eve "of a completely new dimension." Her former teammate agreed, saying that the chief also made the ethnic background of the perpetrators clear.

"He said they were all Arab or North African."

Accusing both women of sounding like the driver, Darian shook his head.

"Anna, tell them about all the great stuff he said."

Although Darian's agitation was growing, he kept quiet long enough for Anna to relay the driver's comments to her friends.

"But you cannot deny that over a thousand women filled out police reports."

"I'm not denying that," Darian said. "What I'm saying is that he, like the police chief, made it about skin colour and ethnic background."

Darian was certain that when the driver looked at him, he saw one of the perpetrators; however, he stopped short of sharing that feeling.

"The media is saying one thousand men, right? I don't even think that number is accurate, but anyway, let's suppose that it was one thousand white German men who were being accused of—"

Anna's former teammate interrupted. She acknowledged that racism remained a problem in some small towns that weren't even worth a visit.

"But Germany is a not a racist country," she argued. "We travelled to the U.S. many times when we were players."

"Yes. Racism is very serious there, but here it's not really a problem," said Anna.

Darian smirked.

"As two white women you're badly placed to make such an assessment," he said. "I doubt people of colour would say that racism doesn't exist here."

Anna's former teammate rebuked his point. She said that all their black teammates never mentioned anything about experiencing racism in Germany.

"They feel like they're treated like everyone else. No difference."

"Now you're gonna tell me what they feel?"

Sensing that Darian and her former teammate were on the verge of an exploding feud, Anna cut in.

"Hey, everyone. Let's take a drink and remember that it's Karneval."

"Actually, he's right," said their host who had remained silent through their tense exchange. She brought up one popular magazine's recent front cover: an image of a white woman's naked body covered by black handprints as if branded.

"And one newspaper printed an illustration of a black arm reaching up between a white woman's legs."

"No way! I thought that kind of racist shit doesn't happen here in Germany," Darian said while looking directly at Anna's former teammate.

"I want to say something about my friend Yusuf," said their host. "And then I hope we can get ready for the party, yes?"

Holding everyone's attention, the Cologne native shifted the energy in the room.

"Yusuf was a French teacher in Syria. He was sent to prison for protesting against the president. He endured months of torture. It left him physically and mentally broken."

Their host inhaled deeply so that she could continue. "After Yusuf was released, a friend told him that Germany was offering sanctuary to Syrians fleeing the war."

Her guests listened without interjecting.

"It was a difficult decision," she said, recalling a distant conversation. "He didn't want to leave his parents and his eight brothers and sisters, but he knew it was too dangerous for him to stay."

She detailed his perilous trek from a refugee camp outside Suruc to Cologne and the remarkable new life he created for himself. When she told them that Yusuf was already fluent in German – and that he was part of a small collective lobbying the local government for greater integration between refugees and locals – Darian, Anna, and her former teammate were amazed.

"But now many people start expressing their hatred, and he told me that he and many others don't feel safe here anymore."

She said more in German. By her expression, Anna's former teammate showed she didn't necessarily disagree but was clearly agitated by the whole conversation.

"And what about the victims?" she asked. "They don't feel safe either."

She spoke some more but in German, her voice rising; then suddenly she reverted to English and announced she was going to the bathroom to get ready. As she walked away, Anna glanced at Darian, who looked surprised. She assured him that in a few minutes her former teammate would be her jovial self again.

"That's how she is sometimes."

Their host meanwhile turned up the music and sang along. Once Anna swallowed the last of her beer, she told the room she was going to change into her costume. On her way, she circled back, leaned into Darian, and kissed him gently on his mouth.

"I didn't see that coming."

"I know."

Anna's cheeks flushed lightly as she retreated to the bedroom. Darian, still taken aback, asked Anna's friend about her costume.

"Today I will be a robber, so I need very little time to change. What will you be?"

"A doctor."

They laughed at their simplicity and pledged to walk into parties together and at a healthy distance ahead of Anna and her former teammate; both were going as fully made-up clowns with juggling balls.

"Maybe we can add something to make our costumes better."

"Nah, I know we won't be the only lazy ones."

Anna's friend smiled at his remark. She rested her bottle on the counter, turned and moved towards the bedroom to put on her costume. Darian reached for her hand. Without saying a word, he held it.

"What's wrong?"

"Nothing, just noticed that you didn't finish your beer."

BARON

The warm water washed away the day's dirt. Lifting his head up from underneath the faucet, he applied and massaged the thick brown liquid into his hair. He adjusted the shabby burgundy hand towel around his shoulders, then paused to look at himself – his foamy head not his flabby torso – before going back under the water to rinse.

As a child, Baron discovered how enjoyable it was to wash his hair at the bathroom sink in front of a mirror. Now, decades past his age of innocence, it was all a matter of habit. And when it came to habits, he had enough for several lifetimes. Over the years the *what, where, when, why, who* and *how* of his daily activities could all be categorized as habits. For instance, once a week he travelled to a neighbouring town by bus to buy fruits when vendors outside the campus offered the same products at the same prices. Perhaps habits, whether trivial or profound, begin as a pleasurable experience that in some way meet a need or desire.

Baron was drying his hair with the shabby burgundy hand towel – housekeeping provided new fluffy white ones that absorbed a lot more water but they weren't part of his routine – when he heard Ahmed enter the dormitory. It was almost thirty minutes into their shift and Baron had yet to make an appearance on the floor. He knew the young Moroccan was only in the room to pick up his water bottle or a football.

"Good weekend?"

"Yes, *alhamdulillah*. How about you?"

There was nothing novel about their exchange, yet Baron was keen. His voice beamed through the bathroom door.

"Same to me, but it always finish too soon."

"Well, we only have five more weeks."

"Thanks God!"

Baron didn't believe in God but often found himself giving thanks with his broken grammar whenever conversing with the young Moroccan. Before leaving, Ahmed told him that their floor leader was in the family room talking with Larry, the head of Residence Hall.

"I'm sure he's telling Larry about us not filling out those stupid sheets."

Baron smirked then said, "Why should we follow him? He likes to make so many papers but it's not a residence hall policy. It's just his own rule, so we don't need to care."

"Exactly. Well, I'm going out to play football. See ya."

"Okay, see you later."

Baron knew that Larry would soon be inquiring about his whereabouts if he hadn't already. For any other Residence Hall teacher on any of the other five floors, this would have been the impetus to be seen working. But not Baron; he got dressed at a speed that suggested he had nowhere in particular to be and nothing in particular to do.

When he finally stepped onto the floor, boarders were arriving on campus from their time spent at home over Friday night and Saturday. Several grade eleven and twelve boys who lived too far to go home on weekends had instead hibernated in their dormitories. In his first year on the job, he would have entered their rooms and attempted a conversation, but now in his fourth year, he didn't even bother glancing at their closed doors as he walked up the long corridor.

"Good afternoon."

The floor leader greeted Baron with his usual business-like tone while sitting at a table, laptop open, in the family room. Whenever on the floor, he sat there appearing fully immersed in his work. Baron knew that, apart from creating a series of forms, which he pinned onto the bulletin board at the start of every week, he wasn't working any harder than anyone else.

Speaking in the local dialect, the floor leader reminded Baron that he and Ahmed needed to write on one of those forms the exact times they entered the dormitories to conduct checks on the students in their section of the floor. Baron smiled and nodded while having no intention of carrying out the task. Before he could walk to the far end of the family room, recline on one of the four sofa chairs, and watch a lecture on *Youku*, the Chinese version of Youtube, the floor leader offered another reminder.

"Jason told me that it was your turn to collect the phone boxes from A Building. I know you forgot, but please make sure that you do it next time."

"Okay no problem. You can tell Jason not to worry I will do it for the rest of the year."

It was no secret that Baron and Jason didn't get along and that they hadn't spoken in months.

"You only need to do it the next two times," said the floor leader.

"The year is almost over, so it doesn't matter."

Despite his courteous smile, Baron was seething. He had thoughts of wrapping his hands around the younger man's neck and squeezing hard. Whenever he was asked what was at the root of his animosity, he pointed to Jason's selfishness and sense of entitlement. His flashy style of dress and affinity for pop culture made Jason the most popular residence hall teacher on the floor—something Baron found irritating.

Born in Shanghai, almost five years after his country had experienced a famine that devoured tens of millions of people, Baron learned about perseverance and sharing. As the oldest of five children, he was also taught many lessons about responsibility. And though luck and faith are fundamentally different in nature, he grasped the teachings about both.

Baron was still in primary school when Chairman Mao sent junior and high school graduates to work as farmers in rural areas. When he entered senior high school, the new government reinstated the national college entrance exam colloquially known as the *gao kao*. This meant academic achievement and not political and family background would be the criterion, at least officially, for admission into institutions of higher learning. The year he graduated from high school, only 280,000 out of the 3.3 million students who wrote the *gao kao* were able to secure a university spot. But by the early 2000s, which is when Jason would have completed the grueling nine-hour exam, the admission rate was over sixty percent.

"Teacher, can you help me to collect my package?"

Baron paused the lecture he was watching and asked the boarder if the package had arrived. The boy had been tracking the package all day and told Baron it would be delivered before nine.

"When it gets here, I can do it if I'm not busy."

Satisfied, the boarder placed his week's milk supply on one of the shelves in the large fridge before dragging his suitcase out of the family room and down the hall to his dormitory.

There was a time when Baron was often accompanying boarders to the front gate where he would then step outside, key whatever password he was given into the automated parcel lockers, and procure the goods. In fact, when he first started working in the residence hall, this simple procedure brought him a certain degree of satisfaction. But that changed once he realized that too many boarders were ungrateful for his service. One eighth grader even asserted that collecting packages was part of the job. (He was the same boy who wondered why the maids couldn't make his bed and throw away his dirty towels since his parents were paying so much in tuition and boarding.) Another annoyance was the amount of luxury items boarders purchased online and had delivered to the campus. Baron was baffled by the boys who bragged about buying a new pair of basketball shoes every week. Each pair had to be trendy and well over one hundred dollars.

With the afternoon sun glaring through the large windows, Baron adjusted the angle of his tablet as he resumed watching the lecture. Seconds in, a call interrupted him. It was an old friend who worked with him at a German industrial equipment maker for more than a decade. Only recently he left the company that had let Baron go five years earlier. Baron knew what his friend wanted to discuss so he rose to his feet and casually walked back to the room he shared with Ahmed.

The floor was far from quiet when he reemerged. Almost all of the boarders had returned and were in their rooms gaming with the sort of intensity that would lead anyone to believe that scores were of vital importance. Sauntering up the corridor, he heard cursing in Mandarin, English, and in the local dialect, but he didn't react.

Although Larry and the principals instructed all the teachers to be vigilant about enforcing the school's zero-tolerance policy towards bad language, he kept walking.

In his first and second year at the school, he'd occasionally let boarders know that their style of speech was inappropriate, but they would either ignore him or bark back. One boy told Baron that he intended to continue expressing himself in whatever way he felt because he read that powerful people never worried about using dirty words. To underline his point, he boasted that his father, who had enough wealth to buy the school, was constantly using foul language.

In the dormitory closest to the elevators, Baron overheard Jason telling a few boys to take their food into the family room. Every boarder knew that it was against the rules to eat and drink anything but water in their room. Yet on almost a daily basis, especially on Sundays when many boys returned to the campus with treats from home or junk food from McDonald's, KFC, or Starbucks, every residence hall teacher on the floor reminded them about the rule. Unlike his colleagues, Baron tended not to barge into a dormitory whenever he suspected there was food, soft drinks, or candy around. Convinced that the food policy was unenforceable much like the one for cell phones – since school leaders were moving away from traditional punishment in favour of giving rule-breakers consequences – he only intervened when the offender was offending in plain sight, a rarity.

Before returning to his sofa chair, he was stopped by the floor leader who passed on information about the assembly and an upcoming staff karaoke night. Everything he mentioned was written in the WeChat group message that Baron read while walking up the corridor. Dryly, he thanked the floor leader then glimpsed at his watch and announced it would soon be time to go to the cafeteria for dinner.

The floor leader had quite a lot to say about dinner; apparently a group of foreign teachers was pressuring school leadership to provide more meatless meals. So when a boarder hurried into the family room complaining about a missing shirt, Baron was relieved. He had no desire to help the eighth grader, who was forever losing clothes and other belongings; however, he knew the floor leader would be eager to assist.

As he was turning towards his sofa chair, Larry stepped out of the elevator.

"Just the man I wanted to see."

Like a game-show host, Larry had one of those booming voices that made everything he said sound interesting.

"Can I have a chat with you?"

That question coming from a superior used to puzzle Baron. He couldn't fathom why a superior would ask for permission to talk with a subordinate. After discussing the matter with several other Chinese colleagues who were equally confused, they concluded that Western principals and heads of departments posed the question to be polite and not necessarily to receive an honest answer.

The two men sat at a table away from the one occupied by the floor leader and the anxious eighth grader. Larry began by inquiring about Baron's weekend.

"It was fine, how about you?"

"Oh! It was a weekend for the ages."

Larry, a middle-aged American, discussed his trek up a mountain located a few hours north of Shanghai and all the pleasant villagers he encountered.

"This is truly an amazing country."

He often made such assertions. Having only been in China for eight months, he seemed to be deeply moved by almost everything.

"So, Baron, we need to talk about punctuality."

The almost remorseful tone Larry employed didn't have any noticeable effect on Baron. His grin stayed present, his posture remained erect, and his shoulders were open.

"I came here earlier but you weren't around."

"Sorry. I was in my room."

Larry insisted that he had stayed on the floor an extra forty-five minutes hoping to see him but left disappointed.

"And this isn't the first time, Baron. I've told you and all the other RHTs that if you're going to be late let me know in advance. It's essential that everyone is on the floor at the right time."

"Yes, I understand."

The American elaborated about every residence hall teacher being important and that parents sent their children to the school because they heard about all the extra attention and care boarders received outside of class time.

"Please remember this, okay?"

"Okay."

The end of this incredibly mild reprimand was cut short by the floor leader and a boarder in grade nine.

"He needs to call his mother," the floor leader reported. Then, with added urgency: "He has a fever and wants to go home."

Larry excused Baron and shifted his attention to the boy who was hunched over with one hand clutching his stomach. Wincing, the student picked up the school phone and dialed with his free hand. At that moment, Jason stepped into the family room with a few of the boarders who loved him the most. He spotted the cringing teenager and asked Larry and the floor leader what was wrong.

Unable to bear being around Jason, Baron gathered his tablet, headphones, and tea bottle and exited the family room. A few months earlier, norovirus had sent over a hundred students and a handful of school staff home sick. Just in case the boy was infected, Baron wanted to be nowhere near him if he vomited.

On the way to the cafeteria, he noticed a young mother and father trying to console their sobbing son. Baron wanted to tell the parents they shouldn't be forcing their kid to live on campus. In fact, he wanted to tell all the parents of students in grade six and under the same thing. But that wasn't his job, or at least that's what he told himself as he watched several parents: some walking with their offspring toward the residence hall and others dropping off their child and striding to the front gate, where they would climb into their expensive car and drive back to their expensive home embedded in an incredibly expensive city.

"I'm hungry!" Ahmed exclaimed, putting a hand on Baron's shoulder as they entered the cafeteria. The two got their food and sat at a table in the section where primary students ate. In his first year as a residence hall teacher, Ahmed had worked on the second floor with the boys from grade one to five. If it were his decision to make, he would have stayed with the primary school boys.

"They aren't controlled by their cell phones yet," Ahmed said, as he waved to a group of younger girls that were in his after-school French club.

"And they show respect to us," Baron added.

More secondary students began filing into the cafeteria while the two men talked about a colleague who was berated by a boarder a week earlier. Although Ahmed wondered if the teenage girl would be suspended, Baron countered that she would only receive a written warning. Larry and the principal, he predicted, weren't willing to deal with the wrath this boarder's parents would unleash if they dared to mention the word "suspension."

"They want to be friends with their child. It's crazy. In Morocco, the parents trust the teachers. If a teacher corrects a child, the teacher knows he's got the support of the parents."

"Same to China, but this school is strange."

Baron pointed out that at his son's school, along with every other public school in China, teachers were supported when they confronted a student. As their exchange of examples picked up momentum, a new message appeared in the staff WeChat group. The boy who was feeling unwell would be placed in quarantine on the sixth floor until his parents could come for him.

"No mention of when they will come," Baron remarked.

"Yeah, exactly! Where do they live?"

"Here, Shanghai."

In the limited online interaction Baron had with the sick teenager's parents, he got the sense they would let their son reside at school 365 days of the year if it were possible. Like many parents he met, they gave their child everything except their attention.

"Some of these kids are really abandoned, man."

"But they're so fashion, right?"

Baron had never learned how to turn the noun "fashion" into an adjective.

Ahmed brought up a compelling video he saw on Youtube about the millions of poor children in rural areas whose parents migrate to urban centers to gain employment.

"They're called the 'left-behind children' and it's really sad, man. There were these two kids who haven't seen their parents in over ten years. I can't imagine that."

Sighing, Baron said, "It's a very big problem."

The Moroccan sent him a link to the video, but he couldn't play it on his phone.

"Oh, you need a VPN to get on Youtube."

"But what about school's WiFi?"

"I don't know. I couldn't get on Youtube and Facebook on Wednesday or Thursday. And today it's still not working."

"Maybe Mr. Xi wants to hide something."

Ahmed chuckled. He argued that President Xi Jinping was not the bogeyman his colleague made him out to be. The young Moroccan praised the leader for investing billions into his country, adding that Chinese citizens no longer needed a visa to visit.

"We've always had a good relationship with you guys and he's making it even better, so I think he's okay."

Baron smiled at his roommate's naiveté before wondering aloud why a staggering number of Chinese people wanted to live abroad.

"C'mon man, don't let these silly British, Canadian, and American teachers get to you. All they do is watch fake news on Fox, CNN, and BBC."

Ahmed told him those same teachers, having absorbed all the Western media's biases and lies, harboured backwards opinions about his country and his religion.

"Do you want to live abroad?" Ahmed asked.

"Sure."

Baron admitted that he had wanted to leave China since he was a boy. He couldn't recall the exact age, but he remembered what triggered the desire to live elsewhere.

"My favourite cousin was much older than me. He just returned from the countryside and so my mother and father were very proud of him. They thought it was great; they thought everything Chairman Mao did was great. So they invited him and his parents to our home for ..."

"Like a welcome back dinner?"

"Yes, exactly, a welcome back dinner."

Baron explained that it was during that meal – while listening to his cousin share stories about his time as a farmer – when he realized he had to get out. He had noted the bitterness in his uncle's voice when he said Mao wanted the masses to be farmers without formal education to make it easier for him to rule.

"But all these years later you're still here."

The two laughed at this undeniable fact.

"I get the chance to visit Indonesia, Thailand, Vietnam but ..."

"You wouldn't move to any of those countries?"

"No, I don't think so. Last year, I went to UK with the school."

"How was it?"

"Just so so."

Ahmed suggested he visit Morocco then presented Canada as a worthy country to visit and possibly move to.

"Canada seems nice but look at what do they do to daughter of Huawei."

Both men laughed before agreeing that Canada needed to stop doing America's dirty work. Baron said he believed that Hong Kong and Taiwan were the most feasible options because of their proximity to Shanghai. More importantly, they were culturally vibrant Chinese hubs offering their citizens the freedom to watch, read, listen, write, and say whatever they wanted, he asserted. Ahmed agreed, saying he did enjoy his time in both regions; but he was quick to describe the protesters in Hong Kong as pawns. For weeks, he had been claiming this by blaming Western nations, namely the United States, for stirring up the unrest.

"During the Arab Spring, they tried to get us to protest and overthrow the government, but it didn't work. We're happy with our King and our leaders."

Baron was frustrated with not knowing what was truly happening in Hong Kong because the only media he had access to was controlled by the Party.

"I just hope President Xi won't use army."

Pausing to consider what a military intervention from Beijing would look like, he insisted that nobody should want to see that again.

The following evening, Baron was absent at the start of study hall. In fact, he didn't arrive on campus until eight—six hours after his shift began. It wasn't his intention to leave his students unsupervised, but the meeting he told only Ahmed about ran longer than expected. The young Moroccan knew Larry had found out about Baron's misconduct and was furious, so he sent his colleague a message of warning before the end of study hall. An hour later, he rushed back to their dorm room. There, Baron was emptying his closet and casually packing his suitcase.

TO FEEL

The winds were too forceful and the rain was too heavy for outdoor activities. In her car, seated behind the steering wheel, Riley did not share in her passenger's gripes about the weather abruptly cancelling their plans. She enjoyed the lake as much as anyone else in the city but wanted to experience something different; something that transcended the mundane duties of her daily routine; something that made her feel like she was doing more than inhaling and exhaling moderately polluted air. Their high-intensity workout met this need. They finished just as heavy ominous clouds invaded the clear sky like a herd of elephants. Sitting comfortably in her car eating a protein bar in her sports bra, tank top, tights, and sneakers also fulfilled this need.

When her passenger asked about a contingency plan, she smiled at him before declaring there was none. As the low puffy clouds continued to unleash a torrent of water, Riley marvelled at the heavens daring to contradict the local forecast. Enthusiastically, she told him it was nice to have surprises in a world where phone applications took many of them away. If the weather could do whatever it wanted, she reasoned, why couldn't she?

Riley knew he didn't harbour the same sentiment. His life was strikingly different. He lived alone, so he had the luxury of arranging everything inside his apartment exactly to his liking. When he returned to his home, there was no role, or roles, he had to play to assure the functioning of the household. He had the same freedom as the weather did; a freedom that she craved.

"I don't want to go home now."

She knew he could understand her native tongue, yet she opted to speak English. She studied the language in school but rarely used it after graduating which was evident by the way she struggled with the wording.

He proposed they go for lunch. She objected, saying the workout left her thirsty, not hungry. In her language, she told him that she was struggling to finish the protein bar he had given her. He suggested going to the aquarium as another option. She laughed and then said they were far too old for the aquarium. Undeterred, he suggested a trip to the cinema for a matinee. She wasn't opposed to watching a movie. She took her phone out of her black gym bag to check what was playing. Showing him her screen, she told him that the only English movie had two time slots in the evening.

"Maybe we can go your home."

She couldn't bear to look at him as she waited for a response. Part of her knew she wouldn't be rejected, but she wasn't certain. In everything she ever learned about Americans via school, films, and social media, they were direct and went after what they wanted. If he wanted to have her at his place, he would have invited her. She figured he might have even made advances in their text messages. The sort of advances that went beyond flirting and were more in the domain of sexual fantasy. Since meeting him a month earlier in spinning class, he had visited her dreams more times than she could rationalize.

The drive to his place lasted less than ten minutes. He continued to talk freely while Riley smiled nervously and kept mostly silent. She felt that they, together, would be something different. Something unscripted. Something unfathomable. Something wild and free.

Entering his housing complex, he directed her to the parking spot closest to his apartment building. Just as they were about to step out of the car and make a quick dash, the skies roared with a power that momentarily paralyzed them. They listened as raindrops crashed onto the car. Their steady pelts were a frenetic arrangement of percussions.

"We cannot shower."

He chuckled in agreement and at her incorrect grammar. She was amusingly unaware that her English sentences often said one thing but meant another. As they braced themselves for the bombardment, he jokingly said it was a pity they didn't have soap to lather up with.

Running at almost full speed, Riley followed him across the lane and down the wide path that led to the entrance of his building. Within seconds her hair, clothes, and sneakers were drenched. They were stunned by how much water was absorbed in less than a minute. Inside the elevator, he twisted the bottom of his t-shirt to add more drops to the puddle he was standing in. Wanting to increase the size of her puddle, she did the same, wringing out her tank top. When they arrived on the fifteenth floor and the elevator doors opened, she forgot about the rain and the pooling water. She stepped into the short hallway, watching him open his door, and was reminded of what she hoped would transpire.

She hesitated long enough for him to notice and ask, "Is everything okay?" Her response didn't come immediately. What she was wanting scared her as much as it excited her and that was something she didn't know how to verbalize. Instead, she smiled politely.

"It's okay," she said.

Riley turned her attention back to the rain and puddles. "I'm sorry my shoes," she said, noticing his clean floors.

"No worries," he replied, smiling. "I'm just happy that you're here."

There was more that he said but she stopped listening. Not in a rude way, of course. She was hopelessly distracted by a yearning and a question she dared not ask. Once his words trailed off, he stopped speaking to look at her, truly look at her, before leaning in. Riley closed her eyes as if she were simultaneously making a wish and accepting its fulfillment. Her lips' reciprocation, timid at first, intensified as he drew closer. Their moist skin and drenched clothes seemed to merge much like their puddles. Silence. Not the orchestrated or imagined kind. Rather, the sort of silence born from a moment desperate to extend its life and rebel against space and time, holding hostage all stillness within itself. She couldn't remember the last time she experienced such silence.

He didn't ask if she wanted to go into his bedroom. With her hand in his, he led her there; her steps fell into his. Opaque curtains were drawn leaving the room shades of black. She welcomed the absence of light, for her body carried secrets and her time with him depended on their survival.

In the shadows, she removed her wet clothes with trepidation. If her nakedness could speak, it would express gratitude before asking for lingering gratification. Instead, her body detected signals sparking the surge and release of pheromones. Smooth were the traces of moisture on her skin as her muscles trembled with anticipation. Once her eyes focused into the darkness, she watched him emerge. Seeing him meant she also could be seen. It was a realization that flooded her with anxiety, prompting her desire to cover up. He seemed to sense her drifting because he squeezed her waist with fervour and brought her back. With every touch and kiss, she shifted from pleasure to tension and back to pleasure. She behaved as though she were ticklish around her stomach—where she stored the extra pounds that made her visit the gym four to five times a week. Then there was the scar; a branding that marked the most remarkable moment of her life.

When Riley graduated from a relatively well-known university in Shanghai, she interned her way into an IT company that was poised for growth. There, she had worked as a software programmer, volunteering countless overtime hours and even weekends just to prove her worth. After several years, she was offered a management position in their newly opened Bangalore office. Instant joy and a profound sense of accomplishment overwhelmed her until thoughts of her life situation dashed everything like rains of a hurricane. It had pained her that she couldn't take the offer because she had recently accepted another.

Lin Yihan had been her second boyfriend and, unlike her first, he had done nothing to break her heart. He was a decent man who believed in stability and loyalty. So when he'd decided that, after three years of dating, marriage was the appropriate next step, she had no reason — other than the fact that she was not in love with him — to refuse his proposal. Once they married, the pressure to deliver to the paternal grandparents a child they could dote over had been incredible. Less than a year into the marriage, Riley was pregnant. She had not dreamed of being a mother so young, but instead figured it was bound to happen at some point.

She had been a few months shy of twenty-five years when she gave birth to their son.

"So soft."

Her remark came after he laid her down on the bed. Riley was accustomed to a much firmer mattress; one that didn't make her feel like she was helplessly sinking. He said something about being unable to get a good night's sleep on a typical Chinese mattress then attempted to redeem himself by adding another point about his ignorance to much of her country's ancient wisdom. She didn't want him talking, especially not in the way that made comprehension more labourious but she knew he was merely reacting to the chatter that was happening between her head and heart. It dawned on her that the worry and doubt darkened her expression and triggered his need for damage control. The possibility that he was as nervous as she was had not entered her mind.

"Gently," she whispered in Mandarin.

She had not been with Lin Yihan since the arrival of their son who was turning five in one week. During those years, a handful of attempts were made, but she simply refused to give herself to a man she had no connection with. They disagreed on everything, including the root of their disagreements. Every argument ended with resentful stares that were followed by days of cold silence which then gave way to a lukewarm make-up exchange that lacked a real resolution. Lin Yihan's mother, who lived with them, much to Riley's chagrin, had urged them to be more patient with one another and to focus on compromising. But Riley believed that all the patience and compromise in the world wouldn't fix their marriage. She had told herself that because of her son, whom she loved in a way that was both strengthening and terrifying, a divorce would have to wait. The waiting, however, was becoming increasingly unbearable. Her time spent at work and the gym served as an escape.

"I love you."

She blurted it out in English as he moved on top of her. There was something about the way he used his hands and mouth that made her feel like she was being stroked by pairs of hands and kissed by many mouths. He said nothing. In that moment, she didn't need him to. In that moment, she wasn't concerned with the veracity of what she had said or even if he heard it. In that moment, she knew that there would be no regrets. How could there be? Considering she had not desired someone or felt desired in such a long time, those three words may have been for herself. To feel lifted. To feel emancipated. To feel alive.

They clung to one another, twisting, undulating, and expanding. Skin melding. Not hers, not his, just skin. For the most part, she kept her eyes open but closed them whenever sensations abiding deeply in the realm of pleasure seized control of her body and caused her to pant and moan.

"I love you!"

FINDING MARIYA

Her astrologist told her it would happen. The middle-aged woman did not predict a cold and dusty warehouse that might not have ever been inventoried, but she did tell Mariya that her work as a marketing manager would never be appreciated by her boss. She also warned her about his destructive tendencies and his inability to adopt a growth mindset. Naturally, the astrologist advised Mariya to look for employment elsewhere, yet stressed that the Universe would not present a new opportunity until she had learned every lesson from her current position. On this morning, this caveat left Mariya unsettled and might have contributed to her exasperation.

"Mariya, I think the warehouse will be good for you," she said, imitating her boss's Dutch accent as she looked for display panels. The longer it took to find an item on the list, the more creative she became with her cursing. She unleashed every offensive noun and adjective available with the kind of venom reserved only for human beings she found despicable. Looking down at the list she was given three days to work through, she contemplated quitting for the second time in as many weeks. She imagined herself entering her boss's office to hand him a recording of her barbs while saying, with all the disdain Mariya felt he deserved, "This is what I think about you." Before exiting the space, she would knock the short and balding man's lavish water fountain off his desk while screaming that he would never experience peace.

As a child and then as a teenager, Mariya did not tolerate disrespect. Even when she and Marina, her twin sister, were university students, she had little difficulty letting people know how she wanted to be treated. Granted, she was duped several times during her freshman and sophomore years which tends to happen when living in a foreign country and operating in foreign languages. Yet, she always rebounded with greater maturity and determination. By her junior year, she was constantly reminding Marina, who was born ten minutes earlier, not to be so naïve. However, Mariya ended up swallowing a mouthful of disrespect after graduation when an employer withheld her salary for almost four months. She might have gone unpaid for longer if Marina didn't fall ill and their mother didn't ask them to move back home.

Being with family amid their town's endless hills, freshwater streams, and towering trees, Mariya felt rejuvenated. She might have stayed permanently if she didn't have a business degree from a reputable Chinese university, ambitions of someday launching a cosmetic company, and a desire to be married with children by thirty.

In the capital, Mariya worked in the logistics department of a relatively new streetwear brand. She wasn't thrilled about some of the more tedious parts of the job, but she was pleased to be earning an income again. Marina, who felt equally restless in their hometown, was hired at a translations company. One night, after the older twin walked into their one-bedroom apartment from an unpleasant date, they talked, cried, and laughed before agreeing to focus on their careers and self-development.

They joined a gym that offered an array of fitness and dance classes. Mariya went to one salsa lesson and knew she had found something truly special. The music and steps made her feel alive in ways she had never felt before. It was also in that first lesson where she met Sergei, a charming salsa enthusiast who was five years older.

They began meeting for coffee before class and then, as the forces that pull two individuals closer to one another grew more intense, they quickly added going for dinner and walks after class. The relationship brought an immense excitement to Mariya's present and illuminated her future with the possibility of forever. Marina appreciated him and the way he made her sister feel. She just couldn't grasp his passion for salsa.

"I think he's obsessed."

Marina made this statement one night after he had driven them home. Despite having to work the next morning, he had announced he was going to a salsa party that was on the other side of the city. She also wasn't fond of him not inviting her sister, but she didn't mention that part. The first time Sergei's mother met Mariya, she told her that even though she loved her son, she knew his selfishness would make him a terrible husband and father. None of these warning signs were ignored. Mariya simply chose to remain on the road that her heart was speeding along.

In the years that followed, nothing could push her off that road; not the slippery patches that resulted from his litany of excuses for not taking a single trip with her; not even her diminished presence caused by his refusal to introduce her to the friends who accompanied him to parties. It wasn't until the start of their fourth year, when his infidelity drove them to a dead end, that she took a deep breath and sought the exit ramp. She accepted the job offer in China that she had been mulling over for weeks but didn't exactly tell Sergei the relationship was over. She simply left one afternoon for the airport. As is the case with matters of the heart, opportunity, not rationality, was most effective.

Her typically stoic boss was satisfied with the launch of the company's first office in China. A relieved Mariya thought his satisfaction meant that after months of overlapping overtime she would be granted at least one day off. However, rather than ask her to take a break, he instead handed her a folder before leaving for the airport. In it were sales targets for the upcoming year, and he urged her to get started on them immediately. There was a small part of her that wanted to throw the folder at him and demand to be treated as a human being and not a workhorse. There was an even larger part of her that admired the small part and mourned the loss of her youthful defiance. Unfortunately, her most dominant parts had succumbed to a numbness that crippled her to inertia.

Living apart from Marina for the first time ever was difficult. Holding on to a fairy-tale ending with a man who did not love her was difficult. Finding a community to belong to in one of the largest cities in the world was difficult. Simply put, life in general or rather the act of living had become difficult. But growing up in a country that was losing its Soviet identity had also been difficult. During those years, when she and her family used to line up for hours with ration coupons in hand to buy bread, butter, and other staples, her mother told her that complaining about the amount of time wasted at food distribution centers didn't change the policies that created food shortages. So whenever Mariya found herself complaining, her mother's voice would arise from the recesses of her memory, and she would promptly stop. She might have sought to explore the sentiments and thoughts that clung to her difficulties if she knew that was a valid option. "It's just how things are," she often repeated to herself, a mantra that was her unofficial coping strategy. It was one that she fully utilized when her boss decided to close the Chinese office without offering her old job back. From time to time, when he was upset with the sales numbers, he threatened to shut down the operation, but Mariya didn't think he would actually do it.

Unsure of whether to return home or remain in China, she kept replaying the angry rants he unleashed whenever a task was not completed the way he wanted. He repeatedly called her incompetent, telling her that she was fortunate to have the attractiveness of a cover girl because her mental faculties were substandard. She didn't believe his words, yet when looking for a new job, she struggled to list her skills and qualities. Luckily, her roommate's best friend had a contact in human resources at a company that supplied functional fittings for kitchen units. The Dutch company was looking to add a new member to their marketing team in China. Her contact arranged for an interview with the managers and she was hired a day later.

It was around the time Mariya started working at Keukeuken Oplossingen that she met a handsome, Cuban, cigar dealer. She was with friends at a popular Latin club when suddenly he appeared. His smile was inviting and the confidence with which he extended his hand seemed to hypnotize Mariya who accepted without glancing at her friends for approval. He held her right hand in his left and placed his right hand on the lowest part of her back. Unsure of where to rest her left hand, she froze until he leaned in and said, "Over my shoulder." Out of habit, she was gearing up to perform salsa steps when she realized he was doing a slow side-to-side two step.

"Listen to the music," he said, gently as he moved his right leg slightly in between hers. Once the first drumbeats pulsated through the speakers, they took a step to the left and then to the right while swaying their hips. With less than an inch of separation, the pair glided from side to side, in circles, backward and forward. During segments without bass beats, they stood pressed together in one place doing slow hip rolls. She had never danced with anyone, much less a stranger, who made her feel the kind of yearning she reserved for the bedroom. Being guided around the crowded dancefloor by an expert who inspired, rather than intimidated as Sergei did, made her feel as though everything was possible. And she felt that way up until the day he revealed that he was about to have a child with his long-time girlfriend.

"How can you say that?" she asked after being tongue-tied for several minutes listening to him profess his unwavering love. Before meeting Sergei, she had had a few moments with a few men but never fully gave herself to anyone. Sergei was the first man she imagined a future with while the Cuban cigar dealer was the first man she ever loved. He had made her feel as though she could trust him, and she did instantly with every part of her being.

Marina shared her sister's shock, disappointment, and anger. For months, all she had heard were glowing reviews, to the extent that she sometimes wished her boyfriend could have been more like the Cuban cigar dealer.

"I feel so stupid," Mariya said, during a video call with her sister.

"C'mon don't say that. He's a fucking asshole."

Mariya agreed, but regardless of what he was or wasn't, she now had to find a way to get through without the man that made the days and nights special.

Work became her refuge. She dedicated most of her waking hours to Keukeuken Oplossingen. By the end of her first year with the company she was promoted to marketing manager. Everyone in the office except her boss offered congratulatory words and was confident in her ability to head the department.

"If Dan didn't have to go back to Holland, you wouldn't be a manager," her boss said, sounding as dismissive and brash as only he could. In the same meeting, he advised her not to even attempt being as successful as the previous marketing manager.

"Marketing was in his blood. It's not in yours."

Determined to prove him wrong, Mariya dedicated herself to marketing by reading several Seth Godin's books and taking an online class designed to sharpen the skills of any marketer. Her efforts paid huge dividends. In her first twelve months as a manager, she established the company's presence on the most popular social media network in China. She created new marketing material. She also developed relationships with two strategic partners. Still, her boss remained unimpressed and took every opportunity to remind her of how much more talented he believed her predecessor was. Desperate for his approval, Mariya worked even harder in her second year. Marina, her close friends, and even a few colleagues urged her to ignore all his comments and to focus on her well-being. She assured them that she would with no real intention of following through. It seemed the more disrespectful her boss's words became, the more her need grew to be recognized as a key asset.

Midway through her second year as a marketing manager, her boss spent one hundred thousand dollars to sponsor a mediocre football club in the country's professional league.

"They will help promote our brand and the sales will follow," he boasted at a staff meeting. So proud he was of his accomplishment, he told Mariya and her marketing team that he hoped they were taking notes on how to think outside of the box.

Mariya was furious. The fact was that Keukeuken Oplossingen's products were unaffordable for the club's fan base. She could have used half of what he wasted to hire social media influencers. After all, it was how she and her team often brought new perspectives to the office; it was how they recently landed a Keukeuken Oplossingen cabinet in the set design of a highly anticipated romantic comedy. She wanted to expose his idiocy but feared what might happen afterwards. Nonetheless, it was in that meeting as she surrendered to silence that Mariya concluded it was time to find a new employer.

Yet, a year later and days away from her thirtieth birthday, she sat on a stool in a cold and dusty warehouse doing inventory of nothing that was on the list she held. Her thoughts hovered around the marriage, children, and career she didn't have. She tried but couldn't stop the tears that streamed down her cheeks. In her grief, she wondered why her astrologist had repeatedly said that the universe would conspire to help her achieve what she wanted. She told herself that maybe the universe had forgotten about her.

Sound blasted. Startled by her ringtone, Mariya looked down at her phone and almost immediately she wished her sister had followed the universe's lead.

"He finally asked me!"

Marina described the best morning of her life. She did it at breakneck speed without taking a breath and without lowering her voice.

"I can't believe this is happening. I have to call mom but I wanted to tell you first."

There was no way for Mariya to match her sister's enthusiasm but she did her best to at least sound supportive.

"I can hear in your voice that something is wrong."

Mariya maintained she was fine, knowing that her sister knew otherwise.

"This is such a happy day for you. Let's talk about it next time," she insisted.

But Marina refused to hang up until her sister revealed what was troubling her. So Mariya began by berating the warehouse and lambasting her boss for sending her there. Then she unloaded everything her astrologist had told her during their last session.

"You seem to trust her more than you trust yourself."

Mariya protested, claiming that her sister's assessment was incorrect.

"You don't understand. I feel lost."

Mariya's voice broke. Misty-eyed and slouching, she just wanted to be alone. Mariya told her sister she would call back in the evening. Before putting down her phone, Marina said, "You've always known what to do."

Mariya stayed on the stool until her eyes were all cried out. She rose to her feet, flung the list on the floor, and walked out of the warehouse.

NONGFU WATER

Squinting to understand the question, the old woman leaned over the counter, giving the shop clerk standing behind the cash register her entire right ear. Jake grinned as the young woman asked the customer, for a second time, how she wanted to pay for the bag of rice.

"How much is it?"

The old woman must not have seen the digits that were flashing on the cash register nor did she hear the shop clerk announce the price.

"Twenty *kuai*."

"How much?"

"Twenty *kuai*."

Jake admired the shop clerk's patience and how she affectionately called the old woman *ayi*, auntie, even though she was holding up the line. The young woman said the price loud enough for everybody in the store to hear. The old woman, having understood, paused, then asked why the rice was so expensive. In a tone that was surely reserved for the elderly, the shop clerk told her that she didn't know how the price of rice was decided but that it hadn't changed in some time.

The old woman reflected on her words for a moment or two. It might have been longer because Jake started to worry about missing the start of the third period. With the score tied at three after two periods of exhilarating play, he had gotten on his bike and rode down to the store at the start of intermission. But as the old woman slowly pondered her next move, he was tempted to jump in front of her.

"I don't want it," the old woman decided as she slowly turned away from the counter. Jake watched the shop clerk smile politely at the back of the old woman's coat while picking up the bag of rice and placing it on the stool behind the counter. The middle-aged man who was standing behind Jake, complaining about how poor the store's service was, swiftly moved in front of him to buy a pack of cigarettes. Having most likely heard the rant before, the shop clerk ignored his disrespectful behaviour until he exited.

"But he'll be back again tomorrow," she said, underneath her breath. Jake looked at the young woman sympathetically but she was busy scanning the bottle of water, dishwashing soap, and laundry detergent he was buying. When she lifted her face up to announce the price, their eyes met and settled in a slow and deliberate manner. Her eyes were a dark brown that could have easily been mistaken for black; his were a shade of green. In that second, they spoke fluently and freely before thought intervened and suggested that such conversation may be inappropriate.

"Nobody delivered the water yesterday," Jake said in a tone merely stating a fact rather than offering another angry assessment of the store's customer service.

"Really?" she asked, looking for the receipt she had written his address on.

"Yeah, nobody came," he continued. His anxious grin matched her anxious paper shuffling.

"Can you tell me your address again?"

She didn't apologize for losing the receipt, perhaps sensing he didn't require her to.

"100 Yihao Jiayuan, Building 42, Apartment 201."

His easy-going tone indicated that he wouldn't have minded dictating his address one hundred more times or whenever she asked for it. While watching Jake place his phone in front of the scanner to pay, she apologized—or more like admitted to being embarrassed by the lapse in service. He assured her that no harm was done before courteously asking for a guarantee that he would receive his two jugs later in the day.

"Yes, today, I promise."

"Great."

"Okay, it will be delivered this evening."

Jake placed the items in his backpack with a smile that was far too wide for what the situation warranted. He knew that his demeanour was possibly revealing much more than he wanted but couldn't control the feelings that her entire being triggered. He imagined an empty store and ample time to verbalize the questions and statements that had been ruminating for months. He imagined there was no third period to watch because there was no hockey team to cheer for. He imagined breaking through the tall walls of fear to grasp whatever was imprisoned. In that moment, he sensed his heart and freedom. These sensations were lost when a shopper bumped him while trying to squeeze by.

"So yeah, I'll be at home waiting," he said, realizing he was now holding up the line.

Jake thanked her then maneuvered the bag onto his back and hurried out of the store. She didn't say, "You're welcome," perhaps because she knew that was something else he didn't require.

The bright sky had vanished by the time Jake awoke. He had dozed off on his sofa after watching his Canucks lose to the Maple Leafs in overtime. His apartment was now almost pitch black and considerably colder. With his lower body still covered by a small blanket, he put on the big sweater that was serving as pillow, then turned on the air conditioner and set it to twenty-eight degrees Celsius.

As warm air began roaring from the large vents of the white rectangular machine occupying one corner of the living room, his stomach rumbled almost as loudly. His night out with colleagues had involved more drinking than he had anticipated, leaving him severely dehydrated and without an appetite for most of the day. Glancing at the empty water bottle he had finished before the end of the game, Jake now regretted only buying one; but he did take solace in knowing that two 19-liter water jugs would soon be arriving.

His stomach rumbled for a second time. There was nothing in his fridge to cook because he had yet to get groceries. He took a few seconds to appreciate being hungry again, then picked up his phone from the coffee table and opened the food delivery app. He placed an order for a set meal consisting of soup, rice, stewed chicken, and broccoli. Stepping into the kitchen while perusing the documented moments of friends on Instagram, he heard a thud in the hallway. He backtracked to his front door and peered through the peephole. The jug of *Nongfu* water looked like a prized trophy at the top of the staircase.

Jake, not wanting to appear eager, decided to wait until the young man who delivered his water brought up the second jug and did his routine loud knocks before opening the door. Walking back into the living room, he connected his phone to the speakers and streamed music. The second thud came as expected but the knocking that followed didn't have its typical weight or sharpness. As he returned to the front door, he wondered what became of the young man's usual aggression.

"Oh! It's you."

Their eyes met again. Hers were still a dark brown that could have easily been mistaken for black. His remained a shade of green. She smiled, a little out of breath, her cheeks rosy with a touch of shyness and exhaustion.

"I should have helped you."

"No, not at all."

That was certainly not what their eyes were saying, but who speaks in sentiments free from the mind's meddling? And once the mind gets involved, even asking "What is your name?" is considered a possible violation. He needed to believe that the only reason she was standing outside his apartment was to deliver water. She was the shop clerk. He was the customer. That was the only certainty in their interaction. Apart from her being a woman and him being a man, of course.

"That's heavy."

He didn't know why he stated the obvious. Maybe that's what happens when beholding the complex, he wondered. Stating the obvious was his way of hanging onto what was safe.

He assumed she was around his age, presumably younger, but couldn't be certain. There were times when her plump round face showed the innocence of hope. Hope that her work at the shop was only temporary. More visible were the strains of knowledge that stiffened her features. Knowledge of class and country and her place in both.

Was she the daughter of the older woman that was regularly behind the cash register in the morning and the older man who often looked inebriated? Or was she their stepdaughter who was married to the young man that usually delivered the water? Or were they simply siblings? But who was the little boy that frequently sat behind the counter doing homework? Was he their son? If he understood their dialect, he would have been able to decipher the nature of all those relationships; in particular, the one between the young shop clerk and the young man. But having only been in the city for five months, he made no attempts to eavesdrop. Observing their interaction, he had never noticed any displays of affection but maybe he was missing subtle cues.

With a slight squat, he easily picked up both jugs and placed them inside his apartment. Aware that her eyes were on him, this performance of strength was for her. If she was impressed, it wasn't expressed with words or reaction. When he straightened his posture their eyes reconnected. Hers were still a dark brown that could have easily been mistaken for black; his remained a shade of green. Stories flourished. There was much to take in.

Unfortunately, the act of following the unknown with confidence was unfamiliar to them. He settled on her hair: straight, shoulder-length and ebony. It glistened just enough to suggest optimal health. Her hair adorned the collar of her red winter coat like precious jewelry. He wanted to manipulate and smell her mane. There was more, much more, that he wanted to do but noticing the fatigue in her smile thwarted a plunge into such fantasies.

"Oh! Yeah."

Recalling his part of the transaction, he quickly moved over to the water dispenser, pulled out the empty jug, and picked up the other one from the floor.

"Here you go."

In his attempt to be overly graceful – handing her the jugs one at a time rather than at once – he made the exchange awkward. She giggled softly at this moment that seemed to epitomize their interaction. Jake found himself mirroring her. He released a chuckle that was almost silent. Then, for at least a dozen heartbeats – it was probably more considering their nervousness – a recognition of opportunity arose. A ballad, in his language, not hers, but a ballad nonetheless. The poetic wanting of the melody and the song had a paralyzing effect. In that moment, or rather within those heartbeats, they conversed with an honesty that words failed to achieve. In a silence that was as peaceful as the music, she left as the song ended.

SHE OWES ME

Bruce had already decided before engaging with the bar owner that he would accept whatever price was quoted. Bargaining would have felt wrong and, considering what he was about to do, he had a strong desire, perhaps even a compulsion, to feel decent.

"Which one?" the bar owner asked.

Bruce was surprised by how casual the man was about their transaction.

"That one?"

His diffident response was drowned out by the music.

"Her or her?"

It was clear the bar owner wanted Bruce to fully acknowledge who he was in the process of acquiring. As subtly as possible, Bruce gestured, but he couldn't get himself to ask the price. Hoping the bar owner would direct the one he didn't choose to sit at another table, he lowered his eyes and stared at his drink. The man blurted out a number that Bruce found fair; then he jokingly offered both for a discounted rate.

"No, one is fine."

"Shuwah?"

The bar owner's English was somewhat fluent, but his pronunciation of certain words like "sure" was authentically Thai.

"I'm sure," Bruce answered. He smiled uneasily, aware that for the second time he was rejecting the less attractive one.

Sensing the bar owner was going to call over a waitress for more drinks, he made up a story about having to leave immediately. He had been living in the country for almost three years and knew all too well about drinking with women they called "bar girls" and then being stuck with the bill at the end of the night. On this night, he did think that prospect would most likely not be the case since the bar owner was sitting and drinking as well, but Bruce wasn't waiting to find out.

He reached into the pocket of his shorts, pulled out a wad of baht, and handed it to the bar owner. While the money was being counted, he opened his book bag, pulled out a few more bills from an envelope, and placed them on the small table. A terse smile and a handshake and the transaction was complete. Relieved, he downed the last bit of his whiskey, wished the bar owner and the two bar girls a goodnight, got onto his motorbike and rode off.

Technically, he could have taken his pick back to his apartment. As the bar owner assured him, she was all his until Monday; but he was worried about bumping into local and foreign colleagues who lived in his housing complex. They knew him as the creative and thoughtful art teacher who spoke in soliloquies about the importance of adding more beauty to daily life. He became one of the more popular teachers at school when he created a stunning mural reflecting what he regarded as the undeniable interdependence of human beings. Bruce knew that being seen with a bar girl would surely ruin their opinions of him.

The following afternoon, he returned to the bar to pick her up. The ambience of the open space was drastically different without the scantily clad barmaids, the loud pop music, and the clientele of overwhelmingly older foreign men. Rays of yellow sunlight replaced the multi-coloured laser lights spotting the tiny dance floor. And gone were the heavily made-up bar girls playing pool, foosball, or drinking games with men just like him.

"*Sawadee Ka*," she said as he approached.

"*Sawadee Krup*," he replied.

"You speak Thai good."

Bruce imagined that she probably complimented all her clients' Thai skills, but he still appreciated the remark. He also appreciated her doing away with the makeup, neon-coloured high heels, and tight clothing. Dressed in a plain white top, sand-coloured shorts, and flip flops, she resembled the average civilian; the kind of woman that would hardly prompt head turning, finger pointing or wild gossiping.

"So tall," she remarked, angling her hands to roughly measure their height difference.

He noted her thick accent, limited vocabulary, and lack of English grammar. She tended to utter short phrases that ended abruptly. She also put a lot of stress on the wrong syllables.

"Why you so tall?"

"I'm not that tall," he said, grinning. "You're just short."

She responded to his quip by punching him in his side and warned him not to make fun of her stature.

"You sa-mile!"

"No, I'm not."

"Yes, you sa-miling."

"No, I'm not smiling, I swear."

As they set off for the bus terminal, she boasted to be one of the taller members in her family which made Bruce chuckle.

She struck him a second time and threatened to do it again if he continued to tease her.

"You take, okaaay?"

She had already pulled the bag off her shoulder. Surprised by her certainty, he forced a smile while extending his left hand. Once he slung her bag onto his right shoulder and realized how light it was, he instantly wanted to ask why she couldn't carry it herself. But then he figured she was committing to her role and merely behaving the way she would in an actual relationship. The idea encouraged him to do the same.

When they reached the end of the block, he slowed his step.

"I have to give you something before we go on."

He lowered his head and leaned in for a kiss, but she moved her face to the side. "Too many people now," she complained.

His attempt at a public display of affection caused her cheeks to flush. Her embarrassment only compounded his humiliation.

"First time you do dis?"

To Bruce, her question sounded more like judgement. In truth, her tone and style of speaking English made most of her questions sound like an appraisal. Assuming that he knew what she meant by "first time," he nodded and replied, "Yeah."

She noted his reservation because she assured him that once they arrived on the island there would be ample time to do whatever he desired. He clung to that promise for the remainder of the walk and throughout the overnight bus ride to Suratthani when the frequent hankering to kiss, caress, and fondle arose. If he was being honest with himself, he would admit that he saw her as his possession and not his equal. It should have been perfectly tolerable, in his mind, if he decided to pounce on her rather than wait until they reached the island. Yet he waited.

They disembarked from the coach hours before the sun began its ascent. Despite sleeping through most of the trip, she complained about needing more sleep. She then complained about the estimated time they were going to spend waiting on the ferry and the lack of seating inside the makeshift departure hall.

Her voice sounded annoyingly loud in the throng of travelers, the vast majority of whom were foreigners. She was not shouting; it was just that everyone else was either silent or using the lowered voice people usually adopted in a dark and quiet environment. Worried that her negativity was ruining the harmonious atmosphere on the trip, he wished hard that she would stop talking. She didn't. She just couldn't find her way out of the pits of irritability – not until she was sitting on the ferry.

"Dis boat niiiiice, Bruce."

Bruce found nothing particularly elaborate or innovative about the vessel, especially in comparison to the ones he had been on during a holiday in Hong Kong. There were three aisles of seating and a row of oval-shaped windows along the right and left side of the lower deck that accommodated a few hundred passengers. On the main deck, several passengers were reclining on the metallic seating in front and behind the bridge. They appeared to be relishing the sunlight dancing across the splendid blue water. Bruce asked her if she was interested in joining him outside. She wasn't. Watching how captivated she was by the blockbuster Marvel film playing on the large pull-down screen, he understood what made the ferry "niiiiice."

On the island, they had breakfast at a British café and took a taxi, which was more like an oversized *tuk tuk*, northbound. He explained they would have the beach to themselves. He went on about the tranquility they were about to experience and the captivating sights they would see while exploring the island on motorbike.

"Have place can go shopping?"

Because her question sounded like a condemnation of his plans, he was thrown off. The bar owner never asked but Bruce had given him details about the trip he planned so he presumed he would have informed her. And even if she wasn't thrilled about the itinerary, he figured that the money he paid for her company was enough for an inclination to pretend.

"Ah, not really. But if you really wanna shop, we can ride back down to where we got off the ferry," he said, slightly deflated. "That area has places to shop."

He had booked a lavish bungalow on the beach. During high season it would have been far too pricey for his budget. Upon arrival, when he pushed opened the mahogany door and entered, her eyes and mouth opened wide.

"Oh my God! Bruce!" she exclaimed repeatedly as she surveyed the interior with childlike exuberance.

She pulled her phone out of her handbag and took several pictures of the towels and facecloths shaped into two swans in the center of the king-size bed. She laid down next to them for a series of selfies and then she found her way to the newly renovated bathroom. Bruce was delighted by her reaction but did wonder when the photo shoot would end. He was apprehensive about being in any of her selfies as he thought about where pictures of a woman like her would end up. Still, had she asked him to participate, he probably would have; but she never did. Instead, she asked him to step outside when she decided to livestream. And when she was ready to show what the view was like outside the bungalow for the audience tuned into her feed, she ushered him back inside. For a moment he did wonder, had he been younger, weighed less, and sported an oily six-pack, if she would be proud to show him off. It was a bit of an insult for him to realize that she as his girlfriend didn't want him as her boyfriend in any of the moments she was capturing.

"Dis place so beautiful," she declared while re-entering the room. "You rich man, Bruce."

Grinning, he agreed that they were in paradise but denied being wealthy.

He closed the door. As she stood at the desk looking for something in her handbag, he embraced her from behind.

"Listening to you speak Thai to all your followers was such a turn on."

With his hands wrapped tightly around her waist, he planted kisses along the sides of her neck. She didn't pull away, but he could sense the sudden tension in her body. Pressing his lips into her ear, he told her to relax and submit.

His hand brushed her hair to the side, and he resumed kissing the nape of her neck.

"You're so sexy. Are you gonna be my little slut?"

His vulgarity sucked the air out of the room. She understood his question but shied away from answering. He repeated the question, bending her forward and aggressively pushing his bulge on her rump. Without asking anymore, his hand went for her breasts and the other one down between her thighs.

"I shower first, okaaaaay."

It sounded like she was making a plea more than a suggestion. Bruce turned her around, both hands groping her buttocks while he placed his lips on hers.

She didn't immediately welcome his tongue into her mouth, and when she did his heightened intensity seemed to unnerve her into a sober silence.

"We can drink first, okaaaaay."

Certain that alcohol would not enhance his performance, Bruce wasn't receptive.

"I don't need a drink. Besides, it's only ten o'clock."

"No problem, have some drink is better for ..."

"Better for sex? No, it's not."

"Shuwah."

Throughout the course of their exchange, she maneuvered out of his grasp.

"Can I join you in the shower?" he asked.

She giggled.

"Tonight, okaaaay?" she answered, grabbing a swan.

"I'm going to make you scream."

She half-smiled then turned and walked into the bathroom.

While she was showering, Bruce left their rental in search of some liquor. The young woman at the front desk told him there were a few bars along the beach that would be open in a few hours. If he wanted some immediately, she advised him to walk back to the main road and get a *tuk tuk* to take him to the liquor shop. When he asked how long it would take to get there on foot, she laughed, saying it could take up to an hour. Abandoning his mission to get his girlfriend what she requested, he inquired about the nearest place to rent a motorbike. The employee explained the many options in the area surrounding the liquor shop.

Before returning to his bungalow, he walked down to the beach to put his feet in the water. He thought he was alone until he heard the faint laughter of children. About one hundred meters away, two boys and a girl were playing a game with the incoming tide. When the sea inhaled, drawing waves inward, the children chased it; and when it exhaled, they sprinted from the rolling water to dry sand. Bruce watched a man, he presumed to be their father, leave a woman's side to join the game. From the way the woman doted and laughed, he guessed she was the mother. Watching the family create a memory had Bruce conjuring several of his own. Soon he had to look away. He didn't want to contend with his feelings alone.

He became a husband and father in his twenties but later got divorced and was relegated to child-support payer in his thirties. Frustrated by what he perceived as the piercing determination of his ex-wife and her family to drive a wedge between him and his daughters, he decided to create actual distance by teaching abroad. He taught two years in Mexico, followed by another four in Abu Dhabi, and then an additional five years in Seoul. Now in his third year in Bangkok, he was having frequent thoughts of returning home. No doubt his daughters were grown, probably independent young adults, so he was under no illusion of rediscovering his role as dad. Over the years, he had seen how some of their social media posts made it abundantly clear that their father could never make up for his absence. Nevertheless, he made reconciling with both girls his goal. He wasn't sure when it would happen but he believed that if he could settle differences with their mother after more than a decade of bitter fighting, then anything was possible. His ex-wife, who had recently remarried, was the one that encouraged him to consider retiring from the international teaching circuit.

"Have sewen eelewen?" asked his girlfriend when he returned. She was sitting on the bed in just a towel

"There's no 7-Eleven around here."

He made it clear that if she wanted to drink, she would have to wait. She didn't appear bothered by that but clearly wished Bruce wasn't so eager.

"I've been waiting all night," he remarked.

He complained about not being able to sleep on the bus because he was so aroused. She found his frustration amusing and pleaded with him to be patient.

"You're so hot," he said as he rubbed his bulge. "I want you now."

Picking up the second swan and passing it to him lightheartedly, she replied, "You go take shower."

Every word that finished with an "er" sounded harsh coming out of her mouth. Bruce accepted the swan but wanted some sort of guarantee of what would transpire once he re-emerged from the bathroom.

"I waiting for you, okaaaaay."

She appeared to be sincere but Bruce had his doubts. He picked up her travel bag from the floor and took it into the bathroom, all the while mumbling something about ensuring she couldn't get dressed. She laughed at the antic and called him crazy. From inside the bathroom, he responded by telling her she was not permitted to fall asleep.

"This crazy man will wake you up if you do."

She laughed. Raising his voice, to make sure he was heard over the running water, he instructed her to put on music.

"Make it sexy," he called out.

When Bruce stepped out of the bathroom a Thai ballad was playing, and she was lying on her back. His towel covered his lower body, but once he joined her on the bed, he invited her to remove it. She ignored his invitation and called him handsome as she caressed his shoulder. He appreciated the gesture but wanted more, a lot more. Sensing that she was not comfortable nor willing to be the initiator, he rolled on top of her, clumsily, and began kissing her collarbone. At the same time, he tried to remove her tightly wrapped towel.

"Can you wait, pleeaaase?"

She blamed fatigue and a lack of alcohol for not being able to give herself to him. Ignoring her request, he plunged his face into her breasts and rubbed her inner thighs. She pleaded with him to exercise restraint. She clutched the top of her towel with one hand and used the other to block his hands.

"C'mon baby, I've been waiting for so long."

"I'm sleepy, okaaaay."

"But you slept on the bus."

"It's not enough. You sleep next to me, okaaaay."

Bruce, trying to contain his annoyance said, "I'm not tired."

She suggested that after their nap they could have lunch on the main road and buy some alcohol.

"You just don't wanna have sex because you can't drink and forget about my flabby body."

"Noooo, you so handsome."

"I'm so handsome? Really?"

"Yessss."

"Okay," he said, jumping to his feet. "Come."

Looking up at him, she didn't move.

"Pim! I'm paying for you to be here! Do you understand that?"

Bruce shouting her name startled her.

"You're here to let me fuck you and do whatever the fuck else I want to do."

He removed his towel and commanded her to fulfill her duties. She didn't budge. After calling her useless, he threatened to get her fired from the bar.

"Come here and get on your knees," he instructed, not as loud this time but firmly. "Can you just give me what I want?"

He was now perched on the edge of the bed, stroking his erection with his back to her. She didn't instantly move, but when she did it was silently and tentatively. Bruce couldn't see her watery eyes, slumped posture, and trembling hands. He couldn't see how barking at her like she was something instead of someone triggered rage in her. When he turned around to look at her, he saw only her slender and firm body that he paid a lot to secure.

Standing in front of him, she slowly removed her towel and let it fall on the floor.

"You want to fuck me?" Her calm and slightly detached tone gave Bruce the impression his tactics had worked. Stepping in between his legs, she took his hands and placed them on her breasts.

"You like that, *farang*?"

Bruce found the force she was applying odd. Seemingly dissatisfied with his mute confirmation, she began moaning.

"You enjoy dis?" she demanded. Her breasts turned noticeably red from the pressure she applied to his hand. Her moaning continued. She grabbed his right hand with both of hers and placed it on her vulva.

"Put finger inside."

He froze. When she started begging uncontrollably, he suggested they take a break.

"Nooooo, now sexy time, *farang*."

Although he wasn't following her directions, she kept urging him.

"Maybe later," Bruce said hesitantly. "This is getting weird."

She suddenly dropped onto her knees, both hands behind her back and positioned her face into his thighs. He found the way she was speaking to his penis unnerving but kept that to himself. When she asked why he kept pushing her head away, he pleaded for a respite. Unfazed by his increasing disengagement, she crawled over to his backpack and went digging. Moments later, she was crawling back to him with a condom in her right hand. She stood up and turned around.

"I'm a bad girl," she whined. "Punish me, okaaaaay."

Bruce couldn't bring himself to slap her bottom. His reluctance appeared only to increase her assertiveness. Turning to face him once again, she ripped open the wrapper and insisted that he tell her all his "dirty" fantasies.

"Tell me, *farang*!"

The rage was overflowing.

"You want to fuck sexy Thai girl, ah *farang*?"

"Why do you keep calling me *farang*?" he protested while fending her off his member. With her wide eyes and flared nostrils, she shouted coarse words in Thai, making it clear that she would never refer to him as Bruce again. All she saw was a foreigner, a *farang*. Tears fell from her eyes as she continued trying to mount him. Realizing that she couldn't overpower him, she walked to the desk, bent over it and yelled, "*Farang*! Want to fuck my pussy like this!"

He caught glimpse of her teary red face and his bare torso in the desk mirror. In that moment, he knew that he was no different from all the men he had been judging since arriving in her country.

"I hate you, *farang*," she said, her voice breaking just a little.

BIG MAN'S BUS

I wanted him to see it in my face. And if he missed it in my face, then in my stance. At any rate, I wanted a threat stimulus to trigger a fear response in the almond-shaped bundle of neurons located in his temporal lobe. This region of the brain would activate the areas that prepared his body to fight or flee. I wanted him to choose flight, because anything else would result in serious injuries and possibly death. It was not my desire to harm or kill him; not in a foreign land where his behaviour may not have been deemed egregious enough to merit the retribution I was equipped to give.

The other passengers had to understand why I was staring down the man who was operating the coach bus like a dictatorship. Most likely they would not have agreed with the means I was willing to go to achieve my goals of justice and peace. But I hoped they understood why my pupils were dilating, my breathing was accelerating, and my heart rate was rising. Perhaps knowing that my vital organs were being flooded with oxygen and nutrients and that my muscles were being pumped with blood, they could have intervened and urged him to retreat.

As futile and far away as the word "should" is, this standoff should never have happened because he should never have been hired as a ticket collector. He didn't have the temperament or the work ethic for the job. This was made abundantly clear the moment I stepped onto the coach and saw him in my seat devouring a large mango. I courteously showed him my ticket, expecting him to jump up with an apology.

"You've made a mistake," he said, without even looking at the seat number on the piece of paper. The certainty in his tone led me to doubt the woman who sold me the higher priced ticket.

"Your seat is there."

He didn't point at any particular seat but from his slight head twitch I concluded that it was behind him and on the left. His dismissive nature stopped me from asking another question or making a polite request. Perhaps if the journey to Dar Es Salaam wasn't so long, I would have settled for one of the empty seats. But when I considered the hours I was going to spend sitting, comfort became paramount. I decided to step off the coach and return to the ticket counter. As soon as the woman who had sold me the ticket days earlier saw me approaching, she smiled. But sensing my confusion and unease as I stood in front of her, she asked if there was a problem. I explained what happened. Without hesitation or seeking more information, she left her post behind the counter and accompanied me back to the coach.

The ticket collector must have seen us coming because when we got on the bus, he was sitting in another seat. He greeted us, grinning widely while cleaning his fingers with a handkerchief. The ticket vendor spoke to him briefly in one of the local tongues then instructed me to claim the seat that cost an extra five dollars.

I watched him follow her off the bus as I stretched my legs out into the additional space that other seats didn't provide. While the passengers in the rows behind me were having conversations in a collection of voices rising and falling, I couldn't help but wonder if they were talking about me and what I'd just done.

It was two in the afternoon when the ticket collector announced in English that we would be leaving shortly. By the time the bus crawled out of Lusaka's busy terminal, we were forty-five minutes behind schedule. Surely, he was aware of the time, yet he offered no explanation or apology for the delay.

Standing in the aisle behind me, he tapped me on my shoulder to get my attention.

"Move here. This seat is more comfortable," he said with a cunning smile.

"But this is my seat."

I knew that my response lacked the firmness required. The problem was, after bringing in the New Year with more spirits and dancing than I thought was humanly possible, my body and mind felt everything except firm. I had a light headache, my stomach felt a bit queasy, and my voice was hoarse.

"No, this will be your seat."

His confidence was deafening. It's possible that, after smelling liquor on me and noticing my tired eyes, and maybe even recalling how gingerly I climbed on and off the bus, he knew I was in no condition to ignore his wishes. The truth was, even at full strength I might not have protested. I understood that my sense of rightness or fairness was, in blatant ways, useless in a foreign land.

The coach stopped about two hours into the journey, just as I was falling asleep. I probably would have been snoring loudly if I had stayed in my seat. But "if" is another one of those words that fail to reflect reality. My legs felt crammed and I thought about going outside to stretch them out until the ticket collector declared the stop was not a bathroom break. We were parked at the gas station long enough so that the few men who had asked permission could relieve themselves in the bushes comfortably. Yet the ticket collector, known as Big Man by several passengers, perhaps due to his size and authority, blocked the door for all but one of them. The passenger allowed to assuage himself in nature returned to the bus with a bottle of Coke for Big Man.

"You are a VIP," he said, accepting the soft drink. The young man, by far the best-dressed passenger, received a literal pat on his back before returning to his seat near the rear of the coach. The woman I was sitting next to, a native of Zimbabwe, told me that it was beneficial to be considered a VIP. I was mildly curious about how to become one and what some of the perks were, but she didn't elaborate. Instead, she returned her gaze to the world outside the window.

Big Man allowed everyone to step off the coach during the second stop. Most passengers, including me, darted for the facilities. After the bathroom, I visited the food stalls stationed outside the small shop that sold bottled water and other beverages, packaged snacks, and cigarettes. I wasn't particularly hungry, but having only eaten a few oranges all day, I bought a meal consisting of *nshima*, pounded white maize, and *ifisashi*, a stew made with greens and peanuts. I watched Big Man as he sat on a plastic stool not too far from mine gobbling down his food at a speed unmatched. He washed down the meal with a Coke he savoured while talking and laughing with the driver. The moment he emptied his bottle, he declared that the break was over and instructed everyone to get back on the coach immediately. I wasn't the only one who didn't finish eating but none of us objected. At least not audibly.

As evening turned into night, the bus gradually became quieter. That is, the passengers were far less chatty.

Big Man, however, continued his highly animated banter with the driver, stretching his legs out comfortably in what was my seat. In truth, the driver didn't contribute much, at least not verbally. Also, his voice was softer and had less resonance, so when he did speak my ears weren't desperate for noise-cancelling headphones. I thought that once the music stopped playing through the bus speakers, the ticket collector would lower his volume and eventually embrace silence. He didn't. He put on a Nollywood film that inspired more loud talk and interjections. His spirited commentary often drowned out the soundtrack, making it difficult for anyone watching to follow the dialogue.

I wasn't particularly interested in the movie but that might have had more to do with the size of the screen than the actual movie. Much like a light fixture, the monitor, which was only a little larger than the ones displayed on the backs of airplane seats, dangled from the roof on a metal rod. Passengers sitting in the rows behind me needed to have bionic vision and hearing if they wanted to grasp what was happening.

"Oh! Oh! She has gone mad."

Big Man only spoke English when he wanted everyone on the bus to understand. Why he felt the need to share his opinion of the female lead was baffling when he knew the majority of us couldn't see the movie.

"She has lost her mind! What has happened to her?"

I wondered if anyone else wished that he would suddenly lose his voice.

It was almost two in the morning when the bus turned off the road, rolled onto a dirt path, and stopped. The driver went out into the darkness, presumably to relieve himself, then returned a few minutes later. He quietly spoke a few words to Big Man who responded with a grunt and a deliberately vocal yawn as he reclined his seat back without any consideration for my knees. There was no announcement but everyone except me seemed to know what was happening. The Zimbabwean on my right, the two men sitting across the aisle on my left, and virtually every passenger in the rows behind me covered their heads and neck with fabric or even an item of clothing. Because we were stationary, the current of air that was keeping the bus comfortably cool stopped. Quickly, the mugginess outside the open windows entered the bus and clung to everything. While I was contemplating removing my thin long-sleeve top, Big Man placed a large handkerchief over his face. I didn't know what everyone was protecting themselves from, but I started to feel as though I was exposing myself to an unknown danger by not doing the same.

The longer we remained parked, the more annoyed I grew with the driver for not getting us back on the road. I figured he would enjoy a short revitalizing sleep then get back to his work, but the moment he began snoring I knew we weren't going anywhere. It surprised me that the bus company only assigned one driver when two would have kept us safe and on time.

My MP3 player was out of battery power and my electronic reader was in my large backpack stored underneath the bus. I don't know if music or literature would have helped ease my restlessness, but it seemed like a better option than sitting in darkness, convinced I was the only person still awake. In addition to feeling crammed and sticky, my stomach began petitioning for food and my bladder started throbbing, sending signals to my brain. I could fend off hunger but not the need to urinate. The problem was, since being parked, I occasionally heard dogs barking in the distance and was worried about encountering them if I ventured out. As irrational as my fear may have been, it kept me in my seat. An hour or so later, a passenger walked down the dark aisle, maneuvered the door open, and stepped off the bus. Without hesitating, I stood up. Then I paused. I wanted to follow him but after considering how he might interpret that, I decided to sit and wait for him to return before going to relieve myself.

"It will open now," the Zimbabwean said as she picked up a plastic bag overflowing with clothes and placed it on her thighs.

"What?" I asked, not fully awake.

"The border," she answered, reaching for another bag that was at her feet.

She was eager to join the other passengers gathering their belongings and rushing off the bus. I quickly picked up my knapsack and got out of my seat to let her go first.

As I was following the woman off the bus, I asked Big Man why the border was closed.

"Because this is Africa, okay!"

He shot me a threatening look, almost daring me to respond. I didn't understand how such an innocent question could generate that much anger. Even the Zimbabwean was taken aback by his posturing. Once he realized that I had no reply, at least not one that I cared to verbalize, he chuckled then said a few words to the driver who was standing by his side. I probably should have turned back to confront Big Man, but I had a border to cross.

Scores of men, women, and children were standing at the large iron gate ahead of me, the Zimbabwean, and the other passengers. I don't know if they were there all night or arrived as the sun was beginning its ascent. Either way, they were the ones who first took off running as soon as a heavily armed soldier opened the structure. Everyone around me followed their lead. Not wanting to get left behind, I found myself running into Tanzania as well. Even parents carrying toddlers were attempting to keep up with the crowd. I needed someone to explain what the apparent rush and panic was about. If I didn't survey the environment, I could have easily thought we were being pursued by someone or something incredibly dangerous.

"Sixty dollars," the customs officer said with a sly smile.

Convinced he was simply testing me, I grinned then placed two twenty-dollar bills on his desk.

"The fee is sixty. You are missing twenty dollars."

The middle-aged man's smile rapidly faded as he leaned forward in his chair.

"But it's supposed to be forty."

"What are you talking about, 'It's supposed to be forty?'" he said. "I am telling that you need to pay sixty to enter my country."

"But all I've got is forty."

I did have one ten-dollar bill in my pocket and a whole lot of Zambian kwachas; however, I wasn't coughing it up without a fight.

I was showing the customs officer the page in my guidebook that listed the fee when Big Man entered the office. He greeted the three uniformed men working in their small space before turning his attention to me and the only other remaining passenger.

"We are leaving in ten minutes," he said, his voice stern and official. "If you're not on the bus, you will be left here."

For whatever reason, he seemed curious to know how close I was to getting an entry stamp. I couldn't understand what they were saying, but it was clear by their hand gesturing and their expressions that my guidebook was being discussed. Pushing the door open to leave, the ticket collector made a parting comment that prompted the customs officers to burst out laughing. Sadly, the one I was standing closest to found nothing amusing about my determination to pay forty bucks.

"If you cannot pay the amount that is required to enter my country, step out of the line. There are many people waiting."

There were several travelers behind me, and I did feel bad about delaying them, but I still had almost ten minutes to negotiate an acceptable price. The customs officer, however, quickly grew tired of my tactics and directed me to move aside as he called the next person in line. When the other remaining passenger from my bus got his travel document stamped and left, I knew I had to act. I told the officer, who was busy with another traveler, that I would be back shortly. Outside the door stood the young man Big Man had called a VIP. He was in the same spot I saw him in when I first walked into the office.

"You need some dollars, my nigga?" he asked with an American accent that was plainly fake.

I knew he remembered how dismissive I had been of his services earlier and could probably see the desperation now on my face.

"Okay, let's do business, my nigga."

I told him I only had Zambian kwachas and needed ten US dollars. He pulled out his phone, did a quick calculation and then asked for 250 kwachas. The exchange rate he gave me was so criminal that under normal circumstances – where I didn't need any American currency – I would have told him all the places he could stick his deal.

"You know you're basically robbing me, right?"

The young man chuckled as he denied any wrongdoing. I gave him the kwachas and he gave me a ten-dollar note.

"This is business, my nigga."

We stayed at the border an hour after the ten minutes I had been given to get back on the bus had expired. Big Man didn't offer an explanation or an excuse for the delay. I might have been the only passenger expecting him to address us. Once we finally left the border, he did stand and rant about the money customs officers gouged from him. Passengers offered sympathetic sighs while I wanted to laugh and shout, "Serves you right!" When he sat down and reclined his seat, I found myself wanting to violently smack the back of his head. The lack of leg room wasn't my only problem. I couldn't stop scratching two mosquito bites on my neck. Noticing this, the Zimbabwean told me that I should have covered myself before sleeping.

"Nobody told me I needed to."

"You don't have mosquitoes in your country?" she asked.

"We do, but we don't camp at borders overnight."

The woman laughed then said "T.I.A."

"Yep, this is Africa."

Later that morning, we got off the highway for a bathroom break. Big Man, repeating that we were behind schedule, gave everyone a mere five minutes. Despite their hunger, each passenger hurried back onto the bus on time. There were a few who managed to buy a snack, but the rest of us returned to our seats empty handed. The ticket collector and his VIP strolled back onto the bus late both with a soft drink and a bag of chips in hand. Judging by the grease on their lips, they must have devoured something else while in the shop.

"I guess you're right about being a VIP."

"It's like this every time," said my seat mate.

As midday arrived without any mention of stopping for a meal, passengers began expressing their displeasure with words, sighs, and loud sucking of teeth. Aware he was losing favour with his populace, Big Man walked up and down the aisle handing out candy and making small talk. When he offered me a lollipop, I told him that I only wanted water and food. He completely ignored me and zeroed in on the Zimbabwean.

"I will give you two, my sista, because you are very close to becoming a VIP."

She thanked him with a gracious smile and when he asked how she was feeling, she calmly told him that she, like everybody else, was hungry.

"We will have lunch soon and it will be wonderful."

When the bus stopped a short while after, I was about to jump to my feet and run to a food vendor until I realized we were still on the highway. There was an accident ahead of us and, as a result, traffic in both directions was halted. The ticket collector didn't have a problem with passengers getting off the bus to take in the scene but stood in front of the open door when I wanted to go outside.

"Excuse me."

Chuckling, he slowly moved out of the way. Feeling slightly agitated, I thought about asking him what his issue was. But the sounds of motorists and passengers reacting to the cement truck that had flipped over captured my attention and led me away from the bus. With the camera on my phone, I took pictures of the rows of cars, trucks, and buses that were backed up for presumably kilometers. Under a generous sun, I weaved through traffic and people, documenting chaos as well as beauty. I forgot about my growling stomach and mosquito bites. Most importantly, the traffic jam allowed me to forget about the ticket collector. The sounds of nature emerging from the forests on both sides of the highway served as a backing track to all the chatter happening inside and outside the vehicles. Despite being stuck and way behind schedule, there was a sense of freedom that arose in me. I wondered if it was a freedom felt by everyone on the highway and every being in the forests. Sadly, when I made my way back to the bus that feeling immediately left me.

"Excuse me."

Considering he knew that he was blocking my access, I struggled to remain courteous.

"You can wait."

Big Man's words and the disparaging tone left my mouth open in shock. He continued to stand on the first step with his back to me while talking in his usual loud manner to the driver.

"I said excuse me!"

He turned, looking down on me with a smugness that surely came from believing he could exercise power over me without resistance.

"What?" he asked rudely.

"I wanna go back to my seat."

"Have I not told you to wait?"

I'm not sure if I paused before acting or maybe I reacted immediately; all I know is that I shoved him out of the way with two hands. He stumbled into the bus door but didn't fall as I climbed the three steps up to my seat. Standing in the aisle, I was prepared for violence. Big Man quickly made his way up the steps but didn't come within striking distance. He returned my aggressive stare with his own. The chatter on the bus was instantaneously drowned out by my heartbeat which sounded loud enough for everyone to hear. In that moment, I was determined that if someone were backing down, it would not be me.

"This man has gone crazy."

He smirked and told the passengers on the bus that I was looking for trouble.

"But all I want is peace, just like all of you."

His imitation of my menacing stare and stance drew some laughter from the rows behind me. As I returned to my seat next to the Zimbabwean, it became clear that he was attempting to come across as the victim of my unprovoked aggression.

"There's a simple word for that. It's called overreacting," he said calmly while sitting in the back of the bus with his VIP and a few other men.

The Zimbabwean ridiculed his manipulative ways.

"He's a great actor," she said quietly while taking in his performance. "He could win the Oscar."

"All this time I just saw him as a brute and underestimated his craftiness."

Looking directly at me, she added, "This is the kind of man that will rule a city and maybe even a state or country."

When I expressed disbelief that the ticket collector or anyone like him could ever hold office, she smiled and said, "Hey, T.I.A."

TREE'S FRUIT

He was not going to rescue them with an answer. In truth, it was best not to assume he was in possession of one. But if he did in fact have a few clever words to pull the students out of their nescience, he was determined to keep them far from his tongue's tip.

Looking directly at everyone sitting in the circle, Mr. Tree waited for a voice to break through. However, because radio silence always feels longer than its actual duration, and because teachers usually prioritized pushing through curriculum, the students waited for Mr. Tree to concede.

"So again, I ask you," he said, holding tight to his belief in education being the key that unlocked the door to freedom. "What is the value of knowing things when we're walking around with the internet inside our heads?"

He reclaimed his seat in the circle, anticipating more silence. Clearly, the exercise was eating up chunks of class time, making it harder by the second to withhold his conclusions and, more importantly, the roads he travelled to arrive at them. The silence grew. The teacher struggled to quell his rolling waves of doubt. It was only his second week at the school. Naturally, he wondered if he were being unreasonable. The last thing he wanted was for students to complain to parents, parents to complain to school leaders, and then school leaders to reprimand him. Yet, he remained stubborn – some might argue righteously stubborn – waiting for someone to contribute.

"By me sitting here and you guys sitting there, the understanding is that you have something to learn, and I have something to teach. Right?"

The words fell squarely on their shoulders and caused a softening of tense muscles. He saw it around their mouths and in the way their bodies shifted. As blank stares narrowed and focused, he sensed an impending response.

"But you don't really want to learn," he asserted, with a sly grin. "You want to pass exams. And I don't really want to teach. I just want a paycheck. Right?"

The students glanced tentatively at each other, unsure if it was okay to laugh or even smile at the unruliest statement they had ever heard from a teacher.

One student never took his eyes off Mr. Tree. Leaning back in his chair, he scowled. He wanted the entire class to know he wasn't amused by the teacher's antics.

"What's your point?"

His question cut through the apprehension permeating the room.

"My point?"

Mr. Tree wanted to hear, so he often pretended to understand less, a lot less. It was a tactic that his former students found terribly annoying, but it always produced the desired result.

"Is this your way of trying to be a cool teacher?"

The shrewd confidence that propelled these cynical questions shocked the other students. Their eyes seemed to travel with the accusation and settled on Mr. Tree. They waited for a fiery retort.

"Good question, Kirk," the teacher said, calmly. He weighed Kirk's words like they were a precious resource to be handled with care. "It might be ... it just might be."

Mr. Tree nodded, letting his response resonate. The bell rang before anyone, namely Kirk, could contribute.

When students inquired about homework, Mr. Tree pointed at the four questions on the board and announced that every night they needed to write down their personal reflections. The students left the classroom looking utterly confused and disappointed. Kirk sighed before concluding aloud that the homework was useless.

The next morning, Mr. Tree strayed from the textbook again. This time, it was to discuss an article he read during his breakfast about human beings and connection. Hoping to spark an in-depth conversation in the second half of the lesson, he handed out a copy of the article to every student and asked if they wanted to read it as a class. Without consulting his classmates, Kirk, who appeared especially frustrated, responded that they would read the article by themselves. After fifteen minutes, Mr. Tree asked each student to tell the classmate to their right something they learned from the reading. Once this was accomplished, he instructed the working pairs to contemplate the feelings conjured from reading the article. For this portion of the exercise, he encouraged them to use their mother tongue, but he warned they would have to revert to English when it was time to share as a group.

Trusting that his students were staying on task, it filled him with joy to watch them engage each other. Therefore, it was deflating to experience once again their silence when he asked for feedback on the article. Desperate to get them talking again, he asked each pair to report to the class the main points of their discussion. In a disjointed and uninspiring manner, they complied. He thanked them, then he asked if anyone felt a need to connect with another human being.

"It's in our DNA, it's in every fiber of our very being … we're hardwired for connection."

Mr. Tree indulged himself, enthusiastically expounding on the article's importance until he was interrupted.

"How can we know if this is true?"

While leaning back in his chair, with his arms folded, Kirk's inquiry sounded like a condemnation of his teacher's rhetoric.

"Hmm, good question! Very good question."

Sensing that perhaps Kirk wasn't the only one doubtful of what the article was saying, Mr. Tree closed his eyes for a few seconds in gratitude. The question, to him, was a demonstration of curiosity—evidence of a free thinker.

"Well?" Kirk asked sharply.

Mr. Tree replied first by thanking him and his classmates for engaging with the article; next he explained his belief was based on intuition but supported by scientific research. He skillfully placed the focus back on his students by asking if they had ever felt loneliness. Many gave slight nods while the others grunted in agreement. Kirk did neither. Mr. Tree thought about continuing with his point but decided instead to pose the question directly to Kirk.

"Maybe I have, maybe I haven't."

His student's dismissive tone was palpable. It was clear to everyone in the circle that Kirk was not interested in being guided down whatever road that question led.

"You seem a little upset. Would you like to express what's happening inside of you?"

"What do you mean?"

"I'd like to know what you're feeling and needing in this moment."

"Why?"

Mr. Tree paused. He knew that to be alive was to be vulnerable. Yet for a moment, he worried about how much of himself he wanted to reveal. There was a time when he would have gone to extremes to keep it concealed. But tragedy, the unmentionable kind, sobered him.

"Because I want to connect with you."

Kirk's body rejected the teacher's plea before he could even formulate a response.

"And why would you want to do that?"

The bell rang. Kirk was the first one to pick up his school bag and spring from his seat. As he exited the class with a few students, he took time to glare at his teacher. Mr. Tree caught the hurt underneath the boy's anger and decided that class wasn't over. He followed Kirk and his classmates into the hallway where the usual quiet and loud activities of high-school kids expanded in all its textures and colours.

Calling out to his students, his hands began to tremble.

"Because if I can hold space for whatever's inside of you and you and you and you," he pleaded, "and if all of you can do the same for each other, then maybe we can make our time here matter." Watching Kirk and the three other students intently, he let his words settle.

His students, along with every other student in the hallway, were dwelling within the crevices of an experience that wasn't generated by a cell phone or tablet. Snapped out of their routine-induced slumber, they shared in a contemplative moment that felt real and important.

"Maybe I don't want it to matter," Kirk said coldly.

With that, the boy turned and walked away, assured that he had delivered a crushing blow to his teacher's appeal. His classmates followed. Their movement, however, relayed varying degrees of reverence to a display that deserved to be acknowledged and remembered.

Mr. Tree watched as the hallway traffic quickly returned to normal. Although the students' attention was reclaimed by the more pressing cares of teenage life, he hoped the moment they shared with their peers would linger. He was well-acquainted with moments that lingered.

Returning to his classroom, he stood at the large window observing students below filing out of the building. He fixated on their movement for a while until his heart started its familiar ache.

First, memories overflowed of the childhood birthdays followed by school recitals and inter-city soccer games. As always, he wondered how the joy could evaporate overnight. Next, came the self-blame that took a firm hold. It would not be the last time he railed against his own weakness in the face of death. Moving back into the circle of chairs, Mr. Tree took a seat. He sat hunched over with his head lowered, crippled once again by a lonely farewell.

MY DARLING NIKKI

It was my seventh morning on the island. My room didn't have the grandest view of the sea but waking up to the sounds of nature's symphony brought a smile to my face for the seventh consecutive morning. There was something stirring about the rhythmic sounds of the tide storming the beach, small tropical birds tweeting, and palm leaves swaying with the gentle winds. As I lay in bed, looking up at the ceiling fan, I embraced my fortune by stretching my arms above my head and releasing a long yawn.

Downstairs, inside the guesthouse's open-air restaurant, I wrote in my journal as I waited for breakfast. Before sitting down, I had told myself today would be the morning I'd eat something other than bacon, sausages, scrambled eggs, toast, and beans; but the minute I got a whiff of all that American-breakfast goodness served to a gentleman at the table on my left, I succumbed.

After breakfast, I usually went back upstairs to exchange my notebook for the novel I was reading. In fact, my feet were moving in that direction when I paused, realizing that I had a lot more to write. Looking out at the sublime white sand and the shades of turquoise water, I thought about the places I could go to continue journaling. I had been meaning to return to the giant rocks at the very end of the beach where, on my second day, I had observed the humbling powers of the sea. As I set off, I began to regret not going back to my room for my baseball cap. Though the climbing sun was showing restraint, I knew that in a few hours its rays would be beaming down in a merciless fashion. Still, I kept walking along the sandy boardwalk at a pace that suggested I was on a mission.

I wasn't too far away from the giant rocks when I noticed her in my peripheral vision. Slowing down, I quickly processed her long cornrows that reminded me of a young Alicia Keys and her smooth golden skin that presumably had a lasting love affair with the sun. I might have paused before I knew that I was pausing. In the same way, I might have turned back and made a beeline toward the beach chair she was reclining on before realizing that I was approaching the most alluring stranger I had ever seen. I would have liked to think I didn't freeze when, sensing my presence, she looked up to settle her bold, hazel eyes on me; but I certainly might have been frozen on the spot. If only I could have had the time to write something eloquent or at least a few minutes to formulate one cohesive statement from the wealth of information I was taking in.

"All I got is hello."

I chuckled nervously at how pathetic the words sounded once they traveled out of my mouth.

"'Hello' is a great start."

Her response was coated in a soft accent that I couldn't place. It gave me the confidence I needed to sit on the beach chair next to her. There, with my notebook in hand, I explained how I was walking toward the giant rocks at the end of the beach to write in my journal.

"So just know that I'm making a sacrifice to be here with you."

Her laugh was not the loudest, but it was the most genuine I had heard in a while. It seemed to fit perfectly with the size and shape of her mouth along with her slender, slightly toned frame. When we finally got around to exchanging names, and I was playfully refusing to share the story behind mine, embarrassment happened. In Nikki's defense, she did warn me about still feeling nauseous from her bout with food poisoning, but I didn't imagine it manifesting itself in such a watery and putrid manner.

"I'm so sorry."

Only a few drops of vomit splashed on my foot; the bulk of what she retched formed a tiny puddle in the sand. I jumped to my feet, rushed to the small shop selling beach attire that was sandwiched between two restaurants, and procured a plastic bag. When I returned, Nikki was sitting up in her chair using her feet to cover the vomit with dry sand. She thanked me for the bag then apologized a second and third time.

The way she retracted and raised the first vowels in words, abbreviated almost everything, and ended most of her sentences with a rising inflection added to a foreignness I found endearing.

"I'll completely understand if you'd rather go on with your day now."

Even though I wasn't glancing down at my flip flops or back at my notebook and pen, she spoke as if I was preparing to leave. She had no idea that it would take a lot more than a bit of regurgitation to drive me away.

Grinning, I said, "If I'm still here in five minutes we just may have something."

For the first couple of minutes, Nikki alternated between hiding her face in her hands in exaggerated shame and begging me to forget what just happened. I asked her, "What incident?" She gave me an appreciative smile but still seemed to be replaying the scene in her head.

"I guess that negativity bias thing is real, huh?"

"Oh my God! So real!"

The excitement in her voice lit up her face and seemed to move down her body like a bolt of lightning.

"I wrote a paper about that last year."

It turned out she was a third-year neuroscience student at Monash University. If I had known that tidbit earlier, I wouldn't have brought up negativity bias to impress her with my knowledge. Not only did she offer a well-crafted definition of the term – her definition made the one I had in my head seem incredibly malnourished – she gave examples of the impact on an individual's health and the overall state of a society. I was shocked when she told me that according to several studies, infants barely half-a-year-old exhibit signs of it when forming social assessments of others.

"You're amazing."

"Me?"

"Yes, you!"

"No, I've always had a fascination with the brain," she explained. "And what I find really exciting is how little we actually know about it, so there's tons to discover."

Nikki confided that because her grandmother on the Australian side of her family suffered from multiple sclerosis, she really wanted to do her future research on neuroinflammatory conditions. I could have listened to her talk for hours about what she was learning in university, or as she called it, "uni," and what she was planning to do after getting her degree.

I was flattered when she inquired about my major. I told her that I graduated from university almost a decade ago which she didn't believe. She asked to see some identification. Then she made me promise to share whatever elixir or beauty tips she swore I had.

"The passion you have is way more valuable than my magic potion."

I admitted that throughout my four years in the Education program, I was never passionate about what was being taught or what I was doing.

"In listening to you, I know that's what was missing."

I told her that those years were uneventful and took her through my teaching career back home and overseas. She appeared to absorb my words as I made it clear that I had no intention of staying in education much longer. When I explained that, in recent weeks, I had been contemplating returning to school to study law, her expression told me my news was well-received.

"Teaching is cool, but I wanna do more, you know?"

Candidly and without antagonism, Nikki asked if a career in law was calling me because I wanted to contribute more to humanity, or did I merely want the salary and prestige that came along with it?

"Yeah, I just wanna buy a Benz and have a kick-ass condo," I said with a chuckle. "Oh, and I wanna travel to all the coolest spots on the planet."

"I knew it!"

We laughed with an ease that usually takes time to develop.

"It's funny because when we think about lawyers, we think about money and—"

"Lying," she added.

"Oh yeah, lying lawyers. So, it's like, money and lies, right?"

"Right."

"But the people I wanna represent might not be able to afford me. So I see myself doing a lot of pro bono work. You know, taking on clients that are being screwed by unjust laws and stuff."

Her eyes widened the more I shared my desire to help the poor and disenfranchised in my hometown. She asked questions and remained patient during my long-winded responses. At some point, she concluded that the world could use more lawyers who believed in protecting and restoring human dignity. It was then that I told her about a recurring dream I had been having for almost a year. In the dream, I travel from country to country helping those indigenous to the land reclaim the resources that have been stolen by corrupt leaders and multinational corporations.

"It's so vivid. I really see myself taking those bastards on."

She nodded in agreement as I ranted about how much better the world would be without certain individuals and institutions.

"Bush and Blair are war criminals. And that fucking Monsanto, has there ever been a more evil company?"

"So true! So, when do you start?"

Chuckling, I answered, "If only it was that easy."

I told her that I hadn't even begun studying for the LSAT much less figured out where I wanted to do my degree. When she replied that any law school would be fortunate to have me, her voice had no inkling of doubt.

"Thank you. Are all you Melbourne people so positive?"

"Absolutely not!"

We shared another laugh. In doing so we continued shedding the surface layers that prevent people from truly being seen and heard.

"Breaking news! It's been five minutes," I announced.

"Way more than five minutes."

"Yep, and I'm still here."

"And I couldn't be any happier."

"Neither could I."

"Neither could I too!"

While I laughed at that, she asserted with complete confidence that good grammar and syntax were overrated. This only made my laughter grow louder, so she responded by striking my shoulder and vowing to stop talking.

"Please don't do that," I said, trying to keep a straight face, "I love how you express yourself".

"But you're still laughing."

"I'm gonna stop, I promise."

We both knew that wasn't true.

"I hate you so much right now."

Once I was done teasing her, I suggested we do something to celebrate our five minutes together. She blurted out an option that I couldn't comprehend, because of her accent. It was only after a third attempt, when she raised her voice and exaggerated her enunciation, that I understood she was inviting me to go for a swim. Out of genuine concern, I asked if she felt up to being in the water. She stood up, did a small hop, and announced she was feeling much better. I didn't necessarily doubt her, but I did ask if she was sure it was a good idea. Nikki dismissed my question, saying there was no need to ever worry about her and the sea. The moment I watched her submerge her entire body into the water I understood her self-assurance. She was undeniably a strong swimmer. It didn't take her much time to distance herself from the shore, where she floated on her back like a star fish, then returned to where I was sitting in the water with my legs stretched out in front of me and my hands at my sides to keep me propped up. She teased me for looking more like a model than a swimmer as I showed no sign of wanting to get my upper body and face wet.

"Can you swim?"

"Ah yeah, I mean, I'm not great, but I can swim."

"So let's see it."

I don't know how many steps I took, but I walked until the water came up to my lower chest. I submerged myself into the sea and began swimming. It's hard to say how many meters I covered, but once I stood up, she was there giggling and mocking my technique. She said it looked like I was trying to beat the water into obedience.

"Whatever," I said, splashing water in her face.

She retaliated, then I did the same. We slapped water at each other like giddy children. After some time, hoping to end the battle as well as touch her – it was difficult not to stare at her wet body adorned with a skimpy white bikini and several tattoos – I picked her up out of the water and threw her back in. Shocked by my show of strength, she promised to get her revenge. She went underwater and began reaching for my legs to trip me up. When she resurfaced, I directed a flurry of splashes at her before escaping. I taunted her as she pursued me onto the beach and around our chairs a few times. She finally relented after I agreed to stop imitating the look she had on her face when I was holding her up in the air above the water.

The long cushions on our chairs had absorbed so much heat from the sun that reclining was unbearable. Neither of us had a watch or a phone but from the sun's position in the increasingly cloudless sky, we surmised that midday had arrived. I offered to show her the giant rocks at the end of the beach and even swore not to throw her off any of them. She said she would have accepted if she didn't have to meet her mother at a nearby spa where lunch, massages, and other self-care activities were on the day's agenda. To make matters worse for me, her mother had made dinner plans with an older couple they met on a boat trip.

"Tomorrow, I'll have brekkie with mum but afterwards I have to see you."

I loved how Nikki called breakfast, "brekkie."

"Oh really?"

"We're spending the day together and it's non-negotiable, hey."

She might have known by how I looked at her that I longed to spend a day, a week, a month and possibly years (hopefully "years" was not plastered across my face), in her company. But not wanting to come across as too eager, I smiled and said, "Sounds good to me."

Away from the sea and the breeze that accompanied it, the heat was having its way with us. I couldn't tell if it was affecting the fish market vendors. They were standing behind their stalls surveying the sea creatures and sea vegetables being carried in large plastic containers, some cylindrical and others rectangular, into the outdoor space by hardworking shirtless men who were surprisingly bone-dry. I couldn't tell if it was bothering the vegetable and fruit sellers. They sat on small stools lining both sides of the road and repeating, in varying volumes, the prices of their fresh and colourful produce. I couldn't tell if the children lamented the heat. (None of them, we noticed, were carrying a book bag or wearing a uniform to suggest going to or coming from school.) They seamlessly navigated their way through an adult world of organized chaos highlighted by frantic commerce and motorized vehicles. Only the dogs, sprawled out at almost every corner, shared in our suffering. Like us, they looked parched and fatigued.

"This is the price we pay to escape that fake world," I said, wiping a layer of sweat off my forehead with the back of my hand.

"Clearly worth it, hey."

For some time, as my wet t-shirt and shorts clung to my body, I was certain she was wrong. But as we continued to explore the densely populated roads and lanes where locals were going about their day in a myriad of ways, I realized how gratifying it was to leave the beach. Our walk was providing me with views of what the island might have looked and felt like before Westerners determined that its white sand beaches were worthy of their encroachment.

She explained how her mother, who was from the capital city a couple of hours away, remembered visiting the island before the establishment of beachfront resorts, boutique hotels, and guesthouses. During those visits, her mother stayed with family friends who taught her about the importance of the sea. They also taught her the local dialect known for its expressions to describe human emotions in ways that the country's official language and English couldn't.

"Mum met Dad here."

"Really?"

"Yeah, but at the time it was so uncommon to see the whole interracial thing so …"

"What happened?"

"She made Dad work really hard."

With a chuckle, I asked if she was going to do the same to me. She smiled and said that her dad made several trips from Australia to convince her mother and the family that he was sincere.

"I already know you're sincere."

The assurance with which she uttered those words almost made me grab her hand and lean in for a kiss. I couldn't tell if she was longing to feel my lips on hers, so I played it safe by pumping my right fist in celebration and saying, "Yes! She thinks I'm sincere." Nikki giggled at my response, then finished what she was saying about her parents' courtship. She admired her mother for not throwing herself at her father just because he owned a large house and a fancy car in an economically advanced country.

"Old dirty white men come here thinking they can have whoever and whatever they want."

Her vitriol was palpable while she expounded on the power dynamics between those foreign men and the local girls.

I processed her claim that loads of them were in the country solely to have sex with underage girls. "That's fucked up," I said. It clearly pained her to think that many of the little girls selling beads, bracelets, and other trinkets along the boardwalk would soon be selling their bodies.

We jumped into the water as soon as we returned to the beach. It didn't take long to start up a second round of playful yet aggressive splashing. Feeling considerably more comfortable with one another, the splashing rapidly turned into wrestling that left both of us breathless.

"This is the bear hug," I said, breathing a lot heavier than usual as I lifted and squeezed her into me.

"I like it."

Everyone and everything around us seemed to ease into a stillness as silence settled—a silence that was more than the mere absence of sounds. It arose from the depths of longing and erased the distance between us. When our hearing returned, only her breath and mine were audible as my eyes navigated hers. I don't know what I was searching for nor what I was discovering. All I knew was that Nikki had the most arresting presence. In surrender, my eyes closed gently while my lips and then tongue spoke. And the way she placed her hands on the sides of my face as we continued our wordless communication made me feel cherished. When our lips unlocked and we found ourselves staring at each other again, I told her that I was fortunate to have met her.

"Ditto."

These utterances only increased the intensity of our exchange. The sea became our sanctuary and neither of us wanted to exit.

When her stomach growled a little after mine began making its demands, we celebrated. Although she had eaten and kept down two meals since getting sick, it was the first time in two days she felt hungry. We held on to each other while discussing our options. There was no shortage of restaurants along the boardwalk. Her only requirements were no seafood and nothing spicy.

Before we got out of the water, I asked her to teach me how to float. I confessed to quitting my swimming classes when I was seven because my instructor attempted to get me into the starfish position. Struggling to contain her excitement, she told me that I would be floating within a few minutes.

"Saltwater makes it way easier."

I felt pretty confident until she asked me to slowly fall back and trust my buoyancy, which she claimed every human being possessed. My doubts multiplied when my lower body began sinking. If it weren't for her hands beneath my lower back, my torso would not have remained afloat. Adopting the calm and soothing tone of a meditation guide, she reminded me to relax and take short breaths that retained as much air as possible in my lungs. I heard the instructions, but my body was still tense. And I could only imagine how much my face was contorting. My hope of overcoming my angst was vanishing when, suddenly, I felt her lips on mine. Her kiss gave me a burst of energy followed by sensations of lightness. It was as if I was experiencing a deeper dimension of the sea. And for what felt like longer than a few moments, the sea did carry me.

"You did it!"

"That was amazing! I really didn't think it was gonna happen."

I told her that she was the best floating coach anyone could ask for and that lunch would be a small token of my appreciation. She accepted but also requested a piggyback ride to whatever restaurant we chose.

We settled on an extravagantly decorated eatery that was closer to my guesthouse than the expensive hotel she was staying at with her mother. It was impossible to miss the large banner at the entrance wishing patrons a 'Happy Valentine's Day', or the rose placed in a glass vase on every table, or the masterful chalk drawing of the naked winged boy with a bow and arrows on the blackboard advertising the day's specials. If that wasn't enough, every employee had a heart sticker on their chest which complemented the Atlantic Starr songs blaring through the speakers.

With only one other couple in the restaurant, a waitress rushed over to us with menus as we sat at a table underneath Cupid. Smiling incessantly, she seemed reluctant to retreat and give us time to survey the options. Eventually, she did.

"I was so worried she was going to wait for us to place our order," Nikki said in a quiet voice.

"Yeah, I was gonna tell her: 'Look, I need at least five minutes.'"

"More like ten for me," she said, blushing slightly. "I'm like the worst when it comes to ordering food."

"It's all good; take your time."

"Awww, that's sweet."

"Well, in case you forgot, it's Valentine's Day."

"Thank you for the remainder, hey."

We laughed but agreed that the festival felt more authentic on the island than it did in our respective countries.

"If a spot back home did all this, it would come across as super cheesy," I said.

"Yeah, totally."

"But here it just works."

"People are always listening to sappy love songs here whereas my mates and I never play that stuff."

We wondered what it said about our own societies when we mocked and dismissed ballads as music for old people or the naïve. When the bubbly waitress returned, we both ordered large wraps – vegetarian for Nikki – a garden salad, and spiked milkshakes.

As All-4-One's "I Swear" played overhead, I remarked that she was my first real Valentine. Naturally, she doubted what I was saying, but once I explained how in the few times I was in a serious relationship it either ended or went on a break by February 14th, she understood. Reaching for my hand, she giggled while telling me that she hoped to be the best Valentine I would ever have. When I inquired about her last Valentine, she laughed nervously before claiming that she couldn't remember. I shot her a suspicious look, which instantly improved her memory.

"Last year."

Something in me did want to know who he was, but I was averse to prying. She asked me what I thought about Cupid who appeared to be watching over our table. I chuckled and said, "Love is dead, and Cupid killed it." A polite smile wasn't the reaction I expected. Nevertheless, I continued to malign Venus's son by making several unsubstantiated statements about his character and life. She didn't laugh nor did she add any of her own outlandish claims. When I asked if something was wrong, looking almost apologetic she said, "He was my boyfriend and still is."

"Huh?"

"Last year's Valentine."

"Oh."

Shock has a way of snuffing out oxygen and even vocabulary for that matter. The waitress came back with our food and drinks still beaming with excitement. Sensing the drastic change in mood, she was quick to dart back to the entrance.

"I'm so sorry."

This was the first of many apologies she would offer during the meal.

"It's okay."

There was more I wanted to say and a lot more that I wanted to ask, yet apart from repeating "it's okay" with a thick layer of indifference, I was unresponsive. She tried to draw a thought, a feeling, anything out of me but soon realized her efforts were futile. Despite how quickly my appetite deflated, I cleaned my plate then waited for her to do the same. Soon after, I took care of the bill and walked out of the restaurant with her following a step or two behind. I could hardly look at her as we stood on the boardwalk. Meanwhile, Whitney Houston's "I Will Always Love You" swelled behind us. Wanting to escape, Nikki suggested we find a quiet place to talk.

"I think I'd rather be alone right now."

That might not have been the truth. I wanted to give her an opportunity to explain herself. I also wanted to pretend she didn't have a boyfriend and continue with our evening plans. But ultimately, I felt betrayed. Even though she hadn't lied to me and didn't owe me anything, knowing that she had a boyfriend was upsetting.

"Maybe we can talk later."

She was about to respond but stopped when she saw me turn and walk away.

I went back to my guesthouse to get some rest; but with my room being directly above the restaurant I frequented every morning for breakfast, it was difficult to block out what sounded like the most romantic playlist ever created. Lying on my back, I reached for my novel and started reading. My eyes were looking at words, spaces, and punctuation marks but my mind was somewhere else. After reading the same page more than twice, I put the book down. For the next little while, I thought about how pathetic it was to be alone in my room on Valentine's Day with the most beautiful beach I had ever seen only a few footsteps away. I didn't want to think about her, but thoughts do what they want when the mind is restless.

There were many internet cafés along the boardwalk, especially east of my guesthouse. The problem was that Nikki's hotel was eastward and I promised myself that I would not walk in that direction for the remainder of my stay on the island.

Travelers were occupying every computer in the first internet café I passed, and so I kept moving. After some time, I found a small establishment with plenty of empty chairs. The computers were a bit older and the internet was a bit slower than at the cafés I usually visited near my guesthouse. Once I finished replying to a few email messages that had been in my inbox for days, I looked at heartbreaking photos and read crushing articles about the recent tsunami that ravaged Thailand, Indonesia, and twelve other countries.

An hour or so later, I sat on the beach and watched the bright orange sun descend into the water, leaving traces of red, pink, and violet in the twilight skies. We were supposed to take in the sunset together. We were also supposed to have dinner on the beach, go dancing at the popular clubs, and end our night on the sand gazing up at the stars.

When I got out of bed the following morning, I noticed small sheets of folded paper on the floor. It was a letter, five pages long, that was tied with decorative twine. I swiftly opened my door, wishing that she would somehow be waiting outside my room. She wasn't and I felt silly for thinking that she would be. I tried to figure out when Nikki had slid it underneath my door. I doubted that she came by after I had returned from my depressing night out. It must have been after the sun rose. Plopping myself down on the bed, I read her sincere apologies for not being forthright about her ongoing relationship with a man she appreciated deeply but claimed not to love. I read excerpts from the colourful, inner dialogue she was having with herself since our first encounter, as well as a detailed account of what she hoped would transpire between us before she departed from the capital city to Australia in two days.

Delaying my breakfast, I practically ran to the internet café that was closest to my guesthouse and sent her an email message expressing my regret over how I had abruptly ended our Valentine's Day. I also agreed to meet her the next day when I passed through the capital city on a 24-hour layover. A few hours later, I received a passionate reply that made me yearn to be where she was. I responded immediately and waited for her to do the same. This continued for some time, until we sensibly decided to further our communication on MSN Messenger.

We spent the entire day and evening immersed in a world of sharing how we felt and acknowledging that we were creating in real time online. Our only moments apart were during lunch and supper. Then again, I carried her with me even while I ate, imagining her doing the same. If the internet cafés didn't have a closing time, I would have been extremely sleepy with my pockets a lot lighter as I made my way to the airport early the next morning.

When Nikki and her uncle picked me up from my hostel, she told me we would be attending her grandfather's birthday party. While we did sing "Happy Birthday" and there was cake, the gathering felt much more like a celebration of what she and I discovered on the same island where her parents met. The entire room greeted me with the warmest smiles and pleasantries. Upon meeting Nikki's mother, I instantly recognized her same great posture and playfulness. They might not have shared any striking resemblances in terms of facial features and body measurements, but it was clear they were mother and daughter. Her aunts outnumbered her uncles, but she had slightly more boy cousins than girl cousins. One aunt, the one she and her mother were staying with, made everyone laugh when she imitated her niece sitting at the computer typing what she believed were love messages to me. She told the room that her niece typically enjoyed going out for street food, shopping, and frequenting the cinema whenever she visited, but yesterday her only interest was me. Her mother chimed in by declaring that I was the reason her daughter recovered so quickly from a terrible bout with food poisoning. We posed for pictures and answered countless questions in tandem.

Later that afternoon, the mood was drastically different as we sat, hand in hand, in the backseat of her uncle's car, trying to postpone the inevitable. Despite all the thoughts swirling in my head and possibly hers, we said very little. Perhaps a few more words might have been shared if her mother and uncle weren't with us but, in truth, what could be said when distance was about to bully its way between us?

The tears, more hers than mine, began as we neared the airport. She sank her head into my chest, her anguish a stifled version of the saddest chord progression in music. I wrapped my arms around her and rested my chin on the top of her head, biting my bottom lip as I tried to repel the effects of her broken notes. Nikki's uncle was reluctant to announce our arrival, but he didn't need to. Even with the windows up, the sound of police officers blowing their whistles and barking commands at drivers who lingered on the platform beckoned our attention. Her uncle explained that because of the recent bombings, he was not allowed to park or even remain on the platform after she was out of the vehicle and had collected her belongings. Her mother, sounding deeply sympathetic as if she already knew the answer, asked him whether I was permitted to enter the terminal. He said I wasn't, which only made Nikki's pain more audible.

Moving at a snail's pace, we made it up the ramp and onto the platform where families and friendships were coping with imminent departures. As soon as the car stopped, she asked me to move with her to Melbourne.

"You can teach there."

When I didn't respond, she, squeezing my hand as we drowned underneath waves of emotions, began begging. Every cell in me wanted to hold on, even with the cars behind us sounding their horns and even with a police officer coming over to remind her uncle of the rule.

I watched Nikki climb out of the vehicle as her mother and uncle said the one word that stayed lodged in my throat: goodbye.

TIME ON THE *GHAT*

He tolerated the pointing and staring but pulled out a sword from his dusty cloth bag and raised it above his head, poised to strike, whenever he caught a passerby taking his picture. These actions were always accompanied by threats that he had absolutely no intention of fulfilling. Threats that were so outrageous, he often had to refrain himself from laughing when he made them.

It would have been presumptuous to call his reaction or response a performance, but it would be just as naïve to assume he truly found those individuals bothersome. From his seated position, on the lower steps of the *ghat*, he had to turn his naked body all the way around or at least look over his shoulder to catch perpetrators. Rarely did he make that effort. As a result, many onlookers were able to steal shots of the back of his head, which was covered with long and dirty matted hair cloaked over his scrawny shoulders. He tended to reprimand the photography enthusiasts who maneuvered down a set of steps at an angle to catch a bit of his profile. Then there was the few who dared to walk down all the steps, stand in front of him, and aim their lens to capture his emaciated face and his nudity. For a moment or two, he glared at those individuals as though he could incinerate them by shooting fire out of his dark penetrating eyes.

Magesh – the name he was given at birth but no longer used – stood out from the other *sadhus* in the city; in particular, those sitting along the riverbank. Rather than yellow or orange fabrics, he covered his body from head to toe with ash that represented death to his worldly life. And while his peers allowed practically anybody to sit and recline with them, Magesh was selective about who he invited.

155

Apart from the occasional traveler — typically a young man or woman with profound questions about life — and except for conversations with the young man who brought him sustenance in the form of fruits and ganja, he observed silence. It was within silence, and solitude for that matter, that he encountered the greatest peace he had ever known.

At various times throughout his days and nights, he found himself wondering if it was a mistake to have abandoned his cave in the Himalayas. There, he could feel his connection with nature in a profoundly tangible manner whether his eyes were open or closed. In contrast, the glory of the Ganges, which drew him to the city along with scores of pilgrims, couldn't upstage the restlessness overwhelming his surrounding environment. He failed to make sense of the endless and often unfair commercial transactions that took place merely steps away from men who encircled the shrouded corpses of their family members burning on neatly stacked pyres while chanting *ram naam satya hair*, God's name is truth.

The mental agitation that Magesh detected in the pilgrims was hard to overlook, especially when he first noticed it within the cows, goats, and dogs that populated the ghats. Fortunately, there was a respite. Every evening at a quarter to seven he closed his eyes and delighted in the sounds emerging from the *puja* being held on one of the larger ghats. Although the ceremony only lasted forty-five minutes, the invocations, prayers, and songs created a devotional atmosphere that hovered for some time, but never long enough, above the riverbank.

Magesh had a similar experience earlier in the year when he and the other men in his order had descended on a nearby city to participate in the country's largest religious festival. The exhilaration that had surged through his body when he had stepped into the waters at the confluence of the Ganges, Yamuna, and Saraswati (an invisible river) was indescribable. Bathing with thousands of other ash-covered men, who had journeyed from the north, south, east, and west to keep the ancient custom alive, had filled his spirit with humility and gratitude. He'd been uplifted by the sea of worshippers, gathered from all segments of society. Eagerly, they had awaited their turn to enter the confluence that was supposed to liberate them from the endless cycle of life and death.

But as the festival had moved into its second and third week, and the crowds grew, these pleasant feelings started to dissipate. Soon, the bulk of the activity on the festival grounds appeared more performative than contemplative. Except for the sages and the pious, everyone turned into spectators once they bathed in the auspicious waters. These legions joined the increasing number of foreigners that were present solely to appreciate the festival from the sideline. Together, with their cameras, phones, and drones, they moved around the grounds trying to document as many moments and images as possible.

After a month, Magesh noticed there was noticeably less space designated for discussions and debates. What attracted the expanding crowds were the displays of startling body control or pain tolerance that added to a well-established belief about certain sadhus possessing magical powers. Scattered across the makeshift tent city were men that hadn't sat down in years; some who held difficult yoga poses for hours and others who demonstrated their skin-stretching abilities. There was one older man who kept his right arm up straight for the last eight years. And a few that wrapped their penises tightly around a stick, then applied pressure by hanging from them heavy objects like stones and baskets filled with food. In a lighthearted moment, Magesh told a member of his order that the throngs of spectators were probably waiting on someone to start levitating or walk on water. His peer laughed and suggested that onlookers would surely appreciate watching one of them survive being buried alive without air or water.

Magesh was even disappointed with those who chose to sit and share the chillum. They appeared to be far more interested in posing for selfies amid the clouds of smoke rather than learning the mantras he and his peers had been chanting to draw closer to Shiva. He observed how those who gave alms were often the ones guilty of trivializing his and his peers' unorthodox lifestyle the most. This, he believed, was done unintentionally and the result of conditioning that transpired in societies obsessed with productivity, entitlement, and entertainment. Having once been a slave to such conditioning, he understood the motivation behind the words and deeds of these individuals trapped in *avidya,* ignorance. Despite his understanding, he still allowed himself to feel annoyed, while at the same time sensing his ultimate unity with them.

The devotees of Shiva from another sect attracted very few onlookers since they were known to meditate on corpses, walk around with a skull, and eat their own bodily wastes. Some even devoured dead human flesh. Those men maintained that all opposites were fundamentally illusory. Therefore, on their path to liberation, they sought to befriend everything that society found abhorrent. Magesh had no genuine interest in their customs, but he admired their commitment to fully embracing everyone and everything.

Unlike the other men in his order, as a teen, Magesh did not abandon his family and friends to immerse himself in a life of meditation, yoga, and religious rituals. He had worked for years as an engineer and had almost married. His parents, who were both staunchly pious, failed to comprehend why their eldest child suddenly wanted to renounce all his earthly possessions and passions. As for his friends, they had initially taken the announcement as a joke and were stunned when he left the city to live in an *akhara*, a place of practice. For the following twelve years, he had undergone a series of tests and some brutal rites, chiefly the weakening of the phallus, to gain complete acceptance into the community.

Whenever family members and friends appeared in his mind, he would immediately send them loving energy. Although he had not seen them in decades, he no longer missed them, for he knew they were in him and he was in them. And so, as he continued to indulge himself in the aftereffects of *puja*, he looked up at the starry skies above the Ganges while chanting *Om shanti shanti shanti*.

WHEN A DREAMER DIES

She stopped dreaming the day her father died. Well, to claim it happened on that precise day, a shortened day, when the skies were tilted farthest away from the sun, might not be entirely accurate. It was during the days and even weeks that followed his passing when Amélie lost the ability to see the beauty in aiming for the unreachable and pondering the unfathomable. After all, such an affliction rarely occurs instantaneously.

Her mother, who was far from being a dreamer, mourned her husband's death but not his bounty of unfulfilled dreams. She thought life was best lived in simplicity and rationality because the country did not have enough room for everyone to dream. And so, her mother made no attempts to convince her to follow in his ambitious footsteps. In fact, as awful as it may sound, she might have found comfort in her daughter's affliction. It was one less thing to worry about, and when it came to Amélie, there had always been reasons for concern. Her dark skin, small eyes, and flat nose — traits she had inherited from her father — placed her outside the acceptable lines of beauty. It was no secret this would only complicate things when the time came to find an appropriate suitor.

Growing up, Amélie often heard her mother tell friends and relatives that if she had not given birth to her, she would not have believed Amélie was her daughter. The intelligence, passion, and curiosity Amélie possessed also came from her father; as did her preference to drink plain, hot water rather than tea, and her ability to recite the poetry of Tang Dynasty legends such as Du Fu, Wang Wei, and Li Bai with great fervour.

Amélie knew that her appearance and character were only a problem because she was a girl. She knew her mother wanted a boy and would have tried having one if the family had the money to pay the steep fine levied by the government for producing a second child.

Her mother began worrying about her not finding a courter on her first day of university. In truth, her worrying had started years earlier but wasn't vocalized until that day.

"No man will want you if you show that you know more than him," she said soberly over the phone. "And remember to stay out of the sun."

On that same phone call, her father, who at that time had no idea cancer cells were spreading across the lining of his small intestine, offered far different counsel.

"Daughter," he said, his tone rich with affection, "don't forget that learning is as high as the mountains and as wide as the seas."

Throughout that semester and the one that followed, he bestowed Amélie with the words of ancestors and sages. Words that had both a transcending and grounding quality. Words that invoked thoughts of birth and death. Words that led to deep reflections on the ephemeral nature of sensations. He offered words that were best digested in bite sizes and savoured like a rich dessert. But when she went back home for the summer, he could offer only an apology. Confined to his bed, he was sorry for keeping his condition a secret and even sorrier for having to leave before she was able to firmly establish her place in the world. Her mother, who in striking contrast didn't apologize for her role in withholding information about her father's health, asserted that she did what they thought was best for her.

The funeral was held in his hometown, under a large makeshift gazebo erected on the grounds of his brother's housing complex. Amélie, sitting on a short plastic stool sandwiched between her mother and aunts, struggled to make sense of the elaborate wreaths of white irises that were placed around her father along with tall, white candles. She failed to understand the offering of food and joss paper and the continuous burning of incense. The white envelopes filled with an odd number of bank notes that mourners handed over to her mother and aunts also baffled her. Indifferent to the supposed bad luck that would follow, Amélie was the only mourner who didn't look away during the closing of the casket. Crying was the only act that felt genuine but even that was adulterated by the excessive wailing of an out-of-work actress—hired by a family member.

The day after the funeral procession to the crematorium, she returned home to fetch her belongings and took the long train ride back to school. Her mother remained with family to continue mourning. She found it nauseating how relatives who knew nothing or very little about her relationship with her father approached her to share what they claimed he wanted her to achieve. According to them, he wanted her to get married, have a child, and earn lots of money. Even her mother, surrounded by people in the community aspiring to offer their sympathies, provided a tearful delivery of what his final wishes were for her. Amélie listened respectfully to everything they said but believed very little of it.

The university campus provided an escape from that contrived space where her identity and future seemed known. Thus, it was there, in her first spoken English class, that she adopted the name Amélie. Up until that morning, she had introduced herself as Jessica to foreigners. But having watched a romantic comedy the night before and then dreaming about the protagonist, she decided to discard Jessica. After all, that name was given to her arbitrarily by her foreign English teacher when she was in grade seven. It carried no real significance.

"Amélie, I'm always here for you, OK?"

Adaze, a medical student from Benin, had the most comforting voice she had ever heard. She loved that he spoke French and said her name better than she ever could. She also loved that he didn't rush to kiss her or hold hands. They had met during her first semester but didn't become a couple until the last few weeks of the second semester. The way he had supported her all summer through text messages and video calls was further confirmation that she had done well by choosing him.

"It's so hard without him."

She would often find herself sharing that sentiment with Adaze and friends. Those words arose out of a sadness that had taken up occupancy all over her body. She stopped reading and reciting poetry because of the tears they produced. She stopped allocating time to reflect on life and all its happenings. She stopped lying on her back to watch her thoughts float by like passing clouds. She stopped wanting to know something new about her friends. There were moments when she wished everything would stop, including school. Despite consistently turning in stellar work and being praised for it by professors, she failed to find meaning in any of it. This, of course, was assuming that meaning was something she was still chasing.

The nature of her relationship with Adaze became far more carnal than conversational. He didn't mention it, but he did notice the change. And there was a part of him that undoubtedly missed the hours they would spend sharing tales and loving stares. But Amélie was desperate to feel more than the numbness caused by her deep sadness. His thrusting transported her to realms of ecstasy that were highly addictive. She began clinging to him, practically demanding her fix daily. He had become much more than simply a boyfriend. As a result, when he graduated in her third year and went back to Benin to practice medicine, she was devastated. Hoping to fill the void created by his departure, she found herself engaging in a series of brief affairs.

Her friends noticed a dominant trend in all her flings and teased her about it.

"But foreigners are the only guys who look at me."

Amélie's defense was accurate. She went through high school without attracting any attention from the opposite sex. Adaze had been the first man who told her she was beautiful and wanted more than friendship.

She'd kept Adaze a secret from her mother and didn't regret it. While she thought that her father would have accepted the relationship, she knew her mother was too traditional to fully embrace him and all he represented. As a result, she never spoke to her mother about boys. Amélie was fine with her believing that her daughter, a twenty-two-year-old university graduate, had yet to have a first kiss.

Although she had secured a decent job at a small engineering firm and was earning more than a living wage, her mother was constantly reminding her about the need to get married.

"I can't bear the thought of my daughter being called a leftover woman."

The reminders intensified as she got closer to twenty-five, which was the unofficial cut-off age for bachelorettes in small, less Westernized cities. Living under her mother's roof, she tolerated, and sadly started to believe, comments about being too heavy and too dark to attract a husband. Amélie's self-esteem dwindled. She had stopped expressing her feelings and thoughts on matters; consequently, her mother stopped accusing her of being too opinionated and too intelligent. Even her hair and clothes were no longer points of contention—she let her hair grow long and exchanged her jeans and t-shirts for dresses and high heels. She looked like a woman primed for marriage.

Since Amélie stopped dreaming, she unconsciously surrendered to the myths and narratives spun by her mother and a hopelessly uninspired society. Most shockingly, she took to storing her confidence in a fairy-tale courtship with a charming man who ticked off all the boxes she was instructed to have; topped with their happily ever after marriage that would produce the child for which her mother longed.

Amélie's acceptance of what she had once considered unacceptable grew with every passing year. Abandoning what was once her unapologetic pursuit of happiness, Amélie was now going on arranged dates with eligible bachelors; each time dolefully wishing that one of them would find her suitable. As the rejections mounted, so did her mother's terror.

"What have I done to deserve this? How can you spend your entire life alone?"

Her questions, which sounded like supplications, were always followed by an almost tearful resolve to find her daughter a husband. It was a resolve that was praised by aunts, uncles, and old family friends. Many of them even dedicated time and other resources to the cause.

"Life for an unmarried woman is too hard," said a relative, who spent much of her time talking to friends about their grandsons.

But nobody seemed concerned about the suffering their tradition was causing Amélie. For the most part, she had become a recluse who rarely smiled or demonstrated any real emotions. Working an inordinate number of overtime hours, she spent her free time in her room sleeping, in her own world watching movies, and on her phone scrolling through other people's lives.

The day Amélie's father died had marked the beginning of her forgetting how to live.

THE FOREIGN GUEST

He didn't consider himself a seasoned traveler. But supposing he was, the Arrivals section still might have been a shock. For starters, there were soldiers. Each one looked to be several birthdays shy of adulthood and patrolled the area in pairs with their long assault rifles and emotionless faces—what could have easily been their way of compensating for the boyish features. Less alarming but still disorientating was that once he got through customs, he was outside, where the sweltering evening heat made him rethink what he was wearing and why he chose to visit the tropical country.

As he waited for his suitcase to appear on the arthritic conveyor machine, he was surprised by the amount of perspiration running out his pores. Yet, it was the bevy of young women, heavily made- up and scantily clad, that he found most notable. They waited, eyes bright, behind the long metal barricade. As he walked down the corridor among several other foreign men, two ladies offered him warm smiles and waved flirtatiously; others blew kisses and cooed over his appearance.

A friend was somewhere in that crowd waiting to pick him up, so he kept pace. At the end of the corridor, he was stopped by a burst of reunions between lovers, friends and relatives. It was there amid all the kissing, hugging, and happy tears that he scanned his environment and saw Maricor. The sense of relief that came over him quickly gave way to elation and then nervousness as he maneuvered his way through huddles to greet her. Stretching out his arms to embrace her, he suddenly realized that she was not alone. Those extra pairs of eyes made him almost retreat which produced an awkwardly brief hug.

"Everybody wanted to meet you," said his friend, with a stiff smile. She had told him that only her uncle would come to the airport and that he would wait in the car to give them a moment in Arrivals.

She first introduced him to her mother who, grinning widely, shook his hand with more exuberance than he expected. Then a little girl with chubby cheeks jumped in front of Maricor to announce that she was the cousin. The child's confidence made all the adults smile.

"I'm this brave girl's father and Maricor's uncle," a man in his forties spoke up as he extended his hand. Feeling more relaxed, Maricor told everyone that she was no longer needed for introductions.

"Hiiii, I'm her big sister and this is my boyfriend."

Smiling, he exchanged handshakes with the couple, then jokingly asked if there was anyone else he needed to meet.

"No way, man! My car is not big enough."

When the uncle added that everybody in their neighborhood wanted to be at the airport to welcome the foreign guest, laughter rose from their circle.

"I said no to maaaany, many people, even my own wife."

The uncle's projection and cadence made him sound like a sports commentator giving the play by play for a highly contested match. His English, in terms of diction and syntax, was distinctly better than Maricor's. She spoke the language slowly and with less confidence. The more he listened to the family, the more the foreign guest realized how different he sounded. He was now the one with an accent; this added to his growing sense of exoticism.

He was considerably larger in stature than every member of his friend's family. Still, in the most inoffensive manner, he had to stave off the uncle's and boyfriend's attempts to roll his suitcase and carry his small backpack to the vehicle. Once he placed his belongings in the trunk, a controversy arose. The uncle figured that a man his size would be more comfortable sitting in the passenger seat. Meanwhile, the mother thought it would be best if he sat next to her daughter in the back since, as she put it, he travelled by plane for almost twenty hours to be in her presence. The uncle suggested that it would be cruel to confine his legs to such a crammed space. The mother dismissed her brother's claim, insisting that the real reason he wanted the foreign guest next to him was to converse. Sensing that he was losing, the uncle asked Maricor to decide where her friend would sit.

"Of course next to me," she said shyly, ending the standoff.

"That's my daughter!"

Everyone, including Maricor's uncle, laughed as they climbed into the minivan.

It was late when they stopped outside a modest two-story house along a hushed road in a poorly lit neighborhood. Just as the foreign guest stepped out of the air-conditioned vehicle and into the muggy night, unsettling thoughts caught his attention. They had visited him on the flight and came back when the family drove him out of the airport parking lot. He knew his thoughts weren't rational but couldn't dismiss them as being utterly preposterous. So he explored them; sensing every sharp turn and twist, along with every bump and sudden drop. Despite the mental exertion, he projected all the calm he could muster by answering questions, smiling, and laughing on cue.

Walking behind Maricor through the front door

without his belongings – the uncle and boyfriend would not be denied a second time – he told himself it was futile to worry. Unless he was willing to somehow make his own way back to the capital – and he wasn't – Maricor's home would be his residence for the next three days.

Even with the fan spinning at its highest setting, the foreigner's forehead was beaded with sweat. It puzzled him how nobody else seemed bothered by the suffocating heat. He thought about asking for some cool air but decided against it. A discreet survey of the living room failed to locate an air conditioner. Sharing the sofa with Maricor, her sister, and her niece, he could feel his boxers succumbing to moisture.

"Everything okay?" From her tone, Maricor's concern was apparent.

"Yeah, I just need to shower. I'm so sticky."

He kept his arms pressed to his body in the hope of trapping whatever odour was smoldering in his armpits. The fear of being detected made it challenging to applaud the cousin's rendition of an Ariana Grande song. Maricor, noticing his discomfort, offered to go into the kitchen to let her mother and uncle know that whatever they had planned needed to be postponed for another night.

"No, no. It's fine."

"You sure?"

"Yeah, it's fine. Really."

Pleased, she assured him that he would be able to shower soon since her uncle needed to take her cousin home. The child was up way past her bedtime. She was inching further into delirium with every song played.

"She will be sleepy at school tomorrow," Maricor's sister added.

Speaking in the local language, the energetic little girl

playfully slapped the sister's hands. Maricor told him that her cousin was having too much fun now to be concerned about school in the morning.

Emerging from the kitchen with bottles of *San Miguel* in both hands, the uncle proudly announced how much of an honour it was to introduce the number one beer in the country to their foreign guest. Moments later, the boyfriend carried into the living room a large bowl of roasted peanuts with garlic and a fizzy drink.

"I didn't make them, but they are really good tasting," said the mother while placing two plates of spring rolls on the coffee table. She apologized for not being able to offer more food but vowed to cook the most delicious dishes during his stay. He thanked everyone, in particular, the mother and uncle for such a warm welcome then implored them not to make a fuss over him.

"Impossible, man. Hospitality is important in our culture," the uncle said as he twisted open a beer and handed it to the foreign guest.

Much like during the ride from the airport, the family's attention shined on him like a generous theatre spotlight beaming onto the main character. The mother awaited his verdict on the peanuts and spring rolls while the uncle urged him to try the pale lager. Considering that he wasn't really hungry, he found the food quite savoury and informed everyone it was a mistake to place the snacks directly in front of him. But it was the cold beer that he found most agreeable—its temperature more than its taste.

"Maricor never have a boyfriend handsome like you before," declared the mother, sitting in the chair across from him.

He had no idea when, much less how, he was given the title of "boyfriend," but not wanting to embarrass

171

Maricor anymore than she already was, he smiled and said he wasn't used to being called handsome. This admission, made with complete sincerity, stunned the family who then found it necessary to shower him with compliments.

"You have so big muscles," the mother gushed.

Meanwhile, the cousin began performing a choreography to a pop song that was blaring through the sister's phone. The child had everyone's eyes on her for most of the memorized routine, until the focus shifted to watching the foreign guest take in her dancing. Worried about freeing his arms and giving Maricor a whiff of what a man in need of a shower smelt like, he applauded the cousin's dance moves in the same wooden manner he applauded her singing.

As the little girl regained her seat on the sister's lap, the mother declared: "I also meet my boyfriend on the internet. So like mother like daughter."

She laughed louder than everyone, especially Maricor. Once her mother started lauding her own boyfriend for being "foreign" and "caring," Maricor barely managed to smile. When the mother alluded to the German's ability to satisfy all her needs, there was a collective and noticeable cringe from all the adults.

"How do you guys handle crazy Trump?"

The uncle, capitalizing on his sister's oversharing, posed the question as though he had been waiting all evening for the American's answer.

"Is our president any better?" By his dismissive tone, it was clear the sister's boyfriend had little respect for the highly controversial leader of their country.

"Good point," the uncle conceded.

"He's a psychopath," the mother maintained, her features losing all traces of a smile for the first time that night.

"Yeah, he's like Trump," the uncle again agreed.

While the boyfriend denounced their president's policies as ruthless one-by-one, the cousin dozed off on the sister's lap. The foreign guest figured the sight of the sleeping child would force the uncle to accept it was time to return home which would bring the gathering to a close and him to a shower. Instead, the uncle instructed the sister to place his daughter on a bed upstairs then opened another beer as he launched into his account of the poor leadership that had plagued his nation since its inception.

"It's really a shame," he concluded.

"There's too much corruption here," the boyfriend added.

"Yeah, and that's why the standard of living is so low."

The mother agreed, saying that her country should not be ravaged by poverty and inequality.

"We are blessed with many resources but cursed with bad leaders."

Their commiseration made the foreign guest forget about bathing. He recognized what a tremendous gift it was to arrive in an unfamiliar country and be welcomed inside the home of a local family offering food, alcohol, and rich information. He accepted another beer, listened more intently, and participated in the conversation with the occasional question.

A few hours later, when the sky was its darkest, the foreign guest stepped out of the shower feeling refreshed and clean but slightly tipsy. Gazing at his reflection in the mirror, he quietly laughed off the inner critic that was admonishing him for losing his inhibitions on his first night in the country. While he dried himself with a towel too small to wrap around his lower body, he replayed the last words Maricor's mother had uttered before wishing him a good night. He was amused by the obvious approval and thought himself lucky to be in the house. It wasn't until he entered the bedroom and saw Maricor tucked underneath the grey sheets that he experienced a moment of clarity; with that, he was thrown by the likelihood of an anticlimactic ending to his night.

"Good shower?"

There was nothing flirtatious in how she posed the question, but that might not have been how he heard it. When she mused that he must be exhausted, he insisted that the water had washed away his desire for sleep.

"So sorry I can't get you away from my uncle and my mother."

It was the second or third time she apologized. For the second or third time, he insisted that she did nothing wrong and didn't need to apologize.

"You know what? It ended up being a lot of fun."

He placed his dirty clothes on top of his suitcase then stood over the bed, posing somewhat like an underwear model. But instead of commenting on his chiseled torso, she thanked him for visiting. Slightly discouraged, he turned off the lights and joined her underneath the sheets. It felt surreal, he admitted, to finally be with her after almost a year of online correspondence. Reaching for the fleshier parts of her body, he wasted no time moving into kissing range. She noted his forwardness and teased him about being intoxicated. Chuckling, he claimed he was sober which made her giggle more.

"Your hands are cold."

"Sorry, it's a bit chilly in here."

She reached for the remote control on the nightstand and pointed it at the air conditioner to bring the room back from what felt like arctic temperatures.

"You were so hot before; that's why I put it on sixteen."

He laughed aloud when she told him that her long sleeves and leggings were her protection from the cold air blowing out of the machine.

"I thought that was your way of letting me know that nothing was going to happen."

She remarked that even if something did happen, he would most likely not be able to recall it in the morning. Vehemently, he rejected this notion, stating that he was fully aware of everything that he was saying and doing. When she asked whether she should believe him, he confidently pressed his lips on hers.

There was nobody next to him when he awoke a few hours before noon. His body could have done with more sleep, but his parched mouth indicated a greater need. As he was putting on his shorts, the mother entered without knocking.

"Oh sorry! You're awake."

Her eyes stayed on his bare chest long enough to be considered staring; all the while, she informed him that breakfast was waiting downstairs.

"The bed was okay?"

Her German boyfriend was around his height and often complained about it not being long enough, she told him.

"He should buy king size for me."

With only meters separating them, he found her loud, nasal tone hard on his morning ears. Before leaving the room, she allowed herself a final look. She smiled and said, "You had a good night, handsome man."

He felt slightly embarrassed, just like he did when she referred to him as Maricor's boyfriend, so he forced a grin but said nothing.

This attention continued later at the small dining table where he devoured a plate of fried fish, garlic rice with green peas and a sunny side up egg.

"It's not enough for him," the sister observed.

"Yeah, he's big man!"

The mother's gaze was one of admiration and intrigue. Before he could say whether he wanted more food, she instructed her youngest daughter to bring over the large pot from the stove. Moving from where she was standing, since the table only sat three – the wall took away space for a fourth chair – Maricor piled more rice onto his plate and asked if he wanted another egg. The mother and sister urged her to cook him more eggs despite his claims that he was satisfied with one.

"My daughter is a good cook."

"Yes! Much better than me."

Although it was just fried eggs, Maricor prepared them as if she was being judged by Gordon Ramsay. The foreign guest however never cooked or ordered his eggs sunny side up because he thought the taste and texture of a runny yolk was slightly revolting. But, as the three women shared a brief exchange in their tongue, he became uneasy with the pressure placed on Maricor. He made up his mind to provide only words of praise the moment he took a bite.

This would not be the first time he withheld a preference or a vexation from the family. And as much as he could say he was simply attempting to be a good guest, the reality was, regardless of how small or seemingly insignificant, every untold truth created greater distance between him and the family. With this distance growing, doubt developed – the kind that preys on the dishonesty of the individual preoccupied with politeness – and soon it lingered. It grew to such an extent that later the same day, he flirted with the idea of telling the sisters he couldn't afford to pay for their groceries. He simply felt there was something contrived about the shock and disappointment they showed when the cashier announced there was an insufficient amount of funds on their bank card. This episode in the supermarket occurred after an entire afternoon of him being asked to pay for just about everything.

The first incident had happened at the pharmacist when Maricor claimed she no longer had the money that she set aside for her prescription because she had given it to her mother. She never came out and requested that he pay, but once she informed him that it was medication for her heart, she knew he would render the cash. Then there was the meal they had eaten at one of the restaurants in the mall. When the waitress came with the bill, which by local standards was high, the sister had declared proudly that it would be settled by their foreign guest. Shortly after leaving the restaurant, the sisters had led him to a popular smoothie shop where he, once again, reached into his wallet.

When they returned to the house in the evening, the mother was sitting on the sofa dejected. In an uncharacteristically sullen voice, she said that her German boyfriend postponed his visit indefinitely because of what he claimed was a hectic and unpredictable schedule at work.

"Last week he tell me he will come next Friday," she moaned.

Her disappointment even had the foreign guest empathizing with her.

"And today he say that work is very busy, so many new contracts."

Looking only at her daughters, she elaborated on what happened during the long-distance phone call. When she spoke in English again it was to assert, in a playful manner, that she needed to get a new boyfriend. Maricor suggested that she get an American before turning to smile at the foreign guest.

While the sisters emptied the grocery bags into the refrigerator and cabinets, the mom kept up her lamenting.

"What will I do now?" she asked as she opened a bag of chips. "I made so many plans." The mother reverted to her native tongue and the two daughters listened with grave concern. Once the mother was done sharing her sadness, the sister made an announcement. At least, that's what he inferred from the tone of her voice and the reaction it generated.

"When did you decide?" Maricor asked.

"Last night."

The mother posed a question, which may have been rhetorical; at any rate, it was followed by a pregnant pause—the type of silence that didn't require interpretation. The sister spoke calmly, in a manner that sought to reassure. He had no idea what she was explaining, but he knew it was serious. Judging by her reaction, Maricor did not support her sister's decision. The mother however, while not excited, nodded, and at times appeared almost pleased by what she was hearing.

When the sister's boyfriend arrived, Maricor, desperate to leave the conversation, called out that it was time for dinner.

"I bring so much chicken, enough to feed so many families," he said, as he placed the street food on the kitchen counter next to Maricor, who stacked five plates. Without taking hers, the sister led her boyfriend upstairs where they could talk in private. The foreign guest wanted to know about the sister's decision but wasn't willing to ask. Instead, he feasted on his vegetable-fried rice and rotisserie chicken that was adorned with a mouth-watering sauce. It wasn't long before the boyfriend emerged from the second floor, straight-faced, and stormed out of the front door without looking at anyone or saying anything. The sister descended into the living room with tears streaming down her face. Both Maricor and the mother rose from the sofa to console and to ask questions. She mumbled a few short responses before collapsing into the chair and deeper into sadness.

That night, while lying in her mother's bed, Maricor told the foreign guest – who had prodded – that her sister would be leaving for Japan in a few weeks.

"Japan! Wow! To do what?"

"Sing and dance."

She said that many young women from her region were doing similar work in Japan. No other details were shared except: "She can get enough money to send back here."

There was a solemnness in Maricor's voice, and her eyes, usually filled with unmeasured optimism, stared wistfully at the ceiling. He was unsure how to navigate around what she was feeling.

"And so you don't want her to go because you're gonna miss her?"

She nodded, yet her objection was rooted in a far more sinister truth.

"Yes, I will miss her."

Jacob knew the answer but asked anyways, hoping that something had changed.

"I already told you," his mother called back from the kitchen, where his baby sister was watching her knead dough for an apple pie. "She said at two. What time is it now?"

It was well after two and Jacob was on the couch holding his tablet and growing restless. He told himself if he and Paolo were allowed at the indoor courts by themselves, they would be battling each other by now in a game of one on one. Jacob figured his friend was sitting around wondering when his mother was going to complete whatever dumb task needed to be completed before she was ready to leave.

Paolo's mother was already in Jacob's bad books because she had scheduled an English test for him at five o'clock in the afternoon. Truth be told, he knew she had nothing to do with the timing of the exam, at least not directly. But she was responsible for enrolling her son in weekend English classes, something which parents around the city, perhaps the country, felt obliged to do. Jacob didn't care about that; all he knew was that the exam was cutting into his usual time on the basketball court and the gaming in his room afterwards.

"They'll be here soon. She just messaged me."

"How soon?"

Jacob didn't want to annoy his mom, but he didn't want to leave her be either. The way he saw it, she was playing the games grown-ups played with language whenever clarity was disadvantageous. Also, he couldn't understand why she wasn't rushing Paolo's mother the way she rushed him in the mornings to be on time for school, and never mind in the evenings when she marshalled him to start his homework. Even on weekends, she had a habit of hanging a metaphorical clock over his head each time she wanted him to do something.

"Soon!"

Success. Her tone confirmed it. He hoped that Paolo was doing the same thing to his mother. In his perfect world, kids could chide adults who didn't respect their time. He believed this would give everyone who enjoyed bossing kids around a taste of their own bitter medicine.

"Is your bag ready?"

"Yeah."

The exasperation circulating through Jacob's body coated that reply.

"You have pants for after you're done?"

He wanted to say yes but knew his bag would be checked before leaving. Not able to come up with an adequate response, Jacob chose silence. Well aware of how agitated his mother became whenever he had a sudden hearing loss, he sat up on the couch, bracing for her reaction.

"Did you hear me?"

Silence. It was the kind of silence that bolstered a false sense of power.

"If I have to come out there," she said calmly.

"Yes."

Fear prompted a more respectful tone.

"Pants?"

He jumped off the couch as if it suddenly caught fire. He ran into his room. It was December and pants were a must-have, unless, he thought, one worked up a sweat playing basketball. But he knew it was pointless, and in this case dangerous, to express his opinion on the matter.

Returning from his room wearing a pair of grey jogging pants over his shorts, he walked back to the couch and plopped himself down to wait some more.

"They're downstairs."

His mother came out of the kitchen with flour-coated hands to share that bit of good news. She stressed the importance of being patient and kind even when life wasn't unfolding the way he wanted. This lecture wasn't the first time he heard such counsel, and he knew it wouldn't be the last. As he hurried to put on his shoes and jacket, he could already imagine himself on the court with Paolo which made listening difficult. He gave his mother the mandatory kiss on the cheek, picked up his bag, and dashed out of the apartment.

Jacob didn't know the price of the white Mercedes Benz he was walking toward, but he knew it was beyond anything his parents could afford. Realizing that something was unaffordable needled him, but like tiny stabs of sadness. Though only in the fifth grade, he understood that his family was part of one demographic and Paolo's family thrived in another.

"Fifty-six points today!"

Paolo was always animated when he shared news about their favourite player, James Harden.

"I know! He's too good!"

"You saw the highlights?"

"Of course!"

Jacob made sure to catch the highlights of every Rockets game. Ever since Tencent started charging a fee that Jacob's dad wasn't willing to pay, watching the replays on his tablet was the closest he got to seeing Harden in action. An NBA League Pass was just one of the many popular items his parents refused to spend money on.

Paolo's mother greeted Jacob warmly once he got into the car. She glimpsed the boys' jovial exchange through the rear-view mirror as she shifted into reverse and exited the parking lot of the apartment complex. Her only interjection was to gently remind Jacob to speak English with her son. To make her point, she brought up Paolo's less-than-great English scores and the upcoming oral exam. The two friends had heard this request before. Each time, Jacob would agree to speak more English while Paolo would playfully object by insisting that communicating in his mother tongue was more fun. When his mother argued that not everything in life could be fun, he usually accepted defeat and kept quiet. But on this occasion, Paolo, adopting a whiney voice, told his mother that because he lived in Barcelona for so many years, he didn't speak Mandarin as well as his peers. He claimed to be embarrassed about Jacob, a non-Chinese, speaking the language better than him. The fib amused Jacob as well as the mother, who promptly rejected it.

"Mom, let me choose the songs."

Paolo's tone wasn't especially courteous nor was it overtly demanding. He spoke with the confidence of a child certain his wishes would be granted. Jacob couldn't recall ever speaking to his mother or father with that sort of self-assurance. His parents provided him with what they believed was a healthy mix of allowances and refusals. But Jacob was convinced they handed out a disproportionate number of refusals; the most recent one had left him suffering for an entire twenty-four hours.

He had wanted the iPhone X since fall but strategically waited until December and the start of the

184

Christmas season (which wasn't officially observed in Wenzhou) to make his request. Tears streamed down his cheeks as soon as his father questioned the wisdom of letting an eleven-year-old own one of the priciest phones in the world. More tears fell when his mother attempted to offset her husband's dismissive tone by offering to buy her son a cheaper brand. The muscles in his throat had tightened and his breath shortened as he sobbed over a phone that he was sure would have elevated his status at school.

Jacob's mother was from Siberia while his father was born in Lagos but later lived in London for many years. They met in Wenzhou. She was working at the front desk of a large hotel. He was teaching English and starting up a small business. One night, they found themselves at the same bar; they talked and began dating from the following day. After moving in together, Jacob was born a few years later. Uncertain about how their biracial son would fare in local kindergarten and primary schools, they contemplated moving to the UK and even the US but ultimately decided that experiencing China and its education system would be most beneficial.

They eventually saw how even Jacob's ability to speak both Mandarin and the local dialect fluently couldn't shield him from unfair treatment. His complexion and features were never accepted. As well, his family's lack of wealth and home address put him on the outside. Almost every student at his school was dropped off and picked up in a luxury car. Almost every student at his school flaunted their parents' money with their clothes, footwear, and smart devices.

Inside the massive facility, which housed a trampoline park, a bowling alley, and an inline skating rink, the basketball courts were occupied. At least, that's what the young employee manning the entrance announced. But when the boys peeked inside through the open door, they spotted a vacant side basket. The worker picked up how keen they were to play, so he told them they could use the rim until the team that had just started its practice switched to full court. Paolo's mother asked how much to pay, but Jacob's hand was already reaching into his bag for the money his mother gave him to cover the entrance fee. The worker opted not to charge them anything, reasoning that their court time wouldn't amount to more than twenty minutes.

Jacob was swift to strip down to his shorts and T-shirt, while Paolo kept his Rockets warm-up top on with matching shorts over his tights. Using Jacob's ball, they started with a few warm-up shots and then began duelling. It was a scoreless game for the first few minutes – not that they ever truly kept score – when Jacob threw up a shot from a bad angle. Hitting the backboard, it went in.

"Ya Ge Bu, great basket!" cheered Paolo.

"I'm Da Hu Zi!" exclaimed Jacob. *Da Hu Zi*, Big Beard, was what the Chinese were calling James Harden.

That's how they played every time. When one of them made a shot worthy of immense praise, he would proclaim himself to be Harden. Of course, it typically proved premature; this was the case on this afternoon when the second basket didn't come for a long while. Jacob went for a steal and couldn't get back in position to block Paolo's five-foot jump shot, which touched nothing but net. Despite their unsuccessful attempts to imitate Harden's signature move – a patented step-back from three-point range – they remained highly spirited and played with an intensity likened to a championship match. Even Paolo's mother, who certainly wished they were speaking English on the court, enjoyed watching. They competed in a way that celebrated effort more than winning. Theirs was a style of competition rooted in comradery; something far from their minds when they first met back in the spring.

Paolo had arrived at Jacob's performing arts school after the Spring Festival. His parents were Chinese nationals and had recently moved the family back to Wenzhou. Paolo's older sister was studying at a top international high school in Shanghai while his little brother was sent to a prestigious kindergarten in the city. Jacob had spotted the new kid from Spain in the hallways and on the playground but didn't truly notice him until the annual Sports Day, when the two boys found themselves lined up next to each other in the 60m finals. The gun sounded and Jacob got off to a terrific start. The race was his until the final ten meters when Paolo not only caught up to him but edged him out at the finish line. The defeat was crushing and left Jacob in tears. He had never lost a race at school or anywhere around the city. He knew he wasn't the best student, or the best musician or actor, but sprinting was his crowning achievement, and it was suddenly taken away from him. Although the newcomer was gracious in his victory, Jacob was furious with him and everyone else who celebrated him being dethroned as the fastest boy in school.

In the days and weeks that followed the race, Jacob watched Paolo's popularity peak. He found it vexing how for years he had tried to gain the acceptance of his peers and teachers; and for years Jacob's mother had to deal with the banal complaints lodged against her son by other parents. In their eyes, he was too demonstrative, too excitable, and too physical. He was too much of everything that the Chinese were not. One schoolmate had the gall to compare his features to those of a chimpanzee, then suggested that, like the great ape, his real home was in Africa. Jacob never told his mother, much less his father, about being called a monkey. There were other words that were ascribed to him, sharp descriptive words, that he never repeated to his parents.

A coach arrived onto the court and told the boys to end their game.

"You can both have one last shot."

Paolo dribbled right, pump-faked, then shot. The ball bounced off the back of the rim and landed right in front of the coach.

"Your turn."

Counting down the clock in his head from five, Jacob dribbled the ball through his legs, did a few crossovers before stepping back to release a long-distance shot that almost went in with one second left.

Sweaty and breathing heavily, the boys sat on the bench, each drinking a bottle of Gatorade Paolo's mother had bought for them. They watched more than a dozen boys around their age do full-court layups, passes, and shooting drills under the scrutiny of two coaches. Jacob couldn't help but imagine himself on the team, learning the skills to become as great as *Da Hu Zi*. He had talked to his parents about joining months ago, but they turned him down by saying it was too expensive. Even Paolo's mother thought it was a bit pricey, but Jacob knew she could afford it.

One of the boys on the team, sporting a pair of the LeBron 16, zoned in on Jacob's shoes and smirked as he jogged by the bench. Paolo was listening to his mother's warnings not to go outside with wet hair, but he saw the taunt and wanted to respond. It was just like when he had once heard schoolmates referring to Jacob as a chimpanzee. Deftly, he had intervened by remarking he looked more like Steph Curry.

"Mom, it's early and I have nothing to study for my English test soooo …"

"Soooo what?"

The mother knew exactly what Paolo, who had his arm around Jacob, was asking for. She smiled and told them they could play video games only if they did it while speaking in English.

"No problem, Mom!"

"Yeah, I will make sure he speaks only English!"

Excited, Jacob jumped to his feet and broke out the dance moves from *Fortnite*. Paolo joined in while his mother quickly pulled out her phone to capture the moment.

THE FLAG

He appeared to be drowning in a sea of remorse. There were the hunched shoulders, the inability to maintain eye contact, and the slightly raised eyebrows. Not to mention his tightly pursed lips that were pulled downward along with the soft and uncertain steps he made to his desk. But if remorse is in fact the echo of a lost virtue, Principal Plumlee might not have been as remorseful as he wanted me to believe.

Unsure of where or how to begin, Principal Plumlee retreated to his mind for several moments as he sat behind his desk. He likely knew that I had been anticipating the meeting all weekend and was eager to hear his deliberation.

"I know this isn't easy," he said, each word sounding like it was smothered with a heap of sympathy.

Aware of his unease, I nodded in appreciation as I leaned back in my chair. Maintaining his I-feel-bad-about-all-of-this tone, Principal Plumlee asked for a summary of the dispute. His asking was certainly more a formality than a genuine desire or need for information; especially since I provided in several voice messages a comprehensive account of what had transpired. It was, after all, those voices messages that prompted Principal Plumlee to call for this early Monday morning tête-à-tête.

"Well," I said, with an exaggerated exhalation. "Basically, I was walking by Jesse's classroom and saw the flag. I was shocked and confused so I called him up and asked him about it. He told me that the flag was just a symbol of state pride. I told him that for me it was a symbol of hate and kindly asked him to take it down. He refused, and so here we are."

I told Principal Plumlee that it was not my intention to bring him into the dispute, but that my colleague gave me no other option. With a shoulder shrug, I expressed my confusion about why the flag remained in the classroom. I sensed my calm and rational delivery surprised him.

Realizing it was his turn to respond, he said, "I appreciate you sharing that." He had told me on Friday that he would confer with his co-principals and the school manager in hopes of arriving at a resolution.

"Once again, I know this isn't easy for you."

I wasn't sure what to make of such an apologetic tone combined with facial expressions and a posture that was plainly pitiful.

"As promised, I talked to my senior leadership team about this and did a lot of thinking on my own," he said, apparently trying to sound a bit more authoritative. "I've decided that I'm not going to ask Jesse to take down the flag because I'm worried about the precedent I would be setting if I did."

My mouth slipped open slightly. My eyes stopped blinking. My torso and limbs became rigid. My entire body was frozen as my brain replayed his words.

"It was hard for me to come to this decision," he continued. "But, in the end, I had to think about precedence."

His utterances hung in the air long enough for me to wish that words were tangible things that I could grab and manipulate before violently stuffing them down his throat. Armed with a deliberate and derogatory look of befuddlement, which was accentuated by a slight head tilt to the right, I allowed my combative nature to speak.

"You're worried about the precedent you'll set if you tell Jesse to take down that flag," I said, with as much restraint as possible. "But what precedent are you setting by letting that flag stay up?"

Principal Plumlee claimed he had considered the question during his deliberation. He added he understood that I found the flag offensive but wasn't prepared to reprimand Jesse.

"It's complicated because, as a leader, I have to consider all sides."

"Yeah but that flag represents hatred, white supremacy … slavery!"

"But it's still his state flag."

"It sure is and it's highly controversial there too, so why bring that flag here?"

I told him that there were many academic institutions in the state of Mississippi that had stopped flying it, and that there have been groups fighting for the creation of a new one.

"I hear what you're saying, but if I tell Jesse to take down that flag, I would be forcing him to deny a part of himself."

He went on to say that he encouraged all staff members to bring who they are into the classroom to create a mosaic of culture on campus. Then, perhaps in his attempt to identify with me, he divulged that he was offended by a flag that was in the librarian's office.

"As a Christian, that rainbow flag goes against my values and what I believe is the right way to live."

I was stunned. Continuing down the road of what he found offensive, he conceded to being uncomfortable with some of the material taught in science classes.

"But what kind of leader would I be if I walked around getting rid of everything that offends me?"

He boasted about his willingness to hire gays and lesbians along with a few Muslims and plenty of atheists from around the world to work alongside local and foreign Christians. If he was looking for me to praise his willingness to employ teachers based on qualifications rather than religion and sexual orientation, he was going to be disappointed. It took a tremendous amount of control not to interrupt him with childish, yet accurate, name-calling.

"I say all this to say that I hope we can come up with something that works for everybody involved."

"What do you mean?"

I knew exactly what he meant but wanted to hear him be more specific.

"Well, maybe I should just come out and ask, what do you want to happen next? What is your solution to all of this?"

I smiled, hoping it revealed the confidence that comes with forming a response deep in the gut and propelling it up and outward.

"Unfortunately, the only acceptable outcome here is seeing that flag come down."

Leaning forward, Principal Plumlee looked like a journalist desperate to get more out of the interview subject. Holding on to silence, I leaned back comfortably with a stare that I knew he wasn't willing to match. I wanted him to recognize that there would be no compromise and that my commitment to having the flag removed was unwavering.

"So, how far do you see this going?"

"To be honest, I'm surprised it's gone this far."

I smirked before continuing.

"I'm shocked and a bit hurt that, in light of all that's been happening in America and the drama with confederate symbols and Charlottesville and Trump, I'm sitting here trying to show you why that flag has no business on campus."

Manipulating his facial muscles, perhaps unconsciously, Principal Plumlee reverted to the pitiable man. Unfortunately for him, I remained unaffected. I told him that everyone I had spoken to about the impasse had expressed outrage and deep sadness.

"None of them could understand why that flag was still up."

"Okay, but I asked Quincy about the flag and he didn't have a problem with it."

With the school year barely two weeks in and being a new hire, I had only spoken to Quincy a few times and didn't know much about his worldview. I surely didn't know what he thought about confederate emblems but wasn't convinced that Principal Plumlee was quoting him accurately.

"So, what are you trying to say?"

I knew very well the point he was attempting to make. And as I felt my ears getting hot, my mouth turning dry, and my body becoming tense, I searched his face for whatever traces of bravery or perhaps idiocy that would accompany his answer.

"That it's not so black and white, because every black person doesn't react to it the same way."

"Did I ever say that every black person feels the way I do about the flag?"

"It was kind of implied in your messages when you said that confederate symbols are offensive to black people."

My anger, heavy and fiery, could not be swallowed.

"What are you trying to do here? I mean, let's say you're right and Quincy doesn't have a problem with the flag; it doesn't change what that flag represents. I've got history backing me up while you try to throw Quincy's opinion in my face. Is that really necessary? Do you think that's gonna help end this?"

"Okay, let's keep a respectful tone."

"My tone is very respectful."

He took a deep breath and conceded that he needed to focus on the reasons why I wanted the flag removed.

"I want you to know that I'm not a fan of the battle flag either, but I do worry about what's happening. It feels like we're trying to whitewash history and I don't like that."

I realized Principal Plumlee actually believed that if all the confederate monuments and memorials were taken down, Americans may soon forget their troubled history.

"And that's why we have museums. But in public places, I and many, many others do not want to have painful reminders of slavery and white supremacy and hate staring down at us. So yes, all that stuff has got to go."

He didn't offer a rebuttal. In truth, he didn't offer any words. He leaned in and listened to my monologue with a seemingly earnest desire to understand. And when I was done, he didn't rush to respond which allowed an impactful silence to arise. Then, in what seemed like an effort to create a more amiable ambience, he said that he was lucky I didn't have a problem with the large flag that was hanging on the wall behind him.

"Actually, I do have a problem with that flag as well," I said, taking a glance at the Star-Spangled Banner above his head. "But I'm not here to talk about all the blood that's on that flag. Just know that one day it will come down."

His face went pink as I declared that black people were and continue to be murdered, terrorized, and

195

marginalized under the American flag. Therefore, anyone who opposed Colin Kaepernick was plainly ignorant, I insisted. I sensed it was more surprise than anger that sparked in him. Most likely, he was wondering how he could have hired someone who proudly condemned a flag he had saluted his entire life.

"I think we'll have to agree to disagree on that," he said, his face showing no sign of returning to its natural colour. "But thank you for your honesty. You've given me a lot to think about."

Our conversation trudged along until the bell signaling the end of first period rang. Principal Plumlee maintained that although we couldn't come up with a solution to the standoff, the dialogue was fruitful and "would pay dividends" in the future. I didn't share his optimism but smiled courteously as we stood up and shook hands. Before I could exit, he pledged to share what we discussed with the senior leadership team and to contact me about a second meeting.

"It's important that we keep talking."

Once again, I disagreed. There was nothing left to talk about.

. That evening, I found myself sitting on my sofa with an urge to expose the school's injudiciousness. I was looking at the picture I had taken of the flag in Jesse's classroom and thought about posting it beneath a headline saying the leaders at my school didn't believe that such a problematic symbol should be taken down. I'd highlight the jarring fact that this controversy was occurring at an international school in China. I saw myself editing my post more times than was probably necessary, wanting to ensure that it was as brief as possible yet focused with all the important details.

Before I clicked on "share," I was already imagining the traction my post would gain. I envisioned whatever clever statement I came up with on Twitter being retweeted by my followers and catching the attention of media outlets back home. I even began mulling over catchy hashtags for Instagram: #antiblackracism #myschoolisracist #theflagmustcomedown #bettychaninternational2018. It was at that moment, while obsessing over hashtags, that I put my phone down and questioned my methodology. I did want to shame Mr. Plumlee into doing what was right, but I also wanted to give people more context. My posts couldn't achieve that.

Dr. Martin Luther King Jr.'s famous "Letter from Birmingham Jail" came to mind. Although I only read it once in an African-American history class at university, I still recalled how he eloquently rebutted the criticisms of white clergymen and condemned them for claiming to support the mission for racial equality while rejecting all attempts at direct action. Evident throughout the letter were his disappointment and frustration with the white moderates' fidelity to the status quo. In no way was I comparable to the great civil rights leader, but I could see that Principal Plumlee was a white moderate who needed to be corrected—publicly.

For more inspiration, I picked up my laptop from the coffee table and did a search for the top ten open letters of all time. "Letter from Birmingham Jail" made the list, as did "J'Accuse!", a spirited rebuke by writer Emile Zola of then French president Felix Faure. Then there was Gandhi's appeal to Hitler in which he urged the Nazi leader to seek peace. The list also included a few recent open letters: one by Emmett Till's family addressed to Lil Wayne and another from Sinead O'Connor to Miley Cyrus. The Till family had reportedly lambasted the rapper for the line "Beat that pussy up like Emmett Till" then challenged him to use his celebrity more responsibly, while the veteran Irish singer had expressed concern that the young American pop star was being "pimped" by the industry.

After reading their letters, I reflected on how I would start mine. In my contemplation, when I became torn over how amicable my tone needed to be, I remembered another open letter. It did not make the list, but I had been moved when I heard a radio personality read it in its entirety a few years ago. I found Alice Walker's entreaty to Alicia Keys and read it. Despite the celebrated writer's staunch opposition to Keys's willingness to perform in Israel, the ethos of her letter was universal love and awareness. By comparing the Israeli occupation of Palestinian territory to Jim Crow South and Apartheid in South Africa, Alice Walker had called on Alicia Keys to survey her moral compass. I was most moved by her concluding paragraph where she had urged the singer to visit the children in Gaza and sing to them about their right not to be harmed simply because they exist.

It was hard for me to see how the fourteen-time Grammy winner could have gone ahead with the concert. I felt, given her humanitarian work, philanthropy, and activism, she should have known about BDS and been embarrassed for even considering crossing the international picket line. But to cross it without any public remorse was shameful.

Equally shameful was how the white church had never truly mobilized behind Martin Luther King Jr., and that after writing "J'Accuse", Emile Zola was convicted of libel and consequently fled to England. Gandhi's letters were powerful, but Hitler had still invaded Poland. Sinead

O'Connor had her struggles with bipolar disorder and other mental issues thrown in her face by none other than Miley Cyrus herself. Lil Wayne's response to Emmett Till's family had fallen short of an apology and he ignored their request for a meeting. Clearly, I concluded, the open letter did not have the best performance record. But I felt compelled, hopefully by righteous indignation more than animosity, to craft one of my own.

I opened with my feelings of disgust and disappointment with Principal Plumlee's handling of the dispute. Aware that the majority of my followers on social media lived outside of China and had little knowledge of how international schools operated, I took a paragraph to discuss my school. I shared its motto and mission along with the mandate of its associated Christian organization based in Hong Kong. This was followed by detailing some of the outrageous comments the principal had made during our meeting that morning, which led me to wonder what happened to the seemingly decent man I had shaken hands with the previous spring.

On that warm afternoon, he had given me a tour of the campus then ushered me into his office for a casual sit down. The framed picture of his family had caught my attention the moment I'd sat down. Noticing where my eyes were, he'd proudly introduced his wife and kids. He'd spent the most time on the only person in the picture who didn't have white skin, blues eyes, and blonde hair.

"We adopted Savannah from Ethiopia."

He didn't mention when, why, or how the adoption happened – I was curious but refrained from prying – instead, he cited a few instances of racism she had encountered in the community.

"On several occasions, people have tried to rub her skin to see if their fingers would turn brown," he said, shaking his head.

He mentioned that a local once approached him in the store and asked if Savannah was as smart as her siblings. The more disappointed I looked, the more he seemed compelled to share.

"All of my kids can speak Chinese but, somehow whenever we go out as a family, people look stunned when Savannah speaks."

I doubt he would have made such remarks to a white or Asian teacher. It was as if he wanted to say that, because of Savannah, he now got it. Not only did he "get it," he was bent on letting me know he empathized with our struggle for equality. Of course, none of this was necessary, but in a way, it was comforting to hear him acknowledge racism. Never would I have imagined that months later, he, the father to an Ethiopian daughter, would allow a flag containing one of the most anti-black symbols in history to hang on a wall in his school.

In my letter, I questioned him on the kind of world he wanted Savannah to inherit. I might have gone too far by challenging him to present the actions he'd taken to ensure that his daughter and everyone who shared her hue could enjoy the same advantages as his white children. If that wasn't enough, I wrote that I was struggling to understand what would motivate a white couple from a small conservative town in Indiana to adopt a child from the cradle of civilization. I asked if the adoption was part of some missionary project at his church and if they had any intention of helping her to explore her roots. It would have been in poor taste for me to accuse them of being like the family in *Get Out*, but I was tempted.

I did accuse him of misquoting Quincy; insisting there's a difference between wanting to stay out of the flag protest and having no problem with the flag. To throw a falsified version of Quincy's response in my face was unscrupulous. It was also quite brainless. Did Principal Plumlee not think that I would contact Quincy? After chiding him for a paragraph, I explained that the vast majority of black people found those confederate symbols racist. However, when living in a racist country where, because of the colour of your skin, the justice system was far from just, and access to employment, education and housing was a constant struggle, protesting a confederate symbol may not have been a priority for everybody. I ended the letter by inviting him to stand with me on the right side of history and order Jesse to remove the flag.

The following morning, while reading over my letter, I was glad that I didn't share it on my social media networks or email it to family and friends. I found nothing wrong with its stinging content, but the rays of the morning sun illuminated a step that I had skipped. In my quest to see the flag come down, I needed to contact HR at the headquarters in Hong Kong and give an account of what was transpiring. If they decided to lend their support to Principal Plumlee and Jesse, it would then be time to post my letter all over the internet.

By midweek, I was growing impatient. HR asked me to give them a week to investigate the matter, but I was beginning to question their sincerity. I emailed them two pictures of the flag hanging on the front wall in Jesse's classroom. What more did they need? A few minutes of research on the internet would have supported all my statements about what the flag represented. I was expressing my frustrations to a colleague when Principal Plumlee knocked on my classroom door. After hearing my approval, he entered and politely asked if he could speak with me alone. My colleague, who was a much-appreciated ally, said she would be waiting outside.

He asked me how I was feeling, but I found his concern disingenuous. Looking into his eyes and trying to keep my anger contained, I asked him to guess.

"I know this can't be easy for you, but I commend you for being a constant professional."

"Okay."

"No, really, I admire that about you."

"Okay."

Realizing I was in no mood for empty pleasantries, he exhaled while preparing to move onto whatever it was that led him into my space.

"Did you reach out to Hong Kong?"

Sounding like he felt betrayed, he said that the head of HR called him the previous evening to discuss the situation with the flag.

"It kind of caught me off guard if you know what I mean?"

"No, I don't know what you mean."

"Well, I thought we agreed to keep talking and come up with a solution together."

I smirked, wishing our conversation was being recorded because my family and friends would not believe that he had the gall to make such a statement.

"We were supposed to deal with this as a community, a family," he continued. "I almost feel like I was stabbed in the back."

It took a great amount of self-restraint to not call him names and implore him to seek psychiatric help.

"With all due respect, after our meeting, there was nothing left to talk about."

"How can you say that?"

"Easy. There was nothing left to talk about. I gave you time to do the right thing and you chose not to … you're still choosing not to."

"But it's—"

"There's no 'but'; you've sided with your BFF, so why don't you go talk to him?"

Principal Plumlee looked a bit stunned. He was probably wondering how much I knew and perhaps who told me. During my conversation with Quincy, he had claimed that our leader would never tell Jesse to take down the flag because they were practically brothers. Apparently, they taught at the same school in the same department for years. Once the bosses of Betty Chan International had appointed him as the leader of a new campus outside of Shanghai, they stopped being colleagues but continued to fortify their bond. They went to the same church and even took their families on holidays together. When Jesse's contract expired at the end of the preceding school year, Principal Plumlee dismissed a qualified teacher to hire him.

"I'm just wondering how far you're willing to take this?"

"Like I said on Monday, the only outcome I can accept is the removal of that flag."

"But—"

"There's no 'but'; I'm not stopping until the flag comes down."

It pleased me to see him withdraw into himself. Before leaving the classroom, he announced that the superintendent would be visiting the school on Friday and was scheduling time to meet with me and Jesse.

"Together?"

"No, separately. Would you be okay with that?"

"Sure."

As he was turning the doorknob, an idea came to me.

"Why don't we have a debate?"

"A debate?"

"Yeah, be it resolved that the Mississippi State flag in Mr. Wallace's classroom should be removed. I'd argue on the 'for' side and Jesse on the 'against'. You could even join him if you like – I don't mind."

I proposed that teachers and upper secondary students would watch the debate and vote for who they felt presented the more convincing case.

"If I lose, the flag stays up but if I win, which I know I will, that flag comes down."

The confidence in my voice and body language appeared to keep him from saying what he was truly thinking.

"I don't think a debate is the best way to solve this."

"Oh c'mon, this is a place of learning. Let's provide a moment of deep learning for everybody who comes."

Principal Plumlee declined my proposal for a second time, then, looking somewhat deflated, walked out the door.

Over the next two days, I passed by Jesse's classroom multiple times hoping, against my better judgment, that his antagonistic symbol would not be there. Seeing it each time, I found myself wanting to end the standoff with my own hands. I would have been fully prepared to confess my guilt to Principal Plumlee and the superintendent for ripping the flag off the wall and burning it on campus.

The superintendent was a middle-aged woman with a noticeable Irish accent and a courteous disposition. She announced that she was not a judge and would not be putting forward a ruling. As we sat across from one another in a spare office, she explained her plan was to listen to my grievances, do the same with Jesse, then make a formal list of recommendations to Principal Plumlee.

"As you probably know," I began, pleased that she was equipped with a pen and notepad, "I'm not American. I was born and raised in Toronto, but my father is from Georgia. So from a very young age I knew what that emblem on Jesse's flag meant, what it means even today. That emblem spoils the entire flag. I understand being proud of where you're from and wanting to share that with your students, but can't he find another symbol? A symbol that doesn't invoke memories of a time when people who looked like me weren't even considered human."

The superintendent filled page after page with notes from my monologue. She only interrupted me to ask for more details or clarifications. Her face revealed very little. I couldn't tell if she agreed with or even understood my point of view. All I knew was that she was listening and did not attempt any defense of the flag. When our time ended, she thanked me for my honesty and promised to send me an email message after her meetings with Jesse and Principal Plumlee.

During the period after lunch, I received a slew of messages from Jesse. He charged me with having no understanding of American history and advised me to educate myself before speaking about his country and state. I found those messages laughable, but when he called me a lowlife for telling staff members that he was a racist – which was something I never did – I responded with a lot more than sarcasm. Despite my refutation, he accused me of lying and implied that he too could file a complaint. I encouraged him to file as many complaints against me as he felt was necessary. Infuriated, he reiterated that I was a horrible person and teacher and that he felt sorry for all my students.

"I'm a man," he said, in his last voice message, "And I'm gonna move on from all of this and I don't care what you think. You wanted to make this into some big thing, and you did. So yeah, whatever. I'm over it!"

After school, I walked over to his classroom. Jesse was not there, and neither was his flag.

LAID OVER

My smile might not have been the biggest, but it was a kind gesture that, considering the context, merited a warmer response.

"Take computer out," the middle-aged woman said with the firmness of a drill sergeant.

Her accent and lack of syntax made the command sound harsher than it was probably intended. At least, that's what I chose to believe. What good would it have done to tell myself that she saw me as an inferior being who merited being barked at? I pulled the thin laptop out of my backpack and placed it on the inspection counter.

"Switch on."

"Why?"

I was in no position to protest but my annoyance grew as I pressed the power button on the top right corner of the keyboard. The instant the screen lit up she said, "Switch off."

If her goal was to agitate me, she had succeeded.

"Are you serious?"

My response was loud enough to draw a few stares from other security agents and passengers. She spoke a few words in her native tongue that were surely directed at me while walking away from the inspection counter.

"This is crazy," I mumbled to myself as I put the laptop back in its sleeve and zipped up my backpack. "Someone has some serious issues."

Standing in the corridor outside security check were Frank and Nisha. They had gone through while I was inquiring about the provisions Aeroflot made for me after canceling the flight to Munich. It had been scheduled to leave in four hours; consequently, they placed me on one that departed at eight o'clock the following morning.

"This is going to be quite a challenge," I said, my eyes wide and giving the impression that I had just endured trauma.

"We've entered *The Twilight Zone*," Nisha added.

Frank, who was the least enthused about our layover during our seven-and-a-half-hours flight from Beijing, said, "Remember we agreed to stay positive."

He was right. Lamentations were not going to alter our situation. I let out a lengthy breath and vowed to regain my composure.

"Switch on ... switch off!" I exclaimed. My impersonation of the security officer delighted my new friends. I repeated her command several times, thoroughly enjoying the hardy laughter it drew. Wondering what was so funny, passengers, shop clerks, and airport staff fixed their eyes on us.

"Alright guys," Frank said, picking up his large duffel bag off the ground. "Where we going?"

Nisha adjusted her handbag over her shoulder and gripped the handle of her carry-on suitcase, signaling that she was ready to move but then she remembered something.

"Did you get your hotel sorted?"

"Yeah, they gotta give you a room?" Frank added.

I told them it took some time for the man behind the counter to understand my request but after making a phone call he announced that the airline was providing me a room at the airport hotel.

"That's what's up," Frank said.

"I have to go to the international transit counter next to gate forty-nine at six-thirty and someone will take me to check in. Hopefully, it's a double room so then I'll just need to get a cot for one of you, and we'll be straight."

Nisha and Frank were surprised by my willingness to share the room. They didn't know how affected I was by our conversation on the flight. On the plane, we had books to read, music to listen to, and movies to watch, yet we chose to ponder the realms of the profound and trivial. And to think we were three strangers who just happened to be assigned seats next to one another.

We walked around the terminal looking for a restaurant that offered something decent to eat, a hot meal rather than cold sandwiches. The terminal's intense quiet was in sharp contrast to our uninhibited chatter.

"We've seriously entered *The Twilight Zone.*"

Nisha's assessment was dramatic, but it might not have been too far off. There was, in fact, a hovering eeriness like a dark cloud before a rainstorm.

"I'm still trying to get someone to smile back at me," I said while beaming at a clerk standing outside a duty-free perfume shop.

Nisha and Frank laughed at the blank stare the clerk gave me. Taking the snub in stride, I declared that I would continue making attempts regardless of how futile they appeared.

We ventured up to the second floor of the terminal and settled on a well-lit restaurant that had large black tables and comfortable looking purple couches. Two women, one presumably in her thirties and another in her forties, were standing behind the counter watching a dramatic program on a small television positioned above the door that led to the kitchen. Despite our enthusiastic greetings — I even said *privet* — they barely acknowledged our presence. With only two other patrons in the restaurant, we had our choice of seats and opted for a table in the back corner that had four couches, one of which was circular and offered a view of passersby. While patiently waiting for one of the women to bring us a menu, we got into discussing what we could do to get some reciprocity from the locals. Frank suggested we download an app to quickly learn some Russian, but Nisha believed that was pointless since I had offered "privet" and still received the steady cold front.

"In *The Twilight Zone*, menus aren't given," she said, unimpressed with the waitress's lack of professionalism.

Growing increasingly agitated, she waved her arm in the air to get the attention of one of the women behind the counter.

"Someone's finally coming," Frank said.

"Good, 'cause I'm starving!"

The younger waitress brought three menus to our table that we graciously accepted, and then she walked off.

"Oh no, we most certainly don't need anything to drink but thanks for asking," Nisha said, her sarcasm making Frank and me laugh.

"I'm going to seriously lose my shit!"

Frank reminded Nisha of the pact we made on the plane. I, adopting a sage-like tone, suggested we all take a few deep breaths.

"Close your eyes and …, " I paused for effect, certain they were hanging on to my every word, "switch on, switch off!"

We erupted into laughter but quieted down once the waitress returned to take our orders. One by one, we pointed to the beverages and the dishes we wanted. She seemed determined to maintain the rigidity in her face and lips while jotting down our choices and speaking in Russian. Before she could escape the table, something she appeared keen on doing, Frank asked for the WiFi password.

"One moment," she said, walking back to the counter and returning with a small piece of paper.

We pulled out our phones, Frank also placed his iPad on the table, and within seconds we were online. And for the first time in at least eight hours we sat in silence, each of us consumed by communication with family and friends, updating timelines, and learning some basic Russian expressions.

When the waitress returned with our beverages, Frank said something that made her blush. She looked at him and asked a question in Russian. He froze, and she walked away smiling.

"Oh my word! Did that really just happen?"

"You must have said something nice to her," I added.

"I just said 'you're *krahseevah*.'"

Frank explained that he told her she was pretty.

"I have no idea what she asked me though. But you guys saw the smile. That's what I do: make the ladies smile."

Clearly pleased with her reaction, the young American announced that he had discovered the secret.

"All I gotta do is let these women know they're krahseevah."

"And what about the men?" Nisha asked.

Frank grinned and said, "That's where you come in as our secret weapon."

"Secret weapon?"

Nisha was puzzled and so was I.

"Yeah, all you gotta do is tell them how handsome they are, and if that fails, show them some cleavage."

"Sure, but only if he's cute."

211

Frank and I laughed as Nisha mockingly expounded on the benefits of having large breasts in an overwhelmingly patriarchal world. I could sense that Frank understood her point but that didn't stop him from playfully asking if she would be willing to change out of her yoga pants into a pair of tight jeans.

"Not a chance. These are way too comfy!"

Her nonchalant tone and an incoming message from her sister discouraged Frank from proceeding. I understood her stance, but I still found myself glancing at her bosom for a half or possibly a full second while she devoted her attention to her virtual conversation. Flying high above frozen land, I had led much of our discussion on discovering one's true identity by ultimately transcending the world of forms. I wondered now if she would have been disappointed with me for looking.

It didn't take long for the waitress to return with our food and beverages. Without a trace of softness in her features, she placed a plate of mushroom spaghetti topped with grated cheese in front of me and Nisha and a plate of chicken Alfredo for Frank. Before she could return to the counter and her television drama, the young American handed her his iPad to take a picture of us. Accepting the device more out of a sense of duty than a willingness to help, she took a step back from the table, raised it up to her chin, and pressed the capture button several times. When she returned it to Frank, he uttered a word, which received another favourable reaction.

"*Spasibo* means thank you," he said proudly, knowing we were impressed. With the addition of spasibo, our collective vocabulary now consisted of three words. I could have added *dasvidanya* to that list, but I hadn't verbalized it yet out of fear that it wasn't part of the daily

212

vernacular and was only used in those trashy Hollywood films that sought to villainize the Russians.

Our food wasn't half bad, but even if it was we wouldn't have really noticed. We spent our time friending each other on various social networking sites, taking selfies, and posting them on our timelines with clever comments.

"Everyone will be asking me about you two after they see this pic," Nisha said, showing Frank and I a shot of the three of us that she was putting on her Instagram.

"I'll be checking the comments," Frank added.

He then asked us if we had the choice, in what country or city would we like to have a seventeen-hour layover. Unlike Frank and Nisha, who chose Brazil and Jamaica respectively, I couldn't think of a specific place.

"Seventeen hours in any warm country where I'm allowed to leave the airport would be sweet," I reasoned.

The more we imagined being elsewhere, the harder it was to appreciate where we were. Even maintaining a fluid conversation became a challenge as incoming social-media alerts consumed more of our attention.

We cleared our plates but were still hungry. Frank suggested we stay on the purple couches and order more food.

"The WiFi here is good, and I think she's starting to feel me," he said, with a cocky smile. Nisha and I doubted the waitress liked any of us, but we jokingly vowed to remain by his side until she offered him her heart.

After settling the bill, we found ourselves back on the terminal's main floor and were once again taken aback by a silence that was unparalleled. Even the automated voice announcing flight departures, delays, and gate changes was hardly audible.

213

"Dare I say it again? We've entered *The Twilight Zone*," Nisha said, as we searched for another eatery. Frank chortled as she hummed a few bars of the show's theme song. Adopting a Captain Kirk cadence, I told them that despite the dreary environment, our mission remained to enjoy the layover. "If we are successful, travelers all over the world shall refer to this moment in history and shall be inspired. My dear comrades, what we do during the next sixteen hours will forever alter the way passengers view the layover."

Laughing uncontrollably, Nisha and Frank pleaded with me to stop. After asking them to pause and observe the international transit counter with reverence, I broke character and burst out laughing.

Next to the international transit counter was a currency exchange booth. With no ATM in the terminal, one after another we handed the stern looking woman behind the glass several 100-yuan notes in return for thousands of rubles.

"I couldn't get that woman to do anything but this," Frank said, looking at me and Nisha with the most stoic face I'd ever seen.

"Did you call her pretty?" Nisha asked.

"Nah."

"Why not?"

"Cause she wasn't! You know I gotta keep it a hundred."

We continued down the corridor and stepped into an Irish pub. Just like the restaurant on the second floor, the pub was nearly vacant. Behind the bar stood three men, each dressed in white shirts and black trousers. They acknowledged us gravely with a few words in Russian.

"Is it just me or are they mean mugging us?" Frank asked as we considered where to sit.

"Well, they're clearly not overjoyed," Nisha answered.

"Privet," I said, grinning widely.

They mumbled the greeting back in our direction then in a low voice resumed their conversation. We settled on the section to the right of the bar where every table was empty. The moment we sat down Nisha proposed that we open the bottle of wine she purchased in the duty-free shop at the Beijing airport.

"Look at all these liquor shops. Let's just buy a bottle of something instead," Frank suggested.

"So, vodka or whiskey?" I asked.

My new friends reasoned that with vodka we would need some sort of mixer whereas none was required for whiskey. I agreed. When the youngest looking of the three men behind the bar felt we had waited long enough and finally brought us menus, Frank prompted Nisha to ask him if we could drink a bottle of duty-free liquor at our table.

"Yes," he answered plainly.

Though I was glad he had no objections to our plan, I found his frosty demeanour unsettling.

"You gave him the warmest smile and still nothing," I said.

"For real! If I was him, I would have been like: 'Hey gurl, whassup!" Frank added.

Giggling, Nisha pointed out that perhaps the waiter didn't find her attractive.

"How could any straight man not think you're hot?"

The words slipped out of my mouth without going through my brain's editing processor. Nisha was, in fact, beautiful. She had the sort of big, round brown eyes that one could spend days, months, years, maybe even a lifetime

215

journeying through. Her full and youthful lips, complemented by straight white teeth and an endearing Manchester accent, made it difficult to not stare at her mouth when she spoke. And when she smiled, her entire face seemed to emanate joy.

"Aw, thank you!" she said.

I was relieved that she didn't react awkwardly to what easily could have been perceived as an advance.

Frank, agreeing with my sentiment said, "He might not be into chicks."

"You guys are too sweet."

For a moment, I wondered who she thought was sweeter. I also wondered if Frank was having similar thoughts.

When the waiter returned, Nisha and Frank ordered whole wheat pancakes with syrup while I asked for potato pancakes with sour cream.

"Man, it was like we were ruining his life by ordering food," I said, shaking my head in disbelief.

"Why are you in my country?" Frank said in his interpretation of a Russian accent.

"That's probably exactly what he's thinking," Nisha said.

With a burst of energy, I rose to my feet and declared that it was time for a drink. My new friends laughed as I walked out of the restaurant humming *The Twilight Zone* theme song.

Duty-free establishments that sold alcohol were all over the terminal. In fact, I couldn't think of another airport with a greater availability of alcohol. I walked into the shop that was across the corridor to the left and honed in on the liquor section. The cheapest bottle of single-malt whisky sold for thirty-five euros. This was a lot more than I could rationalize spending on alcohol. So I opted for the 1.5 liters of Jameson that cost thirteen euros. I returned to the pub reverently holding the bottle up by my chest and walking while maintaining a ceremonial expression.

"My dear comrades," I said, pausing for effect. "All the way from the fairest lands of Ireland, I offer you Jameson."

"We gladly accept your offering," Nisha said, adopting a more official voice.

"Splendid. It is my great hope that this bottle would please you both."

Frank couldn't contain himself anymore and started cracking up, but Nisha managed to continue.

"I am most grateful for your service and sit here with great anticipation for our first glass of Jamie."

Nisha and I carried on while Frank went up to the bar and returned with three short glasses.

"As I pour out this aged substance, which you have referred to as Jamie, my solemn prayer would be that both of you …"

I paused once again, this time longer.

"would …"

Yet another pause.

"Switch on and switch off!"

My impersonation of that security officer had them in stitches.

We were a few sips into our first glass when the waiter brought us our food. He didn't smile, but his comportment was far less chilly. And when Nisha asked for a glass of ice, he nodded his head and said, "Okay" instead of grunting or mumbling something to himself.

"Dare I say progress?"

Nisha went on to label this recent development as a turning point in our mission.

"I don't know about that," Frank protested as he lifted his glass. "If you ask me, this right here was the turning point."

"You mean this right herrrre?" I asked, doing my best Katt Williams impersonation. "This drink right herrrre?"

"This drink right herrrrre is delicious," Frank said, nailing Williams's iconic facial expressions.

We gave Nisha a rundown of the comedian's wildly popular standup routine, so she could understand the reason for our high-pitched duet.

"Is it just me or has the music gotten louder?" Frank asked.

"They know we're trying to turn up!" I said, raising both arms in the air and pumping my fists.

"Turn down for what!" Frank shouted in his best Lil John.

More laughing, eating, and drinking ensued. And as we got louder so did the songs blaring through the speakers. The waiters didn't ask us to quiet down but as more passengers sat at tables and the bar, we figured they might have been trying to drown us out. If this was their intention, it wasn't going to happen by playing a mix of old and recent pop hits. With our plates cleared and Jamie lifting us away from sobriety, several verses and choruses became full-fledged sing-alongs. The other patrons didn't seem to mind our excitement. A young couple sitting at the bar gave us a warm smile.

"Guys, it's almost time."

"So, the plan is to go to your room— "

I interrupted Nisha. "Our room!"

"Ok, so the plan is to go to our room, shower, and then come back here?"

"Turn down for what!" Frank shouted.

"Sounds like plan, Stan," I added.

I wasn't expecting a queue at the international transit counter, but there I was, standing behind eight passengers, all of whom had varying expressions of dejection. After spending the last hour or so drinking, bantering, and belting out pop lyrics, it was difficult to do something as mundane as stand in a line.

Nisha and Frank took seats in the mostly empty waiting area and continued talking at the same volume as we did in the Irish Pub. Because they were no more than three meters away and hadn't adjusted their voices, I was able to follow along and even interject at times; all while attempting to eavesdrop on another conversation between two passengers, possibly a couple, and the airport employee. The line moved along fast enough until the group of four in front of me got to the counter and demanded to be given a hotel room immediately. The young man behind the counter appeared sympathetic to their plight but claimed there was nothing he could do at the present time. He asked them to wait until he received further news from the airline.

"This is not acceptable," said the youngest member of the foursome, clearly frustrated with the responses she was getting. The older man and woman, possibly her parents, and an elderly man who could have been her grandfather listened attentively as she appeared to translate the information she received in English into their language. The group walked away from the counter and went to sit in the far corner of the waiting area.

"Hey, I was told to come here at six-thirty," I said, acting as if I hadn't heard the previous conversation. "The airline said they would put me up in the airport hotel."

I gave the young man who, at this point looked overwhelmed and fatigued, my passport and boarding passes. He took a few moments to gather my flight itinerary then said, "Ah yes, but the airline didn't give confirmation yet." Sounding as sympathetic as he did with the group of four, he suggested that I stick around and wait for an update.

"Can't we just go to the hotel and sort things out there?" I asked, feeling slightly annoyed.

"Yes, you can do that if you like."

His tone and expression seemed to say, "Fat chance, buddy."

"And if for some reason the hotel can't do anything for me, at what time should I come back here?"

"Ten o'clock is ok."

I couldn't believe what I was hearing; neither could Nisha and Frank who were following the exchange from their seats.

"What? That's like three hours from now," Frank said.

"Worst airport ever!" Nisha exclaimed.

I reminded my new friends that until we heard what the hotel could offer, we should remain calm. As we grabbed our belongings and marched out, I tried to follow my own advice. We passed Jamie around as we set off for Terminal E. There was some grumbling about Aeroflot's deplorable customer service, but it subsided the farther away we got from the international transit counter. Playfully, we constructed a list of features that horrible airports had in common. Jamie was doing an admirable job of picking up our spirits.

"Dow, da dow, da dow, da," Frank sang in a traditional shuffle rhythm "Laid over in Moscow. Dow, da dow, da dow, da. Was promised a hotel room."

Nisha and I bent over, laughing.

"Dow, da dow, da dow, da. But worried we won't get one. Dow, da dow, da dow, da. Might have to sleep on the floor. Dow, da dow, da dow, da. And tell Jameson I need some more."

"Dow, da dow, da dow, da," Nisha and I sang once Frank gestured to us.

"Sayin' I got the blues."

"Dow, da dow, da dow, da."

"The Moscow blues."

Our boisterous performance drew many stares from shop clerks. They didn't appear to be annoyed with our conduct but showed no desire to participate. If silent judgment was a currency, they were showering us with large banknotes.

"They need to come and jump on di soca train. Oh gosh," I said, putting on my best Trinidadian accent as I began chipping down the corridor to an imaginary calypso beat.

"I need my rag," Frank declared as he lifted both hands in the air. "It's Carnival!"

The music and vernacular were foreign to Nisha, but that didn't stop her from moving to the rhythm.

"Ride on di soca train," I sang, throwing my hands in the air as well. "Frank and Nisha getting down on dis soca train."

And so there we were, in what had to be one of the world's most unwelcoming airports, walking and dancing to some of the world's most joyous music.

"They gotta bring Carnival back to D.C.," Frank said as he took another sip from the bottle.

The American told us that ever since 2011, he had to drive to Baltimore or up to New York if he wanted to enjoy the bacchanal that transpired at Carnival. Nisha knew of Notting Hill Carnival but had never been.

"I absolutely must go," she announced, smiling euphorically.

"The whole world needs to jump on di soca train," I said, before having more Jamie, "or at least walk around an airport while singing and diluting their blood with alcohol."

For all the criticism we generated about Sheremetyevo International, we all agreed that our whiskey-fueled antics would not have been tolerated at the airports in our countries. Surely, security officers would have confronted us the moment we opened the bottle.

After several wrong turns, each of them accompanied by laughing fits — Jamie seemed to make everything humorous — we found the airport hotel. We might have made a commotion when entering the tiny lobby but, considering the volume level we were using to communicate, that was to be expected. There was a well-dressed man at the reception counter being served, so we parked ourselves on the sofa, which was remarkably comfortable, and waited for him to be handed a room key and walk up the hall.

"Privet," I said, as I sprung up from the sofa. The hotel clerk, who looked to be in her late thirties or early forties, smiled courteously and greeted me in return. I took a few steps toward the counter and commenced a meticulous account of my ordeal.

"The airline cancelled my flight to Munich," I said in a serious but not overbearing tone. "So I now have a seventeen-hour layover, which is tough because I can't leave the airport, but I was told that the airline would put me up in this hotel, so here I am."

"I understand, but right now the hotel is full," the woman said, sounding about as polite as her accent allowed.

"Full?" Nisha asked from the sofa.

Her question sounded more like a condemnation. I was just relieved to turn and see that Jamie had been placed in its bag.

"Yes. Because so many flights are cancelled now, we have many passengers who want a room."

"But the airline promised him a room," Frank said.

"Yeah," Nisha added.

With a confident grin I said, "They sure did."

The woman appeared unfazed by our challenge and asked me for my name. I said it slowly as I handed over my passport. She picked up a sheet of paper and scanned it for several moments before saying, "Your name is not on the list."

She explained that the airline provided the hotel with names of passengers who required a room.

"So, how do I get on the list?"

"The airline must put your name on it."

The woman advised me to return to the international transit counter in Terminal F and wait for someone to resolve my situation.

"Argh, this is not cool at all," I said, turning away from her and facing my friends. While we were deliberating on what to do next, the group of four that had been in front of me at the international transit counter entered. I was tempted to tell them that great minds thought alike, but none of them, especially the one who did all the talking at the desk, appeared to be in the mood for any lightheartedness. Staring down at the hotel clerk, the group's spokesperson said, "Our flight to Bucharest was cancelled and now we have a twenty-hour layover. What can you do for us? The man in charge of transit passengers is useless. He keeps saying we need to wait. But that is unacceptable."

"Can I have your passport?"

The spokesperson reached into her handbag, pulled it out, and handed it over.

"I wonder if her name is on the list," Frank whispered.

"I'm sorry but your name is not on the list."

The hotel clerk gave the woman the same explanation she gave me. I was surprised by the indifference in her voice, considering the group included an elderly man.

"How can our names be added to your list?"

"The airline must do it."

The woman turned to her companions and translated the new information for them. The middle-aged couple and the elderly man appeared increasingly confused and dissatisfied as they listened.

"This is unacceptable!" she shouted while leading her family out of the hotel.

The hotel clerk responded by mumbling something underneath her breath. I found her displeasure slightly offensive since she did little to improve the family's unfortunate predicament.

"I love that chick's accent," Frank said, breaking the rather tense energy in the lobby. "She could definitely get the business."

Looking at Nisha, I laughed and told her to keep Jamie away from our friend.

"I will do no such thing," Nisha playfully protested. "She was actually quite pretty, and she had a lovely accent. I don't know what 'the business' is but I could definitely see myself doing more than just talking to her."

"Touchdown!" Frank exclaimed, throwing his arms straight up in the air.

"I kissed a girl and I liked it," I sang, giving the American a brotherly handshake.

"Oh, my word," Nisha remarked. She seemed amazed at our inability to see the facetious nature of her comments.

"Boys and their lesbian fantasies," she concluded.

"So, you kissed a girl and you didn't like it?" Frank asked, his tone suggesting the question was of primordial importance.

Nisha laughed and called us perverts, saying: "You'll never know."

"C'mon, you can tell us."

I was curious, but unlike Frank I wasn't going to insist on an answer.

"Did it happen when you were at uni?" he asked, trying to imitate her accent.

"Is that you taking the piss? Did it happen for you when you were at uni?"

"Huh?"

"Is that when you kissed a boy and liked it?"

"What?"

"Go on, I'm getting turned on just thinking about it." Nisha fanned herself with her right hand while biting her bottom lip. Although it was clearly a performance, I did find it arousing.

"Okay, okay. I get it," Frank conceded.

"I kissed a boy and I liked it," Nisha sang, enjoying the effect her lyrics were having on him. The American reached for the bottle and took a sip.

"You've got issues, mate," she said. The Manchester native teased him about his outright discomfort. I wondered if he would run off if she sang the line a second time.

"So, do we walk back to Terminal F?" I asked, refocusing the conversation. Nobody was particularly enthusiastic about revisiting that young man at the international transit counter.

"Basically, we need to get your name on that magical list," Nisha concluded.

"Yeah, but you see how they operate here. They'll probably say some bullshit like 'sit down and wait for the airline to contact you.'" Frank's Russian accent was, at best, mediocre, but it made Nisha and me chuckle.

We were far louder than we needed to be. As a result, we probably weren't gaining much favour with the hotel employee. She became increasingly irrelevant as we passed the bottle around, hypothesizing how our night would evolve. We offered Jamie to every traveler entering the lobby, but everyone respectfully declined.

"The whole world needs to jump on di soca train!" I sang.

"Yes! The soca train is back," Nisha said, her hands swaying above her head. "I'm well buzzing!"

"Where's my rag?" Frank asked excitedly. "I need to grab something and wave." The alcohol and the soca train invited us to forget where we were. The more calypso-infused lyrics we made up, the more joyous we became.

"Yes, hello!" the hotel employee interjected, sounding as if she had not been watching us treat the lobby like a bar. "A room is now available, but you'll need to pay eighty-six dollars."

"What?"

I was both disappointed and irritated that she would try to sell me a room.

"We have a cancellation, so you can take the room if you pay eighty-six dollars."

"Eighty-six dollars?" Nisha asked.

"See, there they go with that bullshit," Frank said shaking his head in disgust.

"If my name was on that list, I could have that room for free, right?"

"Yes."

"But because my name is not on the list, you want me to pay eighty-six bucks?"

The hotel employee tried to rationalize the reason, but Nisha interrupted her by asking if that was the only available room.

"Yes."

"So can he book it now, then go and get his name on that list?"

"No, this is not possible."

"So, what you're in fact saying is that you'd rather sell the room than give it to a passenger that's on your list?"

Nisha's line of questioning was frustrating the hotel employee.

"No, you don't understand hotel policy if—"

I cut her off. "We understand very well that it's not really about your little list."

"You're just trying to make money," Frank blurted.

"Exactly!" Nisha exclaimed.

With that said, we picked up our belongings and promptly made up our minds to go back to the international

227

transit counter. Frank and I informed the hotel clerk that we would return, while the Manchester native chimed in, "Only because there's no other hotel in this sham of an airport."

The trek back to Terminal F was exuberant. There was much singing, dancing, and even some interaction with random passengers, the majority of whom supported our comportment. Our biggest encouragement came from a blonde couple that was having a drink at one of the many restaurants in Terminal E. Seated at a table on the right side of the corridor, they had probably been watching our shenanigans – me and Frank performing side heel clicks with Nisha offering dramatic commentary on who was getting the most height and demonstrating the best technique – since we walked out of the hotel.

"Perfect score!" shouted the man, gleefully.

"Which one?" Nisha asked, sounding very much like a television host interacting with her studio audience. "The Canadian or the American?"

"Both!" exclaimed the man's pretty partner.

I halfheartedly protested their judgment by detailing the attributes that made my heel clicks better than Frank's. Not to be outdone, Frank pleaded his case before the judges. With complete sincerity, the blondes told us that we were both winners. They asked Frank if he was okay with not having a clear winner—their lighthearted jab at Americans. I got in there, as my friend challenged their assessment, saying as a Canadian I wasn't okay with it either, which got us all laughing. Moments later, we joined them at their table. I'm not sure who did the inviting, but they seemed happy to drink with us. They were from Sweden and were heading home after traveling around Southeast Asia for the last three months. They had already been at the airport for three hours and had two more to wait. We asked their thoughts on the airport.

Almost in unison, the couple said, "Not the best."

The Swedes were surprised to hear that we three had only met earlier that day. To them, our inside jokes and overall chemistry suggested otherwise.

"Yeah," Frank agreed. "It's like I've known them for years."

"Exactly," I added.

Nisha told the couple that Frank and I had become her brothers. And despite showing apparent signs of intoxication, more than anyone else at the table, there was a sincerity to her words that didn't need to be questioned. I appreciated her sentiment but wondered if it meant there was zero chance of her placing her full lips on mine later in the night. Looking over at Frank as he talked about Nisha being like a sister, I wondered if he was thinking the same thing.

Clearly moved by the fondness we had for one another, the couple suggested that fate had brought us together. "To fate," Frank declared, lifting his beer.

"To fate," the rest of us repeated tapping our pints.

Sensing the conversation was largely focused on the three of us, we got the couple to discuss their impressions about the places and people they met during their trip. They recounted a few tales from their time in Vietnam and Laos then shifted back to us, asking what we were doing in China.

"I'm studying Chinese, which is hard as hell," the American said.

The Manchester native replied next. "I'm a kindergarten teacher, so I spend my days with the little ones."

I told them I taught English at an international high school. They expressed regret about not having visited China and tentatively promised to do so in the future. Being visual artists who did mostly commissioned work and contracts of six to eight months, the couple told us about the amount of time off they have during the year

"Sometimes he has to finish a job and I'm free, so I will take a trip alone," the woman said.

"And sometimes she's the one who has to stay behind, and I go travel."

They described how every trip they'd taken had inspired their art. I enjoyed watching Nisha's visceral reactions as she listened. Her face seemed to radiate her admiration for the apparent peace and understanding that was at the root of the couple's partnership. Considering her revelation during our flight about having never been in love, I couldn't help but think she was longing for such a romance.

It was close to ten when we returned to the international transit counter in Terminal F. We had all drank more beer and whiskey than we intended to and were feeling the consequences.

"I'm shattered!" Nisha declared as she plopped down in a seat along the sidewall.

"There's still a few swigs left," Frank said, angling Jamie for inspection, "but I'm way too faded."

"I'll take care of that."

Because I was at least a decade older than Nisha and Frank, I felt a strange sense of obligation to finish the bottle.

"First I gotta get this hotel room straightened out." I took one deep breath and then another trying to hone my attention to the waiting area and my objective. Looking around the hall, I noted an increase in occupied seats. There were men and women, presumably neglected by Aeroflot like me, sharing their frustrations with one another. The family of four led by the daughter were at the counter making demands while a group of Chinese travelers were asking for an explanation for what was undoubtedly poor customer service by the airline. Amid such dysfunction, it was no wonder that our drunken return didn't cause any commotion. At least, I don't believe it did.

"We should go up there with you," Frank suggested from his seat next to Nisha.

"Yeah, let's get that room. I need to shower and sleep," Nisha added.

Considering my blood alcohol level, I was in no position to judge their level of coherency, but I did anyway and concluded they needed to stay put.

"Cool, but we're here if you need us," the American said as he stretched his legs out.

"And can you please ask where I can have a smoke?"

Nisha said she had quit prior to moving to Beijing, but with cigarette prices shamefully low in China and social acceptability high, she had fallen back into the habit. She claimed the craving for a cigarette was relentless whenever she drank.

"No worries, I got you."

That's not exactly how I felt about her request. Quite the opposite. I wanted no part in facilitating her nicotine fix. However, it would have been silly to use my already weakened cognitive abilities to expound on my anti-cigarette stance when the real objective was to get my name on the list.

I stood behind the group of Chinese travelers and the family of four that was supposed to have been flying home to Bucharest and listened to their grievances. My strategy was to wait patiently for everyone to disperse then engage the overwhelmed worker one on one. Yet, when a minute felt like an hour – alcohol has a way of disrupting my sense of time — waiting proved to be unbearable. So, when the young man behind the desk finally saw me and offered what appeared to be a nod of recognition, I decided to enter the fray. Stepping through the five Chinese passengers, I apologized in Mandarin and told them I would attempt to gain some rectification. Stunned by my linguistic skills, they smiled. There was no need to apologize they remarked and then wished me good luck.

The spokesperson of the family was threatening legal action against the young man and his female colleague, who had just emerged from a closed door behind the long counter, if they were not given a hotel room.

"You people are like robots," she said in disgust. In true bureaucratic fashion, the workers maintained the same volume and tone despite the daughter's heightened, angry rhetoric. I wondered if she was contemplating jumping over the counter when she shouted like someone who was completely out of control: "Can't you see we need a room!"

"And I have told you many times there's nothing I can do because the airline did not put your names on the list," the young man countered before turning to his colleague and speaking in Russian.

"What did you just say?"

"I just told her that all we can do is give all passengers more food and drink vouchers."

Their calm but slightly annoyed mien further infuriated the woman.

"We don't want more vouchers. We want a room, and we want a room now!"

She requested to speak with their superiors, but the colleague asserted that would not be possible since they were off duty. The daughter then turned to her family to translate the exchange. While she was engrossed in conversation, I told the two workers that everybody was exasperated with the situation, not them.

"I know you guys are doing your job, but what is the airline doing?"

"Yes, this is the problem," the young man agreed.

"Can't you call someone from the airline and have them come here and see all the problems they've caused?"

"That is not possible now because they are also off duty."

"Sure, everybody is off duty!" the daughter scoffed. "How can we believe you when you lied so many times already? First, you tell us to come here at four-thirty, then to come back at around eight to get a room, and now it is after ten and we still have no room. You are liars!"

The international, transit-counter workers hardly reacted to the outburst, which might have made the family's spokesperson angrier. She shouted at them in her language before turning to the middle-aged couple and the elderly man, who I presumed were here parents and grandfather, for a quick exchange. Deflated, she ushered them away from the counter.

"This isn't the first time you've seen this?"

Both employees seemed confused by my question.

"I mean, this isn't the first time Aeroflot has cancelled flights and left passengers without a hotel room, right?"

"But all we can do is wait on the airline to put the names on the list."

"No, you could tell your boss about the problem and push them to talk to the airline, and most importantly when passengers like us come here, just tell us the truth about what normally happens."

"But—"

"There's no 'but'," I said, cutting off the young woman. "I mean look around. This isn't right! What do you think we're going to think about Moscow's airport after all this? I know for a fact I have no intention of flying through here again."

"So, what can we do now?"

"Call Aeroflot tell them they need to do something for all of us."

The young man said he wasn't sure what he should tell the airline while his colleague looked uneasy about making the call. Nonetheless, they retrieved the number from a laminated paper on the desk then asked if I had a phone.

"My phone doesn't work here," I said, surprised by the question. "Why don't you just use that phone and let me do the talking?"

I was trying to remain amicable, but I could feel and hear a bit of annoyance edging my voice. If my suggestion sounded more like an order, that was far from my intention. The young man pulled an old Nokia model from his pocket, punched in the number, and handed it to me. I was curious to know why he didn't use the work phone that was next to the computer but kept my question to myself. I put the small device up to my ear, and after three rings a male voice was on the call.

"He's speaking Russian," I said, handing the phone back to the young man. He exchanged a few words with the airline representative then passed the phone back to me. I was expecting to hear an English-speaking representative, but instead my ear met soft classical music.

"I'm on hold."

The two workers and the group of Chinese travelers gave an impression of eagerly awaiting to hear what I would say to the airline. Taking into consideration my inebriated state, it's also conceivable that I was misreading their body language. As I continued to hold, the angry daughter returned. She started filming the two airport employees while giving what sounded like a lively commentary in her native tongue. Wanting to better capture the scene that was unfolding, despite being asked to put down her device, she did a 360-degree pan. She wouldn't comply until both employees threatened to notify airport security.

"I have enough evidence," she said defiantly as she lowered her phone.

"And what can you do with it?" the young man retorted.

"Why do you want to know?"

The family's spokesperson advised him, and by default his colleague, to focus on executing their work duties. Struggling to contain their annoyance, they told her they were doing the best job possible. Unsurprisingly, she laughed sarcastically at that statement and sharply accused them of being delusional. The workers countered by insinuating she was behaving like a child and asked her to rejoin her family near the entrance of the waiting area. She refused to move away from the transfer desk and so the exchange persisted while I was becoming more agitated being on hold.

"Excuse me, where can I go to smoke?"

Nisha had quietly circumvented the crowd and wound up next to one of the Chinese travelers who was standing next to me. The workers told her there was nowhere for her to smoke.

"But I just saw a cleaner go in there and come out a few minutes later," she said, pointing at the closed door on the right side of the long counter. The workers surely knew what transpired behind that door but remained coy.

"I'm sorry. It is forbidden to smoke inside the airport," the young man said, turning his chair away from the spokesperson to face Nisha. He clearly preferred to deal with a passenger craving a cigarette rather than one tearing a strip into him and his colleague.

"Right, but I really need one." My Manchester friend maintained a rational tone and avoided sounding too overbearing.

"Okay, I won't stop you from going there," he said with a smirk, "but I told you it is forbidden, so if the police come it is not my responsibility."

For a second, possibly three, Nisha appeared to consider the risk. Then, having come to a decision, she called out anxiously to the cleaner who may have just finished smoking. Rushing over to him, she borrowed his lighter and hurried off to get her fix.

Minutes later, I was still on hold and the daughter was still ranting when my Manchester friend emerged from behind the staff-only door with a relaxed smile. She thanked the young man behind the counter then asked me if I had spoken to anyone from the airline yet.

"Nope," I answered, trying to remain poised. Watching Frank who was dozing while clutching Jamie she said, "Like Tolle said, it's truly a matter of accepting the is-ness of this moment, innit?"

"Yep, and what is, is that we don't have a room and nobody from the airline is taking my call."

With heavy-lidded eyes, Nisha murmured that she needed to finish reading Eckhart Tolle's book then returned to her seat. All but one of the Chinese travelers had also left the counter area and were now sitting amongst the many dispirited travelers. Even the family's spokesperson appeared to have exhausted her biting criticism and threats. She, like the remaining Chinese traveler and the workers behind the counter, was anticipating the outcome of my exchange with Aeroflot. At least, this was what I gathered from their repeated glances and shared hush.

"Well, I give up," I said, pressing the phone's red icon to terminate the call. I handed the device back to the young man and thanked him. Both he and his colleague sympathetically maintained that someone should have answered.

"Yeah, no one did and so what should have happened doesn't matter."

Sensing my agitation, they suggested that I call back in the next hour.

"And you think someone will suddenly pick up? C'mon, we all know that's not going to happen." I was about to walk away from the counter and rejoin Nisha and Frank, but I took another look around the hall at all the stranded passengers and was stirred to speak.

"It's very clear that Aeroflot sucks! But my thing is, what are you guys doing for all of us? Have you guys pressured your bosses to get us some mats to sleep on? Some blankets? You know, stuff to make this whole situation better."

"I know but—"

"There's no 'but'," I interjected. "Not enough has been done for us and that's why people are so upset. You guys can't keep blaming Aeroflot. The reality is we're stuck here. Now, what can you guys do for us?"

"I'm sorry, we can only give you vouchers for food," the female colleague answered.

Unimpressed, the family's spokesperson stormed off shouting, for the umpteenth time, that she needed a hotel room not more food and beverages. Although I agreed that lodging was our primary requirement, I knew the vouchers would be useful in the morning at breakfast time. The Chinese traveler showed the workers her boarding pass to receive two food and two drink vouchers as well. She also urged her companions to come up and get theirs. Wanting to ensure everyone affected by Aeroflot's poor customer service knew about the hand outs, I made a short announcement before stepping away from the counter.

Frank awoke abruptly from his nap. He noted that the bottle he was holding was empty and that it was too early to embrace sobriety. "We gotta get another bottle," he said, voice groggy.

"Man, I'm done."

I told him that I was going up the second floor to get a bottle of water and offered to bring him one.

"Water? I don't need water … do you need water?" The question was directed at Nisha, but he didn't realize, until he turned to his left, that she was sleeping.

"Wow, she's really passed out," he acknowledged, his eyes still not fully open. "She doesn't need anything but a bed."

"Well, it's pretty late."

"What time is it?"

"It's almost eleven."

"That's early! C'mon, let's get another bottle." He reached into his front pocket and pulled out some rubles. I told him to keep his money and that I'd be back in a few minutes. He smiled and said, "We gonna really turn up now." Leaving the waiting area, I shook my head, thinking he couldn't possibly handle more whiskey.

The walk up to the second floor was noticeably more laboured than when I did it earlier. I laughed at myself for almost stumbling over the last step. No one was around to witness my near collapse, not that my reaction would have been much different if there was. I had consumed a decent amount of poison to reach my altered state, and I was enjoying every minute of it; especially after the way I had just faked being clearheaded at the international transit counter.

Returning to the restaurant with the purple couches brought at smile to my face; maybe more of a smirk, considering how I was replaying the shockingly cold comportment of the waitress that had served us. I hoped that she and the other waitress sitting behind the counter watching TV were still on duty so that they could experience my heightened level of cheer. I wanted to make them even more upset. Nisha, Frank, and I had concluded earlier in the evening that it was our happiness the locals might have found most offensive. And so, upon entering the restaurant, my goal was to be as offensive as possible.

"Privet," I said warmly, as if greeting old friends. Two new waitresses muttered a word or two in my direction then refocused their attention on their television program. Grinning at their frighteningly poor people skills, I opened the refrigerator, grabbed three bottles of water, and placed them on the counter. The shorter, rounder waitress spoke to me in a dismissive tone when I handed her a voucher worth five hundred rubles.

"Sorry, I don't speak Russian," I said, set on retaining my smile.

She examined the piece of paper that looked like a cheque before saying something else. After several moments of failed communication, her colleague turned away from the television and intervened. She stepped around the counter, lifted a chocolate bar from the rack of sweets, and positioned it with the water. Either my calculation was incorrect or for some unknown reason they wanted to give me gift. Or maybe the price of the bottled water was less than what was written on their small sign.

"Spasibo."

I doubt my pronunciation was as accurate as Frank's, but I blurted it out with childlike fervor. Neither of them smiled, though they probably wanted to as they uttered what I presumed must have been "you're welcome." Leaving the restaurant, I jokingly told them I would be back to sleep on a purple sofa. They showed no sign of understanding, not even a desire to understand, my words.

Back at the international transit counter, Frank was snoring loudly with his head tilted backward on the metal support while Nisha was half awake. I gently placed the chocolate bar on the fold of the fluffy sweater she was wearing and waited for her reaction. After fully opening her eyes and spotting the treat on her stomach, she thanked me repeatedly. Ripping open the purple wrapper, she told me that she had been craving chocolate for days. Her first bite looked and sounded like an orgasmic experience. Watching her was moderately stimulating so when she offered me a piece, I almost voiced, "No, but might I have a kiss?" Fortunately, the censoring part of my brain was functioning.

I told her that I avoid eating chocolate for fear of getting pimples. She laughed and asked if I was serious.

"Yeah, I get little red ones here, here, or here," I said, pointing at my forehead and cheeks. Nisha replied that pimples couldn't discourage her from eating chocolate.

"I don't even know why I still get pimples. Is it just me, or weren't we told when we were young that once we get older, we won't have to worry about them? I'm sure that's what my parents told me."

Considering how clear my face was, she found my rant amusing. Her laughter was genuine which, in a world filled with sarcasm, cynicism, and all their offshoots, was refreshing. We wondered aloud if we were being too noisy. Nobody was giving us any looks, but then again, most of the people in the waiting area were sleeping, reading, or listening to something in their headphones.

While we replayed the events of the evening, Frank awoke and asked, "Are we still in Moscow?" Nisha and I chuckled before segueing into his snoring.

"Bruh, it sent trembles throughout the airport."

"Seriously mate. It was freakishly loud."

He told us we were exaggerating — of course we were — and insisted we should have recorded him.

"And risk damaging my phone?" Nisha asked with a soft giggle. "I don't think so."

I handed the American a bottle of water and told him that we had arrived at the halfway mark of our layover. But considering that both he and Nisha had later departure times, it wasn't exactly the halfway mark for them. Nonetheless, feeling a sense of accomplishment for having survived and even enjoyed segments of the last eight hours, we gathered our belongings and embarked on a new mission: explore Terminal D and find a more agreeable area to sleep.

The passageway into Terminal D was near the entry for the airport hotel. In fact, it couldn't have been more than one hundred meters away, but we had decided out of principle that we weren't paying for a room. If Frank wasn't with us, I possibly would have caved when Nisha and I saw the hotel. The thought of sharing a room with her was quite arousing, even though she looked like sleep was going to whisk her away the second her head touched the pillow. I could see myself watching her until I fell into my own slumber. In the morning, our innocence would be lost when a gentle peck turned into steamy kissing and petting. And even with our departure times approaching, we, so engulfed in the flames of passion, would continue to roll around on the bed. Just as I was beginning to imagine the removal of our clothes, Frank interrupted. He wanted to know how much I paid for the bottle of water. Thirstier than he had realized, he finished what I gave him and wanted more. I told my American friend that I was unsure, but my voucher purchased three bottles and a chocolate bar. Seeing no shop around us, Nisha offered him some of her water.

"I'll be fine. Someone will be selling water somewhere over here."

We passed two departure gates and waiting areas; both were vacant. On the left side of the corridor, massive wood panels and plastic sheeting had been erected to seal off ongoing renovations. The lighting was considerably dimmer than in Terminals E and F.

"This would be the perfect place to shoot a thriller," Frank announced. As he described what would transpire in the opening scene, two women wearing dark-coloured, pantsuits emerged from a departure gate farther down the corridor. Maintaining a brisk pace, they walked toward us and passed without glancing in our direction.

"It was almost like they were whispering to each other," I said, surprised by how quietly they conversed.

"Or could it be that we talk too loud?" Nisha wondered.

"Did you say too loud?" Frank asked, exaggerating his volume.

"Maybe those were their night voices," I suggested with a light chuckle.

"Yo, I got a night voice too."

Frank whispered his plans to buy a bottle of water and, for good measure, threw in the few Russian words he knew. Our laughter reverberated like thunder in an unassuming sky.

We spotted a decent number of travelers as we ventured further into the terminal. All of them were either sleeping or attempting to get comfortable on their metal chairs for a snooze. The shops and restaurant we passed were closed, but there was a coffee stand that seemed to be open for business next to a departure gate. Nobody was behind the counter, but the sandwiches, salads, and beverages in the fridge were left uncovered. The bananas and apples sold in a wicker fruit basket placed next to the cash register also led us to believe that an employee would be returning. We inspected the fridge and looked behind the counter but couldn't find any bottled water. I advised Frank to behave as though he were in China and order a cup of hot water. Chuckling, he confessed he wasn't an advocate of drinking plain hot water.

"You gotta put some tea in there or something," he said.

"Same here," Nisha added.

"My dear friends," I calmly said with my right index finger pointed upward to stress the importance of my statement: "If you're not drinking hot water, you're missing out on life … your body, your mind needs the purity of hot water."

They laughed and teased me about having spent too many years in China. Like many other expatriates, Frank and, to a lesser degree, Nisha were not convinced of Traditional Chinese Medicine's claims about the benefits of drinking hot water.

"O ye, of little faith," I said dramatically, pretending to be devastated by their response. "It is a fact that hot water will allow you to sleep better, feel better, look better and even shit better."

Without the British accent, I spoke as though I was performing a Shakespearean soliloquy before an audience of theatre connoisseurs that longed to experience my character's truth.

"Why do you refuse her? Has she not shown herself to be a saviour of all mortals? Like the moon manifesting her love in the night sky, she knocks at the door of our heart hoping we will grant her entrance. Perhaps the bawdy wind that kisses all it meets will speak to you and you. Thus, her greatness … her majesty … has stood … the test of time."

They applauded my improvisation skills and when I refused to break character, they abandoned their seats in the audience to join me onstage.

"Surely, I shall not ignore her any longer," Nisha said, matching my emotion. "She shall become a central figure in this life of mine and for this I say thank you o wise one … you are undoubtedly a respecter of ancient wisdom."

Staring intensely, first at Nisha then me, Frank lifted his right arm and said, "Cannon to the right of them." This was followed by him raising his left arm and bellowing, "Cannon to the left of them, cannon in front of them, volleyed and thundered!" He delivered the lines in the same manner that Geoffrey did on *The Fresh Prince of Bel-Air* which caused Nisha and me to cackle with laughter.

"Quiet my children," he continued. "I have more to share." We could hardly stand straight when he began reciting a nursery rhyme with more conviction than it required. It was at this time that a woman in her mid to late thirties walked behind the counter and shot us the most disapproving look. But we ignored her judgment and continued our improv.

"Can you hear the sound of water?" Frank asked. His eyes were closed, and his fists were clutched tightly on his chest. "Water, water, water … I … need … water." He then stumbled over to a seat and collapsed in the most dramatic fashion. Nisha and I applauded as though we had just witnessed a once-in-a-lifetime performance. Meanwhile the woman behind the counter remained uncaring.

"I think I want some ice cream," Frank said, noticing the three soft-serve, ice cream dispensers that faced the coffee stand. Nisha was considering getting a cup of tea, which she referred to as a "brew" while I wouldn't have minded a cup of hot water. Jumping to his feet, Frank offered the woman a warm "privet" then pointed at the ice cream machines. She immediately walked around the counter to meet him there.

Nisha, seated comfortably next to me, yawned and said, "I'm shattered." I followed up her yawn with my own, admitting that I could also use some sleep, yet it continued to elude me even after Nisha quietly dozed off and Frank, having finished his ice cream, did the same. I wanted to blame my seat's poor ergonomics, but I've fallen asleep in places that were far worse on my back and neck. I wanted to fault the low-frequency buzzing, the kind of sound often heard in a quiet, well-lit stadium or arena, but it was hardly audible. The lighting wasn't bright enough to be a nuisance and the central heating was set at a pleasant temperature, but still the angels of sleep did not carry me away. I closed my eyes, hoping that something other than thoughts would materialize. But the mind does what it wants and mine was stuck on the reasons for *her* absence. It replayed our final conversation and widened a wound that hadn't fully healed.

Glancing over at Nisha and Frank, I wondered if I would have befriended them if she was accompanying me. I imagined us being so excited about traveling together for the first time that we'd pay little attention to anyone else. To cope with the layover, we would have unquestionably secured a hotel room. And in the morning, I saw us having a quick breakfast before boarding our flight to Munich; giving us little chance to make any new acquaintances.

For no obvious reason, I found myself revisiting the itinerary we had made: spend two or three days visiting my cousin and his wife in Munich then tour the country for the remainder of our trip. From that thought, there was nowhere else to go but to the confession she had made a few weeks ago about falling in love with someone in her office and being confused about what or who she wanted. I was appalled, I was hurt, but I didn't end the relationship. She claimed to still love me and continued to spend nights and mornings in my bed. Most importantly, she told me they had never even kissed which might have had more to do with him having a girlfriend that worked in the same building than her not wanting to taste his lips. At any rate, I

246

waited for her to make some sort of decision, but after a week she was still conflicted. That was when I reluctantly chose to make her decision easier by walking away. Unfortunately, she remained in my thoughts and my feelings still orbited around her.

After some time, I left my sleepy friends to explore the rest of the terminal. Not that I was in an exploratory mood, I just knew it was pathetic to sit and relive pain. Returning to the corridor, I was delighted to come across a TGI Friday's. I wasn't particularly hungry but did find myself salivating a bit as I browsed through the menu on top of a podium at the front entrance. I spotted a patron. He was sitting in a booth with his feet resting on the opposing couch while sipping a hot drink and watching something on his tablet. My intention was to continue walking and come back with Nisha and Frank for breakfast; but when the waiter announced that the bar was still open, my plans changed. I followed him into the restaurant and sat at a small round table.

He offered me a drink menu, but I didn't need one. Any single malt whiskey, neat, would do. I watched the waiter go behind the bar and pour the spirit into a short glass before bringing it over. As he smiled cunningly, he set the glass on a square napkin in front of me and told me to enjoy. He seemed pleased to give me a double even though I had only ordered a single.

I cleared my throat and lifted the glass to my mouth. The burning sensation was familiar, but the solitude was not. I was used to drinking with her and marveling at how alcohol seemed to showcase her best qualities. Melancholic horns and keys were the landscape to her colourful reflections. I enjoyed how she talked and laughed a little louder because when sober she was usually inaudible. I took a second sip, closing my eyes to hear her sing. She sang from the parts of her that were most damaged yet made every note sound like love. There, in the bosom of her music, my insecurities took on shapes and sounds that would keep the romantics awake. By my third and fourth sip, the crushing tides of her singing stormed the desolate beaches of my heart. I clutched my glass, resisting our shared history. Many questions remained, but I feared her answers. All my "whys" and "hows" remained trapped within the self-made prison of my thoughts. I took a long sip then reckoned I was done drinking alone.

After leaving the restaurant, I walked farther away from the gate where Nisha and Frank were sleeping. I had the corridor to myself until I saw two tall, dark-skinned men walking in my direction. Judging from a distance the wide grins they flashed, they were pleased to see me. I acknowledged them with a smile as well and slowed down to chat. They asked where I was from. I answered Canada. They both told me they had relatives living there. When I asked whereabouts they were from, they, assuming I knew very little African geography, replied, "West Africa." After hearing that I could list most of the countries on their continent, they told me that Cameroon was home. They were surprised to hear me express a desire to visit their country but told me that I would thoroughly enjoy myself. Naturally, they inquired about where I was traveling to which led me to do the same.

"We're still waiting to go back to our country," the elder of the two said. Because of what they described as visa problems, they had been forced to stay at Sheremetyevo for the past three months. I was shocked and asked how it was possible to live at the airport. Grinning, they told me there were others in the same predicament and even worse. Their ability to smile despite their circumstances was baffling. Here I was complaining about my layover when, apparently, they and others had been living at the airport for months without knowing when they would be flying out.

"This isn't right," I declared.

"Yeah," the elder said with a shoulder shrug, "but this is life."

I had questions, many questions, but they didn't seem interested in discussing their quandary any further, and I didn't want to pry. After a moment or two of silence, the kind born out of uncertainty, we exchanged a few well wishes and said goodbye.

It was almost two in the morning when I rejoined Frank and Nisha. They had been up for a while and wanted to relocate because they felt the chairs would not allow them to have a sound sleep.

"Fifteen, twenty minutes max." Frank said, standing to his feet, "After that you start feeling just how hard it is. There's zero cushion, man."

I suggested we return to the restaurant with the purple couches and sleep until breakfast. Neither Frank nor Nisha was keen on walking back to Terminal F, but they knew it was the best option for sleep. As we were setting off, I told them, with measured confidence, that breakfast would be an absolute treat. Sensing their doubt, I said, "There's a TGI Friday's over there." Frank's face lit up, and he was quick to ask when they opened. Nisha wasn't familiar with the restaurant but tried to share in our enthusiasm for the food we described. When I told them that it was open but only beverages, alcoholic and non-alcoholic, were being served, Frank wondered aloud if returning to Terminal F was a better choice.

"Let's go get some drinks."

"You're more than welcome to go," Nisha said plainly, "but I need sleep, mate."

I added that at this juncture of the layover, reclining on a soft purple sofa was far more appealing than indulging in more liquor.

"Okay, okay," the American said, accepting the aversion to his suggestion. "What time does breakfast start at?"

We were so familiar with the way to Terminal F that we probably could have traversed it blindfolded. There were times where Nisha's eyelids were so low, she might as well have been wearing a blindfold. When Frank and I teased her about being a sleepwalker, she, for our enjoyment, talked about being shattered. She then pointed out a passenger who was sprawled out across three seats and said, "He's completely shattered."

"Why yes, he is utterly and unmistakably shattered," I said, trying to capture Nisha's cadence and accent.

"It's such a great word," Frank added, chuckling at my imitation. "I'm definitely bringing that one back to the US."

"Shattered is a wonderful word," Nisha declared. "One that the whole world should adopt."

"So, you prefer saying 'shattered' instead of…what's the other one?" Frank asked.

"Knackered?"

"Yeah, knackered. That's the one."

While Nisha was expounding on her affinity for the word "shattered," I noticed something that I had missed during the previous walkabouts: men and women lying on the floor in sleeping bags inside a space sectioned off by glass partitions. There had to be at least a dozen passengers camped out in the small area located on the left side of the wide corridor, behind rows and rows of chairs.

"Look at all of them," I said, urging my friends to stop and observe.

Frank and Nisha paused to glance over at the passengers.

"They're most definitely shattered," Frank said with a chuckle.

"Yes, completely shattered," Nisha confirmed.

"I'm wondering if the two Cameroonians I met are in there," I said as we resumed our walk. Born in Sierra Leone, Frank was quick to ask about the men I brought up. I told him and Nisha that I had a short exchange with them outside of TGI Friday's.

"They told me they've been living at the airport since November."

"What? That's like three months!" Frank exclaimed.

"Oh, my word!" Nisha added.

"Trust me, I was thinking the same thing. They said they had some visa problems and once that's sorted out, they'll be able to fly home."

Frank believed there was no way the Cameroonians would be in the same predicament if they held passports from a rich country.

"Can you imagine the Russians trying to do that to a few Americans? Or Canadians? Or Brits?" Frank asked rhetorically. "They know that wouldn't fly, but with Africans they feel like they can do whatever they want. I hate that bullshit."

Nisha and I wholeheartedly agreed. As we resumed our walk, I gave an account of what I thought was discrimination against Southeast Asian and African passport holders that had transpired at the customs checkpoint when I was traveling a year ago overland from Mainland China into Hong Kong. Nisha recounted her aunt's and uncle's experience with customs officers at Heathrow airport last fall. Being Pakistani passport holders, they were held in a backroom for additional questioning that went on for over an hour.

"And when they were finally allowed to go, they weren't given any sort of explanation."

"It's all bullshit, man!" Frank asserted.

"Yep, and when it's not the country on your passport, it's your last name or even your first name or your skin colour or head wrap. There's always something—"

"That's used against all of us who aren't white," Frank interjected.

"It's incredibly frustrating," Nisha agreed.

Shaking my head, I smirked and said, "White is still the only colour that is always right."

Entering Terminal F, Nisha wondered aloud about change. She wondered if change would ever come to all of us who have been racialized and marginalized.

"Can we actually say that things are improving when we have Brexit and this surge in support for right-wing parties in Europe that are flat out racist?" she asked, visibly bothered by the current state of affairs. "And don't get me started on Trump."

I acknowledged the obvious: it was hard to be optimistic about change when we were all being bombarded with news stories that demonstrated how humanity was moving backwards. Nonetheless, I maintained that a life without hope was not one that I could live.

"Man, I wanna be hopeful, but goddamn," Frank sighed as he reflected on the ways of the world. "We're still getting shitted on."

Frank revealed that the reason he was flying home was to support his cousin in a court case against the city of Washington D.C. His announcement captured our complete attention. Transporting us back to the night of September 11, 2015, he presented a detailed account of how his cousin was slammed to the ground, verbally abused, and falsely arrested by police.

"Some white lady felt 'uneasy' at this ATM that he was at and called the cops. She said he was standing around a bit too long. When really, security footage showed him pausing to hold the door open for a couple with a stroller. And after that, you can see him on his phone not bothering nobody."

"That's messed up!" I exclaimed.

"But why was he arrested?" Nisha asked.

Frank believed the dispatcher had given the officers the impression that a robbery was in progress or had just occurred.

"So, when they spotted him walking towards the metro, they jumped out of their SUV as if he was some criminal that needed to be apprehended right away. Luckily, someone across the street pulled out his phone to catch those pigs doing what they do. They had him screaming in pain and didn't give a damn. His face was all bruised up, his neck, his back … I couldn't even watch the whole video."

My American friend remarked that his cousin was traumatized by the ordeal and had yet to resume his university studies.

"He didn't deserve that; nobody does. But in America, we've been terrorized like this since slavery, and so

I'm thinking, even if we win this lawsuit and stick it to the police, what happens next? Will that stop them from harassing us? From beating us? From shooting us? Will they finally realize that our lives matter?"

There was layered silence. Perhaps we all needed to absorb the poignancy of these questions.

We arrived at the restaurant. Although the waitress sitting behind the counter was far more interested in her phone than in greeting us, we were elated at the sight of more than a dozen vacant purple couches.

"For some reason, she doesn't seem thrilled to see me again," I said, pretending to be surprised.

"Man, I'm so done with these people," Frank grunted as he led us to the three couches farthest from the waitress. There, we plopped ourselves down as if our bodies had completely run out of fuel and needed replenishment. Considering how comfortable the couches were, we wondered why other passengers were not spending the night on them. We got our answer a few minutes into our rest when the waitress came over.

"No sleep here," she said, with incomprehensible contempt.

Slightly startled by her presence, Nisha and I sat up and cordially asked why sleeping was forbidden. Rather than giving us the reason, she simply repeated: "No sleep here."

Once she left, I looked over to my left and told Frank, who was lying on his back, that he could stop pretending to be asleep. When he didn't budge, Nisha, who was occupying the sofa on my right, remarked that he was shattered. Aware that I had yet to shut my eyes at any point during the layover, she asked how I was able to stay awake. I could have told her about the girl. I could have told her about the frightening neighbourhoods my insecurities had me visiting since our heartbreaking end. I could have told her that the loneliness I felt was almost as terrifying as those neighbourhoods. Instead, I grinned and suggested that I may not be human. Letting out a long yawn, Nisha said that nobody would believe she was anything but human. She then asked if I thought the waitress would return as she abandoned her resolve to comply and stretched out on the couch.

"Get some sleep," I said while I watched her get comfortable. "If she comes back, I won't let her bother you."

With her eyes closed, Nisha thanked me and declared that I was the best. Hyperbolic or not, her words made me feel appreciated. I reached into my backpack and grabbed my electronic reader. I was reading "The Lady with the Dog" on my way to the airport in Beijing and had not returned to it since then. A day before the trip, I had uploaded a collection of Anton Chekhov's most celebrated works to my device. I read "The Lottery Ticket" in school but didn't enjoy it as much as my teacher and some of my classmates. But there was something poetic about reading Chekhov's oeuvres while being in his homeland.

Unfortunately, I only got through a few pages before the waitress marched toward Nisha and said, "No sleep, no sleep." Feeling protective, I sternly told her that my friend was tired and that she was being rude for waking her up. Visibly annoyed by the woman's refusal to let her sleep, Nisha asked: "Who am I harming by sleeping here?" I'm not convinced she understood the question. Nonetheless she continued to demand that my friend refrain from sleeping. Frank's snoring distracted her for a moment. But looking over at him, she didn't dare to wake him up.

"Look, we're not bothering anybody so please leave us alone," I said, praying for her retreat.

"You must sit," the waitress maintained while refocusing on Nisha.

"No, what must happen is you must leave me alone so that I can close my eyes and sleep!"

The waitress reacted by threatening to notify the police. Nisha dared her to make the call.

"Okay, I call the police."

"Call them. I am not going anywhere!"

The woman began talking to herself in Russian before commanding Nisha to sit up.

"Why are you still here? Go call the police and tell them that I'm committing a crime by wanting to sleep."

Once again, I'm not certain how much the woman understood, but she responded by yelling at Nisha in Russian.

"You're clearly a mad woman. Go call the police. Do you want me to call them for you?" I asked.

"I call police!"

"Go and call them already! And while you're at it, call the mayor; heck, you can even give your buddy Putin a call. I'm sure Putin would love to come and put us in our place. You have his number, right?"

The smugness in my body language and the condescension in my voice needed no translation. It was clear that my intention was to insult her and her leader. She fixed her eyes on me then unleashed what surely must have been a venomous scolding.

"You do realize I don't understand anything you're saying? I don't know why you're still talking to us. You should be calling the police," I said with a chuckle.

"Why you no speak Russian? This is Russia you must speak Russian?"

I laughed and so did Nisha.

"Right, I should learn Russian because it's such a useful language."

She might not have grasped my words, but the sarcasm was hard to overlook.

"This is Russia … Russia is for Russian people. Why you are here?"

"Trust me, I'm asking myself the same question. But hey, you don't want us in your country, and we don't wanna be in your country, so we have something in common. How about that?"

I told the woman that in the morning we would happily fly away then asked if she would happily find new passengers to disturb. Looking like she had heard enough, she stormed off while mumbling to herself.

Nisha thanked me, then wondered if the waitress would notify the police. I believed she was bluffing and encouraged my friend to get the rest she yearned. Pensive while lying comfortably on her back, she asked how a person could become so unreasonable. I wanted to resume my reading, but her question was followed by several others.

"Don't you think that if she wasn't playing the role of employee, it all could have been avoided?"

"Sure, so long as we had stepped out of our roles as international passengers," I added.

She reckoned that identifying deeply with the roles we play prevent us from experiencing empathy for one another. I agreed and invited her to reflect on the occasions when she wasn't playing a role.

"That's rare, but I do feel incredibly human right now."

"I do too."

"Why can't it always be like this?"

I didn't have an answer, and I don't think she was expecting one.

"I was listening to a lecture online and the woman said that each one of us comes into this world with unique worth ... a unique soul. But we're socialized to never really uncover it because we're taught to pay attention to everything else ... everything that has to do with the roles we play or will play. And so, she said that we all suffer from ADD."

"Attention deficit disorder?"

"No," I answered, knowing that she would assume that. "Well maybe we do, but she defined ADD as Authenticity Deficit Disorder."

"Wow! That's brilliant!"

We reflected on the ways we could be more authentic and decided that individuals who don't suffer from ADD have a greater chance at happiness. I also pointed out that despite living in an accelerated world, people aren't any happier. I even speculated that humankind might be more miserable than it had ever been.

"Slow needs to become the new fast," I said, believing, perhaps naively, that contentment was more likely if we decreased the speed at which we live our days.

"We value how fast a person can get from one moment to the next because the present moment is never quite good enough. But isn't that madness? Each moment doesn't have to be a means to some other end ... each moment can be a means unto itself, right?"

When Nisha didn't respond, I smiled, realizing that I was reasoning with myself. I lifted the electronic reader up to a comfortable viewing position and reentered Chekhov's world.

ACKNOWLEDGEMENTS

Pastel Remembrances is not the book I thought I would write, but it turned out to be the book I needed to write. When the time came to have my manuscript edited, I knew that I wanted Saada Branker to do the job. Saada, I'm grateful for your tireless work and eagerness to show me the finer points of the English language. Collaborating with you has been an absolute pleasure. You have to edit my next book; it's not even up for debate.

Last year, I came home after spending sixteen years abroad. The transition has been incredibly smooth, and I believe that has a lot do with the love and support I receive from my family. I'm incredibly fortunate to have a family that believes in my dreams and never tries to convince me to get a conventional job. They never bore me with questions about RRSPs (I don't have any), badger me about "settling down", or dissuade me from exercising my freedom to be me. So I want to give a huge thank you to my 100-year-old grandmother, Carmen; my mother, Claudette; my father, Mitch; my four sisters: Wusua, Kemba, Sassa, and Cheeka, as well as my six nieces and nephews: Jahleesha, Nyeesha, Melissah, Mehki, Malika, and Maharli. I'm so glad to be back home with all of you.

When writing a book, inspiration is vital. Lucky for me, my friends are a constant source of inspiration and so I'd like to give a big shout out to every one of them. I feel the need to give an extra special salute to all the friends who have been with me through all the changes. Ricky, Ron, and Ray, I know we don't stay in touch like we would like to, but the bond is always there. I'm grateful for all the great times, and I look forward to sharing more moments with you guys.

Femi, from the Bryant Building to China to Colombia, we're doing exactly what we said we would do: Real Livin' for life! Let's continue to make the most of every moment. I can't wait to meet Moremi and see Elymar again. Chris, I'm so glad Deon put us in touch back in 2004. We've explored Asia together; after Covid, let's get back on the road. But for now, let's continue to question everything and make music. Henry, we've come a long way from Canilx and "flatlines". My time in Wenzhou wouldn't have been as fun if you hadn't showed up. When are you guys coming to Canada? David, you did my first website and now I get to work on your movie. Keep making art; the world needs it and remember Turn Out!

Larry, I don't know if I would have gotten into Communications if it wasn't for you, and I definitely wouldn't have survived that internship at CTV without you. Your level of discipline and focus motivates me to push harder. Harry, you helped to make my first book launch something memorable. The way I see it, we should take it to the next level with Pastel Remembrances. All I wanna know is when we gonna do the "dkd" and "creep" again? Sarah, I'm glad you know how much your voice matters. *Do Health* didn't happen in 2020, but hopefully we can make it a reality this year. Sonia, thank you for always believing in my storytelling abilities and for schooling me on what marketing is all about. I'm excited to see what this new season will bring you and your family.

Finally, I'd like to thank you, the reader, for taking the time to read my words. I hope you've enjoyed these tales and will support my future projects. There's much more to come.